RELIQUARY OF THE DEAD
WAR OF THE GODS, BOOK 1

David A. Falk

Lagomorph Rampant Studios
Vancouver | Canada

Published by Lagomorph Rampant Studios
www.lagomorph-rampant.com

ISBN 978-1-0692160-0-7

This book is dedicated to those who believe "there are more things in Heaven and Earth… than are dreamt of in our philosophies…"

… and to my father …

Bruno Ronald Falk (1938-2025)

CHAPTER ONE

History is more than mere recollection. It reconstructs the past based upon value judgements, prioritizing what we think is important to preserve. Those who attempt to approach history thinking they have no bias fail to see it stare back at them in the mirror. — **"Princes of Thebes: A Festschrift Celebrating the Career of Dawn Chauvet" by Andrew Montet**

A drop of water traced down the fogged window of the office with plaster walls stained yellow with years of condensation. What good ever came out of this office? Pierre Gulet sat there, waiting for the hammer to drop. Cairo was especially hot and humid that day, and perspiration rolled from his slightly receding blond hairline. He removed his round wire-framed spectacles from his dark brown eyes and folded them gently, then inserted them into the vest pocket of his white cotton shirt. It didn't matter. With all the humidity, he couldn't see out of them anyway. He felt he had been waiting for hours in the cheap folding chair that punished his tailbone. The room was littered with chests, glass display cases, stelae, ancient pots and votive statues, a pharaoh's hoard of the afterlife, from digs across Egypt, and not even the fineness of the loot, piled upon each other in seemingly random order, could distract Pierre from his misery. The heat only punished the injury with insult.

The door swung open, and Gerard, Deputy Director of the Antiquities Ministry, a rotund over-tanned windbag of a man, blustered into the room. Pierre stood up, a stack of file folders in his arms. Papers burst from their manila leaves and splashed to the floor. He bent down to pick up the papers. Not his finest moment.

Gerard watched Pierre grovel on the floor, and a wry smile crept to the corners of his mouth. When Pierre composed himself, Gerard took a seat across from him in a large oak chair with high arms that itself was an antique from the 1920s when the academic chair was more than a metaphor for endowment. He took a deep breath and spoke.

"You know why you're here," said Gerard.

Pierre, of course, knew why. The reasons kept rehearsing in his head, every failure repeated over and over, and every mistake. He could not let it go, and Gerard and the entire Antiquities Ministry reminded him of every detail of his incompetence.

"I know mistakes were made at the Naqada fort," said Pierre with a slight stutter. Even though he was more than half a foot taller than Gerard, he felt half his height. "But we can get the project back on track."

"I'm going to get right to the point," said Gerard. "The concession is being assigned to someone else."

Pierre crumpled back into the folding chair. He exhaled, the wind left him empty and deflated. "Why? I've only worked there three seasons."

Gerard rested his elbows on the desk, folded his hands, and leaned forward. "Your field reports are below the quality the ministry demands. This is no longer the 20th century. Field reports matter." Gerard was, of course, correct. The days of Mariette and treasure hunting were long gone. And even viewing the monuments as purely vehicles of tourism, the so-called *real work* popular in the 21st century, was passé. A lot had changed in the past four hundred years: pandemics, wars, flip-flopping between socialism and capitalism, and the ever-steady march of science and engineering.

The nuclear industry saw a revival not seen since the 1950s, and no nuclear plant had experienced a fatal accident in over 150 years. This did not mean all was peaceful—far from it. Tactical nuclear exchanges were made against enemies both foreign and domestic. One American President evaporated his political opponent, earning his party forever the *nuclear option* moniker, and thankfully never rose to power again. The opposition, however, did not fare better. They became the big-tent party of indolence and incompetence. Today, the USA persists as a two-party system, just two different parties.

Amid all this, archaeology also changed. While digging would forever remain a part of archaeology, non-destructive methods had become highly sophisticated. Ground penetrating radar and ultrasound technologies can now peer below the surface without turning a spade of dirt. Magnetic resonance machines tied to powerful 3D modelling computers were now available as affordable wand-like devices, which can scan the interior of a mummy without unwrapping it.

But more than the technological change was the administrative change. Archeological digs were now mired by mountains of paperwork: environmental impact studies, ethical assessments, diversity and compliance affidavits, compensation remittance forms for indigenous populations, and the ever-dreaded quarterly preliminary reports.

"I know," said Pierre. Standing up, he fumbled for several loose papers among his packet of mangled file folders. "Those preliminary reports were a start. The interim reports are looking more promising. And I have a new data management system, so I'm finally starting to get a handle on all the data."

"It's not the reports," admitted Gerard who somehow managed to remain perfectly dry and cool despite the office sauna. Even the few remaining wisps of tar black hair he had slicked back to cover his mostly bald head had the sheen of dry plastic. "The management of your concession has been… let me come out and say it… a disaster."

"We hired a local to keep the goats from the marker flags only to have him sleep on the job," said Pierre. "The flash flooding that washed the backfill into the trenches—it was the first rainfall in a hundred years. Who could have predicted that?" Truth be told, the goats had not done half as much damage to the site as the local workers did when they thought they might find another Narmer Palette under the sand. Another handful of papers hit the floor with a swoosh.

"The decision has already been made. You will no longer be managing the site."

"Who will be replacing me?" Pierre sat back down.

"A delicate point." Gerard twiddled his fingers. "I am assigning the dig to Mahmoud."

Pierre's face blanched white. They both knew Mahmoud had been placed on his dig at the Deputy Director's insistence. "Mahmoud is a fine assistant and will someday make a good archaeologist. But won't the fact that he's your nephew and lacks the academic qualifications raise some questions?"

"This is Egypt." Gerard's face flushed red. "Egyptian digs should be managed by Egyptian citizens." He leaned back in the chair like a king on his throne, royal as one could expect from a squat little man handing out favors to his courtiers. "The lack of qualifications might have raised concerns if your reputation had not preceded him."

"What?" said Pierre.

"Reports have been sent to the Minister for months. Every detail of your incompetence." Gerard tapped his fingers on the arms of the chair. "Unlike you, the person who wrote those reports was quite thorough."

"Why?" Pierre could not believe his ears.

"You don't have what it takes. You made Mahmoud look like he was rescuing the dig from incompetence. And to be honest, you're not likeable. Some placed bets you were going to make full professor, but *smarter money* shorted your perceived value. And perception is truth." The rotund man shook his head slowly and spoke in a low soft voice. "You will never work in Egypt again."

"What now?" Pierre began to see the implications of what Gerard had done to him. Gerard had silently thrust a metaphorical knife between his ribs, and Pierre had not even realized he was still bleeding out.

"About that." Gerard reached into his desk, drew out a #10 envelope, and slid it across the old oak desktop.

"What's this?" Pierre was hesitant to accept anything from his betrayer.

"A one-way ticket. If you leave quietly and don't make a fuss over what happened, you get a job and transportation out of Egypt, and I will write you the last recommendation that you will ever need."

Pierre squinted at Gerard.

"The European Space Agency said that they need an expert in ancient history. Perhaps, they need a schoolteacher. Don't know. Don't care." Gerard paused for a moment. He grinned and then resumed. "The ESA has established several small colonies on the exoplanets."

"The what?"

"For a hundred and seventy-five years, they have sent pilgrims to habitable worlds outside our solar system." Gerard snorted and fanned himself with a file folder. "At least, they call them habitable. Don't seem habitable to me."

Then it hit Pierre. His jaw dropped open. Gerard confirmed it with his next sentence.

"People go out and never come back." Gerard chuckled. "This takes care of all my problems in one tidy package. You on the other hand… Whatever it is they want, I doubt it has much to do with archaeology. Better pack a lot of ebooks."

"You expect me to go to some alien planet?" Pierre stood and began walking to the door. Gerard leapt to his feet.

"I don't expect you to do anything," said Gerard with the quiet assurance of a coiled viper.

Pierre stopped. His hand was on the doorknob.

"I'd be thrilled if you made a stink and died penniless in the streets of Paris." Gerard picked up the envelope and walked over to Pierre. He looked Pierre in the face. "Sending you off-world was the Minister's idea. You can burn the last bridge you have or take the ticket. Either one works great for me."

Pierre looked hard at the envelope Gerard held in his hand. He shook his head slowly.

"Your reputation here is finished. That ticket is your last chance."

"I would rather sell pencils in front of the library."

Gerard flapped the envelope with one hand. He folded it in half and stuffed it into Pierre's shirt pocket. Gerard waddled back to his desk and belted out a harsh laugh that would have frightened a hyena. "Sooner or later, you are going to realize that there is no place left on Earth for you."

Pierre opened the door to the office and walked across the threshold.

"Just one more matter," said Gerard. He pulled a cigarette from a gold case and tapped the open end against the metal. He lit the cigarette and took a deep draw. The red ember creeped halfway down the cigarette. "My agents have contacted your landlord and your creditors. I think you are going to need to find a place to sleep for the night."

* * *

Pierre stared at the shiny wood finish of the bar. Expats drank here to forget their woes. The hookah smoking doomed the atmosphere into perpetual dark and dank smog. A place where the sophistication of society evaporated into an alcohol fueled haze. He had ordered a drink he had no way of paying for. His elbows rested on the ledge, and his head was in his hands. Before him were two fingers of smoky whisky he had not even touched.

Beside him was Sarah, a pudgy brunette in a tight single piece black dress. Pierre had called her earlier in the evening but was unsure if she was going to show.

"Tough break," said Sarah. She took a sniff from her unmixed Rosso Vermouth chilled in a tall martini glass. Pierre could predict what Sarah was going to experience as he had drunk Rosso Vermouth many times himself. The elixir had hints of raisin and orange peel. You could just take a small sip and let the layers of flavor unfold in your mouth.

"You've already heard?" Pierre lifted his face. After what happened, he was happy to see a familiar face. She was as close as he had to a friend in this city.

"The whole city knows." Sarah rubbed the rim of her glass. "Cairo never changes: the pyramids, the donkey carts, the unfinished high rises, the rancid stench of garbage, the systemic corruption. Gossip runs wild in a town like this."

"Your connections at the university?"

"The cabbie told me. They're always the first to know."

Pierre took a swig of the whisky. "How's George?"

"The divorce was finalized five years ago." She smiled and cocked her head.

"You know, when I was an undergrad, I held quite a flame for you."

"I knew," said Sarah. "I was ten years your senior and a teaching assistant. And I loved a narcissist."

"What happened?"

"Caught him fucking his grad student," she said and raised her glass. "Good riddance to garbage, human and other types." Pierre raised his glass to meet Sarah's.

"I appreciate you letting me use your couch," said Pierre.

"One night only," she said. A dye-red lock of hair fell in front of her moon-shaped face. "I have no desire for a man. It's to sleep only. And only for tonight."

"Didn't we have something once?"

"Do you think *that* because I used you for moral support?"

Pierre winced as her words sank in, feeling foolish. He looked deep into his drink.

Sarah took a breath and exhaled slowly. She clenched her fingers together as though she was holding a cigarette. "You are toxic to everyone around you. Gerard is an ass, but he is probably the best-connected ass in Cairo. A lot of people are in his pocket."

"I know."

"Tonight, the cabbies all know you've been blacklisted. Tomorrow, the bartenders will know." The bartender stopped drying glasses and glowered at Pierre. Sarah reached into her purse and laid a thousand-pound note on the bar, enough to buy five drinks. "By the end of the week, those begging for *baksheesh* will know."

"What could I do?" He shrugged his shoulders.

Sarah took another swallow of her drink. "Take the deal."

Pierre's face blanched.

"Oh, don't be so surprised." Sarah rolled her eyes. "The Minister called me an hour ago. I wasn't going to return your call. He asked me to put you up for the night and to try to talk some sense into you."

"I thought you were my friend." Pierre shook his head in disbelief.

"Only a friend can betray a friend. George hurt me more than you could imagine. You were a younger, kinder George. I never loved you. You remind me of those days." She paused for a moment, then continued. "Still don't understand why the Minister is giving you the time of day."

Pierre knew why. He descended from a long pedigree of French archaeologists: Lacau, Naville, Montet, Gulet. And the Minister came from a long line of politicians. Favors exchanged between grandfathers. Debts were never openly discussed but also never forgotten. Clearly, the Minister was squaring accounts with Pierre's grandfather. But as powerful as the Minister was, he dared not go against Gerard's network of influence, the influence of a spider in his web.

Pierre picked up the nearly empty glass. He swirled the remaining golden liquor which clung to the walls of the tumbler like honey. "I could always retire to the classroom—"

"Gerard won't allow you a graceful retirement," she interrupted. "There may be nothing for an archaeologist on the exoplanets. But you are a Ph.D. and can reinvent yourself."

"But an exoplanet?"

"I hear the colonies are growing by the year."

"What would I do out there?"

"The Minister said they only wanted someone with archaeological experience in the ancient Near East." Sarah thought hard for a moment and then added, "That seems oddly specific."

"Life never evolved on the exoplanets."

"It's preposterous," said Sarah, "which is why I think that they want you as a social studies instructor."

"A high school teacher?"

"That's what I think," she said. "Look, mommy and daddy colonists have mommy and daddy time, and soon make baby colonists. Who is going to teach baby colonists the history of planet Earth? These people are making history. But if they aren't careful, they risk losing their historical identities. It can happen after only two generations. I'm thinking they want their kids to have a balanced education. Someday, they will build schools and universities. They might need teachers to pass the knowledge on in the interim."

"Who'd want to leave Earth for that?" Pierre took another sip of the whisky. His taste buds were past the burning phase and the enjoyment stage. It now tasted like water.

"Considered it myself."

"Really?"

"Considered a lot of things after George."

"Why?"

"Why did I? Or why didn't I?"

"Why didn't you?"

"Exceeded the weight limit. Too fat, they said." She snorted. "Many people would like to be in your shoes right now. Earth is not the resort destination it once was, and a lot of people are looking to escape for a simpler life the exoplanets promise. A home, a garden, a tight-knit community. Spots on the trip are in high demand and the qualifications are stringent. Few are accepted."

"You sound like a sales rep," said Pierre.

"Perhaps you need one."

"What do you mean?"

Sarah slammed down the last of her Vermouth, then ordered her usual Merlot. The bartender set before her a large globular crystal glass, sparkling with ruby reflections. The wine was deep, red, and translucent. She picked up the glass, took a sip, nodded, and set the glass right in front of her.

"You don't always do what is good for you or even know when you've lost," she said, glaring at him with a harsh stare. "One of your two character flaws. You don't even realize how done you are." She looked into Pierre's eyes. He wilted as he sank deep into her green eyes. Crow's feet had taken over skin, once porcelain, smooth and pale. Her oil-slick hair had gone gray at the temples. Her stare communicated no compassion and not the slightest hint of regret. Deep in the pit of his stomach he knew he was nothing to her.

"Gerard knows the editors of every Egyptology journal in the Northern Hemisphere," she said. "Not only will you never work again, but you will also never publish again in this field. And you are too old to start over."

"I see."

"I still don't understand why Gerard was interested in taking your concession in the first place. I heard that it was an unremarkable Old Kingdom fort." She rubbed the edge of her glass with her index finger.

Pierre averted his gaze back to his almost empty whisky. "The fort itself was unremarkable. Dozens like them all over Egypt. Cesium magnetometry revealed that underneath the fort was the profile of a temple complex. About half as long as Amenhotep III's at Thebes."

"Under the Old Kingdom fort?"

"Site proofing showed that the temple dates to the Naqada III period. Potentially, this is the largest Dynasty 0 temple ever discovered. It could rewrite what we know about the first three dynasties. It would be scientifically more important than the Great Pyramid at Giza." Pierre raised his glass and downed the last of the whisky then slammed the tumbler onto the countertop.

"Explains why he wants you gone. If you hang around Cairo or even a Western university, everyone in the field will know that Mahmoud didn't discover the temple himself." She shook her head. "The only way people would buy that story is if he was able to convince the community you voluntarily left the project. A transfer to an exoplanet would convince many you left for something better."

"Fucking Mahmoud stole my scans."

"Typical." Sarah shook her head in disgust. "Get the expat to find the discovery and then use your buddies to dig it up and claim the media prize."

"I was too trusting," he said. "You'd think someday I would get stabbed in the back so many times all that trust would leak out onto the floor where my pride has built a mud hut for itself."

"When it comes to people, you never learn. That's your other character flaw."

Pierre motioned the bartender. Another whisky. He raised his hand.

Sarah pushed his hand down. "No more for him."

The bartender walked over to Sarah.

"Look," said Sarah to the bartender. "He's got no money. I'm covering his drinks tonight, but I'm cutting him off."

"I'll ring you up," said the Bartender.

Sarah grabbed Pierre's shoulder. Pierre snapped to attention.

"Do you want any sort of future?" said Sarah. "Do you want to get through this?"

Pierre frowned then nodded his head.

"You're an inconvenience for Gerard," said Sarah. "Gerard is many things but he's not a murderer. But I wouldn't want to put that to the test. An exoplanet wants someone with your qualifications for a reason I'll never figure out. The Minister claims you have a pre-cleared pass to that brighter tomorrow. Earth has nothing more to offer you."

CHAPTER TWO

Have you reached the top of your field? Were you among the few and proud of your branch of military service? Are you driven by personal achievement and development? Are you looking for the next great challenge? If you want to help mankind expand to the stars, consider joining the European Space Agency. — **"An Invitation to the Stars":
ESA Recruitment Literature**

A taxi, yellow and dented, with streaks of barn red rust running down to dirty tires, pulled up to the broken concrete curb. Pierre stepped out onto a curb showing similar signs of municipal neglect. The patchwork sidewalk was lifted and split, a disheveled mess of black stained concrete. Weeds poked through seams. The small herbs desperately strived to bridge soil and sky.

All Pierre had was a tan canvas backpack, which he carried by a frayed green strap. He had haggled his way back into his apartment to pick up a change of clothing, a few electronic book pads, his laptop, some important papers, and a few hundred in cash. Fortunately, enough for the ferry to Italy and a ticket for a Vestral train, the late twenty-fifth century replacement for the antiquated Cagliari rail system. Sardinia had hosted a rocket launch site since the 1960s. And now, he stood before a shining plastoglass and alumasteel geodesic dome that filled the skyline, modernized for 25th century space exploration, all of which could have been mistaken for a botanical garden.

He looked over his shoulder, catching a glimpse of the cab speeding off into the fog of midday traffic. Cagliari was a bustling metropolis of 8 million people and could have passed for any large European city:

Rome, Paris, Prague, or Vienna. A mix of thousand-year-old plastered architecture sprinkled with ultra-modern plastoglass office buildings. Compared with his chosen occupation, a thousand years was recent events, but he was going to have to change his way of thinking. He could no longer dig in the soothing warm sands of Upper Egypt looking for four-thousand-year-old artifacts. Frankly, he knew sod all about outer space. But one learns to pick up a variety of diverse skills for one's research. How difficult could it be to pick up other skills?

For a minute, he scanned the street for taxis or buses. Anything he could catch or hitchhike his way out of this fate. Second thoughts flooded his mind. What he read about space travel on the way had not filled him with confidence. The average colonist could expect to live about 36 years. Clearly, injury rates were being omitted from the promotional brochures.

But no traffic stopped for him. Pierre pivoted on his feet, shifting his weight forward. He sighed and took a cautious step forward. It was only a short walk from the ruined sidewalk to the front door of the ESA. An automatic door slid open before him. He stepped inside the geodesic dome.

The dome's interior was at least twenty meters tall. Palm trees, banana trees, rubber plants, citrus, as well as a selection of native plants like madder pink peonies and the peeling trunks of cork oak forested the lobby. White leather chairs were planted among the tree trunks. The floor was paved in white Carrera marble. The sweet scent of lemon nectar tinted the air. And yet, for the money spent on the elaborate lobby, it was devoid of people.

Pierre was greeted by a diorama to his immediate right. A lunar surface with a man, or at least the wax figurine of a man, who spanned well over six feet tall. He was dressed in a space suit with a bulbous helmet tilted backwards. He held the European Space Agency flag in an outstretched arm. The massive brass plaque at the base of the diorama proclaimed, "Captain Joel Edmundson CBE, founder of the first human colony on Ross 128 b, AD 2305." Behind the figure of Edmundson loomed the statue of a tall woman, about half a foot taller than Edmundson, also dressed in a space suit but without a helmet. She had a long white face, almost canine, with shoulder-length white hair and gold pads under her eyes and around her neck—an android. Since the Armistice of World War IV, humans rarely encountered androids anymore—it was forbidden for civilians to interact with androids. About the only time one sees an android anymore is in a museum or a diorama like this even though they used to be everywhere in society. Seeing the android made Pierre uneasy.

At the far end of the dome was a light tan burl wood desk with a thick glass top and brushed steel trim. Behind the counter was a young woman with bronze colored hair cut to shoulder length. She was wearing a black pants suit with a bright red patch over her heart. She stepped out from behind the counter and marched towards him. Her stiletto heels tapped against the stone tile.

This was a nice place, a place for nice people. He was wearing a torn and stained plaid work shirt and jeans. Pierre realized how out of place he was. He did not even own nice clothes. This was going to be another embarrassment and failure for him. He had to leave and leave now. He turned around and walked towards the door.

The young woman, however, was faster than she seemed at first glance. She intercepted Pierre at the door. "Doctor Gulet?" she asked.

Pierre was taken aback. He had not heard anyone use his earned title pretty much since he graduated from the University of Swansea. He almost said, *who?*

"I... I... I am," Pierre stuttered.

"I am Tiffany, your intake clerk," said the woman.

"I was expected?"

"Your arrival has been planned." Tiffany frowned at him. "You're late."

"I didn't even know when I was supposed to arrive."

"Poor planning won't make friends here." She pointed at the massive wood desk with one hand. Her other hand was on her hip. "You should have arrived here thirty months ago for the normal intake process. Candidates accepted into the program normally require thirty-six months of training. Your departure has been moved up and your training will be accelerated. And the fact that you have important friends that can pull strings will earn you no more favors."

"My invite letter must have been lost in the mail," said Pierre. "Is it normally this quiet?"

"I would also advise you not to change the subject or deviate from your instructions," she chided him. "Follow me."

Tiffany led Pierre to the back of the geodesic dome. She swiped a keycard and opened the security door. Behind the door was a hallway of glossy white floors, glossy white walls, and glossy white ceilings. The stark white was disorienting. Tiffany opened an office door and stepped inside.

The office had a white glass desk with a terminal and two chairs on opposite sides of the desk. She inserted her key card into a NextCompZ terminal, and her desktop appeared on the screen. She sat at the desk and shook the mouse. A moment of navigating and she pulled up a page that had the intake form and Pierre's records.

"Now, I'm sure that you've thoroughly familiarized yourself with the Arish Colony on Gliese," said Tiffany.

"Is that where I'm being sent?" said Pierre.

"Are you trying to be funny?" Her brow furrowed.

"No." Pierre's ignorance couldn't have been more genuine. "I didn't receive much information."

"Oh, so you're dead weight."

"What?"

"Political exiles, criminals… useless people."

"No, I'm an archaeologist. My presence was requested." He tried to gather his bearings. The whole situation was confusing. Too much contradictory information, too fast. He knew this was his final chance, if he could make some sense of it.

"More useless," she sneered. "Nevertheless, every candidate is subject to a questionnaire prior to formal acceptance. Your suitability and credentials have already been verified, but this is a final screening before training begins."

"Fair enough, but let's assume that I have not received the materials and know nothing about the… what's it called? Gliese?" He paused in the doorway and walked over to the other side of the desk. He gently lowered his backpack to the floor and sat down.

"Don't you watch MoreTube videos?" The prim Tiffany sounded gobsmacked.

"Let's say I've been too engrossed in my work to watch a lot of videos." He rolled his shoulders forward and placed both hands between his knees. He did not like being asked questions, even impersonal questions. He much preferred being the interrogator than the interrogated.

"Completely unorthodox," she complained. "Nothing about this intake has been normal." She flipped past a few screens. "You do know you are about to take a one-way space flight, right?"

"That much I was able to figure out on my own."

"So you do know something." She clicked a few more icons. "You are scheduled to go to an exoplanet known as Gliese 832 c, which orbits a red dwarf star. The planet is 16.16 light years away, and the journey takes twenty-three years."

"Did you say twenty-three years?" Pierre winced. "Do you mean this request for an archaeologist is over sixteen years old?"

"Oh yes," said Tiffany. "Actually, they requested it twenty years ago. When a colony asks for additional personnel and aid, protocol demands they confirm that request every six months. For unusual requests, there is an approval process that takes four years. This ensures they recognize what they ask for is necessary."

"I take it that a faster-than-light drive still has not been invented?"

"Do you know how relativity works?" She flicked a lock of brown hair with the back of her hand.

"I'm an archaeologist. Of course not."

"Okay, our interstellar ships have a maximum velocity of 70% the speed of light." She shook her head. "And we tweaked every law of physics to make that work. However, while the dilated time on board would be a little over 16 years, you'll arrive at Gliese 832 c in about 23 years from our frame of reference."

"If I arrive after about forty years, how do we know they will remember I'm coming?"

"Mission Control sends them a message every few months, reminding them of their requests and pending arrivals." Tiffany pointed at the desk. "It is part of the concord. They receive our messages, and we send them care packages. Every ounce is precious, and dead weight is a sore point. They will receive notice of your pending arrival seven years before you get there, which will be repeated until you *actually* arrive there. It is unlikely they will forget about you."

"Isn't sixteen years a long time to be on a space vessel?"

"You won't be conscious for the trip." Tiffany laughed at him. "We're going to put you into a medically induced coma and pump you with drugs that slow your metabolism to a crawl. You won't require food and water and won't age. And that's all I can tell you without reading you into the program. We can continue or you can walk away now?"

"By all means, read me into the program." Pierre winced at being treated like a child, but it wasn't as if Pierre had anywhere to go. "It all sounds terribly complicated. Why not just freeze the crew?"

"Ever dropped an ice cube into a warm cup of water and heard it crack?"

"Yes…"

"Want that to happen to your brain?"

"Not really." Now, he felt stupid *and* condescended.

"It is probably best to start with the intake interview, and if you have any concerns, you can raise them along the way."

"That's fine."

"What is your age?"

"I'm forty-five."

"You realize this is older than we normally accept?"

"I'm sure it is."

"The admissions committee on rare occasions accepts exceptionally qualified individuals, and you might be one of them." Tiffany sniffed her nose. "I don't necessarily agree with those decisions."

"It must be a great responsibility to have that prerogative at your paygrade." Pierre immediately picked up that Tiffany had no decision-making power and was little more than the night guard who saw herself as the Agency Director.

"You'd probably be surprised to learn that you have not been our oldest candidate or our most qualified." She snapped back to put Pierre in his place.

"You don't say." Pierre thought it best not to antagonize her further. While she might not be able to disqualify him from the program, she could make his life miserable for his short stay in Cagliari.

"Any health problems?"

"Not really."

"Diabetic?"

"No," he said.

"I see you wear glasses," she said. "Why did you never have corrective surgery?"

"It was never a problem."

"We will fix that before you leave. What is your reason for joining the Gliese Colony?"

"Vocational exile," he drolly remarked.

"Political exile," she corrected him.

"Say what?"

"Political exile," she repeated. "Colonization of Gliese is a United Nations initiative, for which the ESA handles the logistics. One hundred and twenty countries have signed on to the project, contributing over 20 trillion US dollars. A perk these countries get in return is the option to send up to one political prisoner to a colony every fifty years without question, without examination, as long as they are not a danger to the colonists and meet health and humanitarian concerns."

"Really?"

"The only countries so far that have exercised this option have been Russia, India, Iran, Taiwan, Canada, and with you, now, Egypt. Most countries never exercise this option, preferring to keep it in reserve."

"I didn't think I rated so high."

"Well, it looks like Egypt's option to send someone was about to expire. I can't think of a better way of letting someone else deal with your trash." Tiffany pushed a lock of hair behind her ear that had fallen out of place. "Are you married?"

"No."

"Impotent?"

"No!" Pierre was shocked how personal this was getting.

"If you are, we will find out," said Tiffany. "Children?"

"Sadly no."

"Averse to having children?" Tiffany interrupted before he could answer. "You need to be aware that if you embark on this mission you agree to a contract to be a colonist. You will be required to couple with a person of the opposite sex for the purpose of producing offspring within a period of two Gliesian solar years, 22 of their months, upon landing upon the planet. Failure to do this is punished by exile, and I hear exile on Gliese is a death sentence. Is that understood?"

"Let me understand this correctly," said Pierre. "Do I have to couple? Or do I have to produce offspring within two years? Because no one can promise the latter."

Tiffany straightened up and clarified. "We mean the former of course. If you are making a good faith effort to produce offspring, that is all the contract requires. But you should know colony officials might require evidence you and your mate are coupling."

"Watch me undergo the sex act?"

Tiffany fidgeted uncomfortably for a moment.

Pierre observed her body language and realized how serious they took this provision of the contract. "I will do my best to produce offspring."

Tiffany cleared her throat. "I'm glad to hear that. Next of kin?"

"None."

"Okay, then in the case of death and accidental dismemberment, notification of your death will be posted for the public in the Daily Ledger."

"Does death and accidental dismemberment occur often?"

"More often than you think," said Tiffany. "Space is a dangerous place. If you didn't realize it, Arish colony on Gliese is an agricultural settlement. Farming accidents and incidents with heavy machinery are common, and medical facilities are limited."

"Ah, I get it. Don't get hurt."

"That would be best." Tiffany clicked on the submit button. She then moved the monitor aside. "You will be going to the Arish colony. Half the people on the transport vessel will be assigned to Basra colony. You will receive detailed colony information at the briefings. At this point, you need to sign the health and confidentiality waiver." She turned the monitor to face Pierre. On the screen was a box for a signature and a pad for a thumbprint scan. "Enter your signature and thumbprint for our records."

Pierre signed his name with his finger and pressed his thumb against the screen. A scan of his thumbprint remained on the screen after he removed his hand. "So what is this contract that I'm signing?"

"You've already signed it," said Tiffany.

"What sort of contract is signed without being seen?"

"The top-secret kind," said Tiffany. "You do not have the security clearance to see the contract you're signing."

"How am I supposed to know the content of what I signed?" This felt like trouble to Pierre, but it was not like he had any other option but blind trust.

Tiffany handed Pierre a half-sheet declassified synopsis that said, if he was to enter the Gliese program, he would have to fulfill the terms of the contract, and disqualification, ejection, resignation, or recall by extradition from the program would carry the maximum penalties allowed by law, not excluding the death penalty. After reading it, Pierre shrugged. "My student loan agreement frankly had scarier language."

"I noticed that you brought a backpack. Would you please place it on the table?" She pointed to the bag at his feet.

Pierre picked up the backpack and placed it on the table. He turned the bag around to face her and unzipped it. The khaki cloth backpack had been well-traveled and suffered from long wear and the distinct odor of mildew. She held the back of her hand up to her nose. She reached and pulled a trash can close to her.

"We practice strict quarantine and weight allowances." She pulled his clothes out of the bag and tossed them directly into the trash. "From now on, you will not be permitted to leave the facility. We cannot have you contract any strange diseases during the observational period. Your weight allowance will be limited to 500 grams. You will only wear the clothes we provide. Your new clothing is designed to meet project specifications. It is light, durable, and creates a sense of unit cohesion."

"A uniform," said Pierre.

"Informal mission wear," she corrected him. She next pulled out the laptop. "Your laptop will be sent to the IT department. They will copy your files into a virtual machine they will set up for you, and you will have full access to all your programs and data. The hardware will be scrapped."

"I paid a thousand quid for that laptop."

Tiffany glanced over at the brushed silver laptop. Raised an eyebrow. Cocked her head and said, "Antiquated junk."

"Don't you at least need my password?"

"Won't be necessary." She then opened the backpack and continued to pull out items. The book pads went directly into the trash.

"I bought those." Pierre protested, waving his arms. He settled back into the chair while she trashed his stuff.

"Heavy items are prohibited," she declared. She then pulled out a large envelope. "What are these?"

"My degrees, certs, transcripts, and identification." He wanted to get up and walk out. But where would he go?

"I'll send these to archiving," said Tiffany, setting them aside. "The documents will be scanned as high resolution, digitally signed electronic documents. The originals will be stored at the ESA vault in Geneva."

"I see." Pierre's back went rigid as a pole. He frowned at her.

"You've got three pounds of documents here," said Tiffany. "You cannot take them with you. Look at the bright side. You'll never need a document notarized ever again. Simply send a copy of the file, not that you'll need any documents where you're going. No call for IDs or any other documents on Gliese."

"Suppose not." He slumped in the chair.

"Toughen up." Tiffany frowned. "Everyone thinks it is so wonderful to be able to travel to an exoplanet, but few will make the sacrifice. Sacrifice hurts. It's supposed to hurt."

"I know. But do I have to like it?"

"And no one said you had to." She removed a small satchel of archaeological tools from the backpack and estimated the weight in her hand. "That you can keep." She dumped the rest of the backpack into the trash. "We're done here. Shall we get you measured and suited up?"

* * *

In the morning, Pierre sat up on the cot attached to the wall of his so-called room. The walls painted in glossy gray closed in on him. There was a small cubby hole for a gray toilet. A tiny closet also painted in glossy gray held his uniforms. Drab, glossy, and diminutive, a place to sleep. A lifeless hole meant to drain the last vestige of personal identity. In a prison context, such accommodations would have been a human rights offense.

The polo shirt and matching chinos he was given was his size according to the tags. The shirt, pants, shoes, belt, and underwear were all in black embroidered with the Gliese program logo. Being skin and bones, Pierre was uncomfortable in more relaxed cuts of clothing, swimming inside them like he was wearing a potato sack.

He heard a knock at the door. When Pierre emerged from his room, he adjusted the collar on his new polo shirt. He could not wait to get out of that room. Tiffany was waiting in the corridor for him.

"You're up early," said Pierre.

Tiffany checked her watch. "Regulations have a 5am assembly time for all personnel." She led the way along the corridor. "You're thirty minutes late."

"You could've told me that. Fortunately, I'm a morning person."

"You aren't going to get far if you need to be told everything." She scowled at him as if he was being an inconvenience. "Did you enjoy your accommodation?"

"A step up from my old apartment." Pierre wanted to deny her even a pinch of sadistic pleasure.

"That will change." She smirked as they rounded the corner into the mess hall.

The otherwise empty room was designed to hold no more than a dozen people. A communal table with a kiosk held a lone plastic covered tray. Pierre's smile dropped.

"This is where you eat twice a day," she said.

His eyebrows raised. "Aren't there nearly a thousand people here training to go to the colonies?"

"All missions are isolated from each other. And each mission gets individual instruction by experts who specialize in its destination world."

"Twice a day?" The prospect of eating every day in what looked like a clinic more than a cafeteria did not inspire him. But he was encouraged by the fact he would only have to do it for twelve weeks.

Tiffany walked over to the kiosk, grabbed the lone tray, and handed it to Pierre. The tray was no larger than a single croissant. Pierre opened the tray. In the center of the white plastic tray was a square blob of blue jelly.

"What is this?" said Pierre.

"That is breakfast, and you could also call it lunch." Tiffany grinned widely and squinted. "Bon appétit."

"You're kidding. This is not food."

"Technically no. It's *nutrition*." She escorted Pierre to one of the tables and they sat down. "While in the training facility, you will be taught to live on subsistence rations. That is Gelatinous Nutrition Konglomerate or GNK. In it you receive all your daily vital nutrients. Every necessary vitamin, mineral, and synthetic protein. You get one ration of this per day."

"You mentioned there would be two meals per day."

"The second consists of food crops being grown right now on Gliese. Are you a vegetarian?"

"No, of course not," he said. "I've lived in Egypt for the past decade. Beef is the only palatable food to eat. Veggies are cooked to mush so you won't get explosive diarrhea for a fortnight."

"Sucks to be you," she declared. "There's no livestock on Gliese. All the *meat* is reconstructed from plant protein."

"Any cannibalism?"

"That's not funny." She scowled at him, exposing her needle teeth. They were the teeth of a child: small, delicate, and immature.

"Got it. Long pig, not on the menu," said Pierre slowly. He was not surprised Tiffany had no sense of humor. "Care to tell me what is on the menu?"

"Beans, barley, and when available leafy green vegetables."

"Sounds delicious." He held the tray to his nose. He smelled the GNK deeply, a rancid stench. His gastric juices welled up. He did all he could to keep from vomiting. He shook his head to keep from dry heaving.

Tiffany frowned and pursed her lips. "This program is voluntary. No one is forcing you to be here."

Pierre squinted at the food then at her. "I guess that's a matter of perspective."

"It is a privilege to go to Gliese. Everyone here wants to be here. But if you want to stay, you had better get with the program."

"I'm convinced," said Pierre. Malcontents and the politically inconvenient have always been shipped off to the stars, a modern Botany Bay. A criticism leveled against the program since its inception two hundred years ago. But now he was in the program and an inconvenient malcontent. And if he wanted to stay in the program, he had to start becoming a team player.

"Why are you here?"

"Did you think I was joking when I said vocational exile? I study ancient civilizations. I am being shipped off to a planet that has never had life let alone a civilization." He folded his arms and slouched in the chair.

Tiffany nodded. "You didn't answer my question. You told me what you did as a profession. But I want to know, *why are you here?* What is it that you are looking for?"

Pierre dropped the attitude and reflected upon her question. He remembered being driven by his parents to achieve, channeled into a profession because he was good at ancient languages. His professors had steered him into taking courses then entire degrees. But no one before had ever asked him what he wanted.

Pierre stroked his chin a moment. "I guess I want to make a great discovery that for once, just once, no one can steal from me."

"Colonists were the first people ever to set foot on an alien planet. They say the facts from the air are different from the facts on the ground. This was never truer than with Gliese." Tiffany rested her elbows on the table. "If you can't find something worthy of discovery in all that, then you are nothing more than dead weight."

"Some way of encouraging people."

"Not my job," she snapped and stuck her middle finger in his face. "My job is to motivate useless prima donnas with Ph.D.s to get with the program." She stood up and straightened out her black slacks. "You're sixty days behind in your classes and briefings. You were accepted on the grounds you would be able to catch up. I'm not so sure that you are up to the challenge." Tiffany shook her head.

"It would be a mistake to doubt my abilities," said Pierre with as much spite and animus as he could muster.

"Eat your GNK, and I'll introduce you to the accelerated curriculum."

Pierre could see Tiffany did not care why he went along with the program, just as long as he did.

CHAPTER THREE

The European Space Agency (ESA) was founded in 1975 with the goal to promote for exclusively peaceful purposes, cooperation among European States in space research and technology and their space applications…. After four and a half centuries, the ESA can boast more successes, including the permanent colonization of exoplanets, than any other space agency in the history of mankind. — **"Presser Celebrating the 450th year of the Founding of the European Space Agency"**

Pierre entered what must have been the smallest classroom he had ever seen. Seats for a dozen people crammed into a fourteen by eighteen-foot room. The tables were arranged in a u-shape, and a lectern stood in the center of the class. Even though the class had not yet started, the other eleven members of the mission were already present and seated. Pierre took the only chair available to him which happened to be closest to the door. This was the first time he met his fellow colonists: five men and six women. The mission instructor was dressed like a mission volunteer except his polo shirt was a burgundy color with the same red mission patch.

"Welcome again to the Tuesday mission briefing," said the man in his early sixties. He was clearly an academic: tall, thin, spectacled with male-pattern baldness. "We have a twelfth member for the mission, Dr. Pierre Gulet. I am Prof. Roger Woodbridge, your mission instructor. I won't introduce you to the others at this time as we only have an hour for the briefing. But this completes the mission complement."

Roger turned on a large video screen to show his slides. With a sweep of the hand, he moved through the slides to his topic for the day, ecology.

"One of the most important issues you will be engaging when exploring Gliese 832 c is the changing ecology," said Roger.

"What do you mean changing?" said Pierre. "Planetary meteorology is not my strong suit. But isn't the atmosphere 12% oxygen and 5% carbon dioxide, and the surface air pressure around 0.93 atmospheres?"

"That was certainly true 200 years ago when the early probes measured the atmosphere. But in 2317, the Intrepid rover found that the methane levels had fluctuated over time."

"I'm sorry," said Pierre. "What are you saying?"

"We accidentally introduced bacteria into the ecosystem. That bacterium has been processing nitrogen bearing minerals into molecular nitrogen. The other kind of bacteria appears to be blue-green algae."

"You mean pond scum?" said Pierre incredulously. "Our gift to the exoplanet was pond scum?" The students in the room laughed.

"You laugh, but it was a gift." Roger stepped to the side of the lectern. He advanced the slides to a chemical cycle and explained, "The cyanobacteria thrived in the Gliese environment which was rich in carbon dioxide, methane, and strong light. Within a little over a century and a half, the atmosphere was transformed into 83% nitrogen, 15% oxygen, and 2% carbon dioxide and methane."

"I may be a bit thick," said Pierre. "But that is still not exactly a comfortable atmosphere. Is everything being done in biodomes?"

"Not exactly. The atmosphere is within safe tolerances. Pressurized domes are now being used as little as possible. Much of the agriculture is being done in the exposed soil outside."

"How?"

"Plants adapt fine to the air. The difficulty is the heat. Temperatures range from -40°C to 64°C. Don't forget your parka and sunscreen."

"I meant people." Pierre waved his hand. "Don't they need space suits to go outside?"

"A little behind, are we?" Roger smirked. "Colonists don't need pressurized suits. When the need arises, the air is rich enough they can use lithium hydroxide rebreathers to strip out the excess CO_2 and pressurize the air to enhance oxygen uptake."

"Thank you," said Pierre.

"And that is why some at mission headquarters are concerned." Roger continued with his main lecture. "The environment of Gliese is changing more rapidly than anyone anticipated. And when an environment changes that fast, the results are unpredictable."

A man in the middle of the classroom raised his hand. He had a chiseled physique and a square chin, hard like stone. A regulation military buzz cut of blonde hair. Not a thread out of place on his uniform. Pierre quickly sized him up as the type who could chew glass. "Terrance Brandt, mission commander," he introduced himself, posturing to the new guy.

"What is it, Terry?" Roger sighed and shook his head, piquing Pierre's interest.

"Hasn't the environmental trend shown that the atmosphere is progressing towards being Earth-like? Why the concern?"

"That is one possibility," said Roger. "But perhaps not the most likely outcome. What if the atmosphere conversion overshoots Earth norms?"

"I don't get it," said Terry. He ran his hand through a brush of thick blonde hair. No way could he have been more than twenty-seven. His body builder frame scarcely squeezed into the issued uniforms, clearly the lead alpha male in the room. Terry must have been a football quarterback who had failed to make it at the state level. Pierre smirked.

"Unintended consequences," said Pierre. "That's what Roger is driving at."

"Why yes," said Roger. He stammered for a moment, taken aback by a student who got what he was saying. "Precisely what I mean. Would you care to elaborate?"

"Certainly," said Pierre. "It's simple. We sent probes to explore the existing Gliese environment and introduced a colony of bacteria instead. This is an unintended consequence as well as a macroscopic application of the Heisenberg Uncertainty Principle, that is, you cannot measure something without affecting its result."

"Show off," piped the ruddy redhead in the corner. The class laughed. "Alicia Stripes, physician and not a pompous ass." She was short and stout, with freckles, and shaped like a barrel. She had hazel eyes, deeply set and unremarkable, and she looked the type that would have struggled with her weight, but exercise and bloody-minded determination kept it in check through an athletic program rivalling any Olympian. Underneath a layer of baby fat was a muscled machine that could put almost any man to shame, except maybe Terry. But unlike Terry who had an unfair natural advantage, for Alicia it was all work.

Pierre laughed weakly along with the class then continued. "The bacteria broke apart the structure of the rock, releasing gases, increasing atmospheric pressure, and making the atmosphere more appropriate for humans. So what did we do? We added agriculture and human settlement to an ecosystem already in constant flux. What are the potential consequences of this activity in an ecosystem that is potentially more fragile than Earth's? That would be difficult to predict."

"Even with all our mathematical modeling?" Terry lifted his nose in the air. "I find that hard to believe. How can we not predict the results? We have artificial intelligences running round the clock, calculating every conceivable mathematical model about the planet."

"Might I remind you, Terry, that mathematical models are only as good as our knowledge of the variables." Roger resumed control over the class. "Dr. Gulet is correct. We cannot necessarily calculate every eventuality. We try. Certainly. But data always has limits. We have assumed a lot about Gliese. The planet seems simple on the surface, a quiescent, empty, lifeless rock, like Mars. But Gliese has secrets. No native bacteria were discovered on Gliese. But the bacteria from Earth found in the soil today is behaving in unexpected ways, epigenetically adapting to the conditions on Gliese."

"Why is that important?" said Terry.

"It's important," said Roger, "since if anyone ever returned to Earth from an exoplanet, they could potentially bring back with them an epigenetic plague for which humanity has no immunity. One reason the Gliese Project is a one-way trip." The eyebrows of the class were raised at the prospect. Roger seemed to expect the reaction of the class, and if he didn't, he never let it show. "Let's say that bacteria creating deadly strains is not an immediate concern. Let's say that the proportion of oxygen to carbon dioxide would continue to rise. And the air pressure and oxygen levels take a saddle curve. What would happen?"

"Sounds good," said Terry. "Never liked wearing rebreathers anyway." He laughed and the class laughed with him.

"Would it be good?" said Roger. He shifted from side to side. His legs trembled a bit. "The nitrogen could decline, and carbon dioxide could rise past 5%, meaning you'd still need rebreathers. But other things might happen. Create a static electric spark with your feet on a carpet and start a fire. The domes are constructed with rubber seals. Those gaskets normally have a lifespan of fifty years but are vulnerable to rubber rot. Steel tools would corrode faster. It could put the colony in jeopardy. Moreover, planetary temperatures could rise, and the planet could start to bake like Venus."

"We are talking about a possibility," said Terry. "Besides, why isn't everything made with alumasteel that never corrodes and is stronger than stainless steel?"

"What if the mining droids or the metallurgy processing units at the colony break down? And you cannot get parts from the home world? Are you going to stop using metal altogether until new parts arrive in forty years? Think about it. Wouldn't you revert to using simpler alloys that can be made on site without advanced technology?"

Terry looked at his notebook and did not respond.

"That is why you are being instructed," the professor chided. "You are being briefed on what the situation is on the planet, *and what challenges you may face.*" He enunciated the last phrase with deliberate emphasis. He looked at the digital clock on the wall. It was a bit past 11am. "Time's up. Your next instructional block is engineering. Pierre, please remain behind for a few minutes."

Pierre stood up to let the others leave the classroom behind him. As they walked by, one of them bumped Pierre's exposed back with his elbow. Pierre winced at the shock lurching forward a bit. He pivoted to see who had hit him. Terry returned a satisfied grin. When the last student filed out, Roger removed his smart card from the projector and stepped towards Pierre.

Roger stretched out his hand. Pierre shook it, a bit surprised.

"So good to have someone like you on the program," said Roger. "I hope you don't mind taking out a few moments to talk."

"Mind?" said Pierre. "Of course not. But won't they miss me in engineering?"

"I wouldn't think so," said the older academic. "Frankly, if it comes to you having to fix a star drive, let's say the mission is then more than doomed."

"Your vote of confidence is reassuring."

"It would be good for you to be there, of course. But you wouldn't be missing much. Besides, the others have been taking those modules for nearly three years. Catching up on thirty months of classes on the architecture of star drives might be challenging even for you."

"Okay." Pierre saw the problem. If the star drive broke down and he was the only one to fix it, they would be quite screwed.

"I wanted to take a moment of your time to orient you a bit on the personalities that you'll be dealing with on the voyage," said Roger.

"Any help would be appreciated."

"I figured it might be." Roger pulled a chair and sat down. "I need to sit. My knees are shot. Too much water polo in my youth." He took a moment and rubbed his knees.

"Take your time, Dr. Woodbridge," said Pierre.

"Just Roger please."

"What is your academic specialization?"

"Ionosphere formation of exoplanetary bodies," said Roger. He had said it so often that it rolled off the tongue with no thought. "You?"

Pierre chuckled and sighed. He said, "Prophetic utterance in Egyptian Middle Kingdom burials."

"Figured it might be something like that," said Roger. "Look, you are a unique asset on this mission. I've read some of your work. You have problem solving skills the others can only dream of having. Leverage those skills. Don't let them disrespect you. Don't be a prig about your education. But never let them look down on you for having one either. Show them your contribution has value."

"I don't want to be a fifth wheel. At the same time, I want to pursue a meaningful line of research."

"That's what I figured." Roger shuffled uncomfortably in the chair. "That's why I wanted to share two things with you before you head to Gliese. First, I noticed that there is some friction between you and Terry."

"We only just met."

"He's taken an instant dislike to you. He's vindictive. And that could present a problem for you."

"How so?"

"He's technically commander of the flight from Moon Orbital to Gliese even though most of your flight time will be in hibernation," said Roger. "Commanders do not like their authority questioned. You one-upped him. He won't ever forget it. What's worse is that, even though he isn't well liked, he is a natural leader."

"I'm not trying to make waves," said Pierre.

"The others will be behind Terry. You need to understand that the eleven began the program together, and you are the outsider. They will be loyal to him."

"Ah..."

"The power dynamics may change once you are on Gliese. Once you are in orbit at the docking station at Gliese, six of you will take a lander to Arish and the other six to Basra. From that point onwards, you'll probably never have to deal with Terry again."

That sounded too good to be true.

Roger continued, "Then James Gardiner, the colony governor, will be in charge. Terry will do his best to make your life miserable for the next twelve weeks. Nevertheless, you will still have to work with him daily."

"I will do my best to get along."

"Just understand what you are in for."

Pierre nodded and paused for a moment. "You said two things. What's the second?"

"About those unintended consequences," said Roger. "That wasn't exactly hypothetical. Something strange is happening on Gliese, damn strange." Roger lowered his voice. "The others don't know it, but there is a problem with the planet. Gardiner said he needed someone with problem-solving skills when he put in your personnel request."

"What kind of problem?"

"I don't know. Gardiner insisted we don't send another biologist, meteorologist, geologist, mineralogist, or physical scientist of any kind."

"What's so significant about that?"

"Gliese does not have a remarkable climate. The planet doesn't even have tectonic plates. You see, Earth gets earthquakes and volcanoes because continental plates rub against each other." Roger rubbed the sides of hands together to explain. "We also have oceans and tides. Gliese has none of that."

"Well, maybe it's those pesky bacteria chipping away at the minerals." Pierre tried to inject a little dry humor into the conversation.

"Don't think so." Roger put his elbows on the table. "Bacteria are capable of incredible feats but not usually on that scale."

"What do you think is going on?" said Pierre.

"With your minor in geology, we're hoping you can tell us."

"That was decades ago in my undergrad," said Pierre. Then it occurred to him: "You've been reading my transcripts." He glared at Roger.

"It was part of your background check."

"Learn anything else important from snooping into my past?" Pierre made a fist and shook it.

Roger nodded. "We learned you are quite the generalist. Your undergrad included a mix of hard sciences and humanities. You have training in a dozen different disciplines from computer science and biochemistry to linguistics. Formal training in thirteen languages."

"Should any of that matter?"

"It so happens ancient Near Eastern specialists have one skill where they excel beyond any other academic."

"Which is?"

"A keen sense of observation," said Roger with the pride of presenting a precious gemstone. He shuffled uncomfortably. "You have a rare skill. We fed your information to the MegaAI sitting in orbit. It concluded that, over the last five years, you have shown extraordinary use of inference and intuition."

"How exactly does a computer measure 'intuition'?" Pierre said with incredulity.

"Well, your use of the word *counterintuitive* is… let's say overrepresented… in your 47 publications. It's found in 85% of your papers." Roger shrugged. "I do have to admit a man with 12 years in the field having 38 single-author publications is impressive. You've been active."

"I like keeping busy."

"And yet, you never landed a tenure track position?"

"Merit is no longer considered when awarding teaching positions," said Pierre. He resented they were talking about why he had failed to break into academia. A sore point for him.

"We realize that too," said Roger. He opened his posture. "Look, our group on Gliese is overrepresented by agricultural specialists, engineers, and scientists. What we would normally call essential staff. They make the food that keeps them fed. They fix things when they break. And they are tough when lives are on the line. They are all skilled and talented, but they have encountered an issue requiring a more nuanced skill set. They are simply not equipped to observe or deduce in ways you are."

"What is it that you want me to do?"

"If we are going to get to the bottom of this and the other puzzles Gliese is throwing at us, we need you to be our investigative contact there."

"I'm not a spy."

"Of course, not. You are an observer." Roger smirked. "When you find the underlying causes of whatever is happening on Gliese, just send us back a report with your findings. That's all we ask."

"My reputation and career are in tatters." Pierre shook his head. Why were they playing this game with him? "I don't like being manipulated. No one is telling me what is going on or what I am really in for on Gliese."

"Some of the administrative staff may know." Roger shrugged.

They know and are keeping it secret? He couldn't believe what he was hearing. Rage welled up inside of him. "I have half a mind to walk out right now." His vocal tone turned to frost.

"It's not so easy to leave." Roger stood. He steadied himself with the chair.

"It's easy. Let me demonstrate. I am here. There is the door. I put one foot in front of the other until I am on the other side of the door. Then repeat until I have exited the facility."

"That won't happen," said Roger.

"Why not?" Pierre shook his fist in Roger's face. Even though he was not a fighter, he was angry enough to deck the man.

"You signed the State Secrets Act as part of your paperwork."

"What are you talking about? The European Space Agency is a civilian organization."

"Which undertakes military contracts for Earth Central Command," said Roger. "When you signed your name and scanned your thumb, your person entered into those state secrets. The dome of this facility also serves as a sniper nest. Should any human asset attempt to leave the facility, those secrets would not travel far."

Pierre's face flushed red. He hated being manipulated and used. And this smacked of both. Worst of all, his hands were tied.

"I would suggest that you look at the bright side," said Roger.

"There's a bright side?"

"Well, you will get to dig in the sand again. Just not on Earth." Roger put his hand on Pierre's shoulder. "Only difference is there are probably more discoveries to be made in one cup of Gliesian dirt than in all of Egypt. Are you up for it?"

"I hate you," said Pierre. His anger subsided with a laugh, and he grinned at the prospect of doing real research again.

"Good, use that hate as motivation," said Roger. "But I'm merely a contractor. I didn't choose you to be here. And CrimsonCloud hypercube MegaAI L002 believes you will be a superior selection over hundreds of thousands of other candidates that wanted into the program."

"I thought I was being exiled by the Republic of Misr, Egypt."

"That too."

"How inspiring," said Pierre. Who didn't want him gone? His expression dropped, becoming as drab as the waiting room décor of a dental office. "Would I still get credit should I discover anything? Or will the MegaAI claim credit for that too?"

"Like all research today, once it passes peer-review and is cleared by the MegaAI, it will be auctioned to the journals, and the highest bidder will publish it. Rest assured, Pierre, we have no interest in stealing your research. We *need* you to front your discoveries. The world still needs to know that human innovators are out there conducting ground-breaking research."

"I don't trust you."

"Don't blame you. But by having you investigate and report back… we have what we want."

"No choice but to press forward?"

"That's thinking clearly," said Roger sternly. "Just know your limits, and you can do your research for a long time to come."

Pierre took the warning for what it was. He was not about to risk this opportunity by rubbing these people the wrong way. Besides, what better opportunity would come along in his lifetime?

The older professor looked at his watch and noticed that it was after noon. "Oh my, you missed the engineering session. It's meal period now. You better hurry off and grab your food ration. Great chat. We'll have to do it again before you blast off."

* * *

The control panel glowed blue against the star field of the cockpit, which cast a deathly pale light into Alicia's face. She wore a headset over her frizzy red hair. A seatbelt harness secured her into a swiveling chair. Backlit buttons and navigation controls covered the interior of the cockpit like a pallid wreath of glowing tiles.

Having grown up on a farm, Alicia had operated combines, tractors, and harvesters, so she gravitated naturally to operating a space-faring vessel. The controls of the transport vessel were not especially complicated. Most of the complex calculations were done by the programmers and engineers at mission control. The glowing buttons of the control panel reminded her of tasteless hard candy pasted to a gray metal board. The controls did little more than compensate in the event the class A navigator was incapacitated or was unable to steer the vessel.

Terry stood behind Alicia. He hovered over her shoulder. She shifted in her seat. Terry had the intellect of a sack of potatoes, and she resented his command. She had served with men like him in the Marine Corps. He was the sort of commander that got people killed. As a physician, Alicia stitched too many broken young men and women whose lives were shattered by the decisions of bad leaders like Terry.

A yellow light flickered on the panel. Alicia typed up the error log. Lines of gray text zoomed across the small computer screen. She paused the screen to read the messages.

"What is it?" said Terry.

"Fault in a cooling system," said Alicia. She continued to read the messages.

"Subsystem?"

"Don't know," she said and continued to read the screen. She shook her head. "Got a system address. Cross referencing."

The ship banked hard to starboard. Terry lurched to the left, hitting his head against the ceiling storage cabinet. A cut opened across his temple. The jerk should have been seat-belted in the command chair instead of lurking over her like a vampire. Blood coursed down his forehead and into his eyes. He wiped away the blood with one sweep of his left sleeve.

"What was that?" said Terry.

"Are you okay?" Alicia turned to see if he was all right.

"The panel." Terry pointed to the panel that lit up red. "Focus on the fucking panel!"

Alicia winced as she absorbed his chide. She regretted giving a damn. She madly pushed buttons to filter output from non-vital subsystems. Even with extraneous systems turned off, text scrolled off the screen faster than she could read it. She paused the screen intermittently and read what she could.

Terry grabbed a handrail and squeezed till his knuckles blanched white. "Well?"

"Everything is throwing errors." Alicia began to panic. "Cooling offline, power offline, computer network down, oxygen recyc offline. No response from the navigator. Fucking everything is down."

"Don't be stupid," said Terry. "It can't all be down. Pinpoint the fault."

She shook her head. She hammered the panel with her fist. "I can't!"

"Who's the general duty officer?"

Alicia looked at the current duty roster on a screen. "Pierre."

"Can't be," said Terry. "Where's Parsons?"

"Parsons is no longer onboard." Alicia shook her head.

"What are you talking about?" Terry stepped over to the intercom. He pressed the button, opening a channel to the entire ship. "Action stations. We've lost helm and navigation control."

Terry left the cockpit and marched to the engineering section through the starboard gangway to the anterior of the ship. The hallway was lined with conduits and pipes. Steam billowed across the metal grated decking. Red emergency lighting lit the hallway, a dying submarine lost in the depths of an ocean abyss.

When Terry arrived on the engineering deck, he found Pierre working on a terminal. Overheating engines hazed the room with smoke. Emergency valves whistled, releasing pressure from the damaged cooling subsystem.

"Where's Parsons?"

"I think he's dead, sir." Pierre hedged his bets, even though he knew Parsons must be dead. "He was on the larboard gangway when the side of the ship blew out."

"Blew out? Can't be," said Terry. "We're flying blind. I need helm and attitude control."

Pierre looked around and saw some control panels at the end of the hall. He ran down the hall of the engine room and read the control panels. He saw the flashing panels and quickly read the indicators. Even with his limited knowledge, he knew the situation was dire.

"Radiation is off the chart." Pierre double-checked the readings. No doubt about it. Radiation saturated the ship, and he was helpless to stop it.

"The engines?"

"All pulse engines are running at full speed. But we can't control them."

"Bleed through," said Terry. "Damn, half the reactor must have melted away. I need navigation control. Now!"

"According to the computer, we are still on course and picking up speed," said Pierre. He thought about the implications for the moment. "Oh, this is bad."

"What?" said Terry.

"Controls are frozen. We are a radioactive missile rocketing straight into Gliese," said Pierre. He recalled the training manual. "According to the emergency manual, we need to separate the engine compartment."

"You can't do that," said Terry. "We'll all die."

"We're dead already." Pierre looked around the maintenance section. "Radiation is at fatal levels. Mission directives say we must jettison the engine and drives." A large relay switch was mounted against the wall, leading to a series of charges designed to separate the engines from the crew quarters. A glass pane covered the relay switch. The protective pane normally retracted automatically when the system received the imminent destruction message; however, the pane was stuck, only partially open. Pierre tried to grasp the pane with his fingers. It refused to budge.

In the corner of his eye, he saw a small fire extinguisher. Pierre grabbed the extinguisher and smashed the glass over the relay switch. He put the extinguisher down and cleared the glass with the sleeve of his jump suit.

"Don't flip that switch," commanded Terry. "The entire crew will be stranded in interstitial space. No rescue mission can reach us this far out."

"Mission directives say if we lose navigation control, radiation exceeds fatal levels, and we are maintaining a trajectory to the destination, we become a clear danger to the Gliese Colony." Pierre shook his head. "We must separate the ship because in minutes everyone on board will be dead."

"We have time to get the systems back online and make repairs." Terry scrambled around the engineering deck looking for any tool he could find.

"There's no allowance for repairs," said Pierre. "Everything is so irradiated we could never go near Gliese."

"Okay, you're right. It needs to be done." Terry stepped up next to Pierre.

Pierre nodded. He paused for a moment and turned towards the relay switch. He looked back at Terry. A red tube of metal smashed into his face. Pierre hit the floor—his head spinning and vision blurred. He saw Terry holding the fire extinguisher standing over him. Terry stepped over Pierre and raised the fire extinguisher to hit him a second time.

A bright white light appeared, and a siren rang. "Simulation complete. All personnel are required to exit the simulator immediately for debriefing." A split-second later, men in yellow jumpsuits rushed into the simulator.

Pierre passed out.

* * *

Pierre woke up. His head was swimming. He was wearing a blue patient gown and was lying in the infirmary at Mission Control. A bright white sheet covered him up to his chest. A bandage was wrapped around his head. He recognized the white paneling that was everywhere in Mission Control. After being captive in the transport vessel simulator a week, he slipped easily into believing he had been aboard a real spaceship.

"You're awake," said Tiffany who was sitting at his bedside.

"What day is it?" said Pierre.

"Wednesday," she said.

"Three days. I must have been hit harder than I thought." Pierre turned over on his side. He tried to get up only to fall back into bed.

"You were sedated. Don't try to get up." Tiffany picked up a computer tablet. "The medic has you under observation for concussion."

"I see." Pierre settled back into bed.

"I need your report from the simulator."

"Didn't you record everything?"

"We record sensors on the vehicle. There's a lot that the video cameras cannot record." She turned on the recorder and pulled up the mission file. "We find the debriefing speaks to factors such as thought processes and motivations."

"Where do you want me to begin?" said Pierre.

"After the critical event, what do you say happened?"

Pierre struggled for a moment to remember what happened. "I was assigned to the duty deck by Parsons who had to do maintenance on the larboard gangway. Twenty-five minutes later the sirens went off. I felt the ship lurch."

"Then what?"

"Terry entered the engine room. I was instructed to check the engine room monitors."

"What were you thinking?"

"My first thought was to rescue Parsons, but the gangway hatch was emergency bolted and Parsons was probably dead." He paused, stuck out his lower lip, nodded for a moment, then continued: "It was hard to not even check if he was alive. But when I checked the course bearing, we were on a direct course towards Gliese."

"What did you do then?"

"Terry said the helm had lost navigation control and half the reactor had melted down. I informed him we were headed for Gliese and radiation had reached lethal levels, sufficient to kill the crew in hours."

"What does that mean?" said Tiffany. Why was she asking? Wasn't she familiar with the program used in the simulation?

"I took it to mean the transport vessel was an imminent threat to the Gliese colonies. Mission directives said we had to jettison the engines from the rest of the ship."

"And was there an incident between you and Commander Brandt?"

"I suppose," said Pierre. There was a long moment of silence.

"Care to elaborate?"

"I broke the safety glass on the relay switch," said Pierre. "I was about to trip the relay and separate the engineering section when Terry tried to stop me from tripping the relay. Tried to stop? He did stop me by cracking my head with a fire extinguisher."

Tiffany frowned and turned her head. Her cheeks wrinkled like brittle leather exposed to the sun.

"What?" he said.

"That does not agree with the official report."

"What official report?"

"The report by Commander Brandt," she said. "As mission commander, his log is the official version of events. His version differs from yours."

"How so?"

"He claims he gave you a direct order. He tried to save the crew and the ship, but you jumped the gun."

"The manual says mission directives override any order given by the commanding officer, and it is impossible to save a crew that is already dead by lethal radiation poisoning."

"You've been reading the operation manuals?" Tiffany raised her eyebrows. "Not everything is written in the manual. The staff has noticed friction between you and Brandt. We are concerned your actions provoked this incident."

"My actions?" said Pierre. "My actions? He beamed me in the head with a fire extinguisher."

"What's the proof that happened? The report states that the commander passively restrained you."

"By restrain you of course mean take a heavy metal tube and bash my skull with it?" Pierre scowled, clenching his fists until they shook. The ESA's martinet bureaucracy always prized pre-vetting more than the truth.

"The official report states your injuries were sustained when the ship simulator banked." Tiffany flipped through the pages of the report on the computer tablet. "It's all right here."

"The report can't be wrong, and Terry can't be a liar." He held up the palm of his hand, sweeping away the unthinkable.

"Watch your words," warned Tiffany. "I know you have not been acculturated as the rest of the crew, so perhaps you don't realize that slandering a mission commander is insubordination. The commander's word is always assumed to be the final word on mission reports. Your report could subject you to disciplinary action."

"Let me revise my report." He shook his head, the hair bristling on the back of his neck. "The official report presents an incomplete view of events."

"That sounds like a better report," said Tiffany.

"The official report may say I was given a direct order, and yet I still followed the mission directive."

"Did you disobey a direct order?"

"No," said Pierre. "I reconciled the order with the context of the situation. Brandt acknowledged the mission directive. Then I was incapacitated by a foreign object. How's that report?"

"That report sounds very truthful."

"I'm certain that *truth* will owe a debt to the future. When can I report back to duty?"

* * *

Roger Woodbridge was sitting at his desk reading some notes, when Pierre stepped into his office. The old professor sat at a prefabricated sheet metal desk painted with gray enamel. He looked up and noticed the slender Frenchman. He nodded and set the electronic note pad on the desk and ushered Pierre forward. Nearly a month had passed since his time on the simulator.

"Pierre," said Roger. "Good of you to drop by. Come on in and close the door."

"What can I do for you?" Pierre stepped inside and closed the door behind him. He was now wearing the official mission BDUs. After wearing the mission polo shirt and chinos for six weeks, Pierre enjoyed

47

the option of the new khaki green clothing. The BDUs were ironically a slender cut, feeling like a second skin, a part of him. He took a seat in a gray metal folding chair.

"I see from your test scores you've made excellent progress. Better than we could have hoped for. You are easily on par with most of the crew members." Roger flipped through the test results. "A few deficiencies, but that's to be expected."

"Thank you, sir," said Pierre.

"You've even managed to pick up the etiquette."

"I feel a *however* in the future of this conversation."

"There is," said Roger. "We noticed you are not working well with Terry Brandt."

"I do all I can to avoid him," said Pierre.

"That's not the same as working with him."

"He beamed me in the head with a fire extinguisher." Pierre pulled his hair back to expose the welt on the side of his head. He shrugged his shoulders.

"That wasn't in the official report."

"I was told reporting the incident would work against my interests."

"Damn officious corruption," said Roger. "Brandt must have powerful friends. Makes sense given his lack of aptitude." He shook his head. "Nothing changes."

"I afford Brandt every courtesy."

"He wants you off the mission. He thinks you challenge his authority. And he is the mission commander."

"Brandt is a walking sack of testosterone." Pierre leaned back in the chair. "He lacks ability, sound judgement, and is insecure. He is a danger to the mission."

"The administration won't change a vetted commander on your say alone." Roger picked up a file folder and looked at the dossier. "Normally, the commander has the final say as to who is on the mission or not."

"I'm not asking for Brandt to be replaced," said Pierre.

"Brandt is not the issue here. You are." Roger slapped the file folder on his desk. "The colony wants someone like you on Gliese. The Egyptian government is adamant it wants you off the planet. Brandt wants you off the mission. Is there anyone you haven't pissed off?"

"Call it a natural talent?" Pierre twiddled his thumbs.

Roger gave a hearty laugh. "Brandt's going to cause you problems in the future. But I don't see how you are interfering with his command. Brandt needs to realize that you're only a passenger. Earth Central Command is slow to adapt to civilian needs, and this situation calls for that distinction. He may also be threatened that a Ph.D. has an equivalent rank to a colonel as far as military courtesies and hierarchy are concerned."

"I'm not part of the hierarchy." Pierre clenched his fist. "I'm a scholar. Why can't they leave me alone to do my research?"

Roger chuckled. "You are exactly what Gliese needs. They might not know what they are asking for, but that's not my problem. I am denying Brandt's request."

"Isn't that going to be a problem?"

"It could be," said Roger. "That is why I'm going to confine you to quarters during remainder of your training. Consider yourself under house arrest until your arrival on Gliese."

"At least I can catch up on my reading," said Pierre. "And here I was worried that I was going to be punished."

CHAPTER FOUR

Despite our advances in electronics, robotics, and even interstellar space flight, one area of space transit has remained essentially unchanged for four hundred years, and that is our ability to escape Earth's gravity. Even today, we still depend upon large amounts of high-energy rocket propellant to get a person (or cargo) into orbit. While space mining operations have defrayed some of the need for moving all raw materials from the gravity well of Earth into orbit, humans generally begin their lives and training on Earth. — **"The Current State of the Space Flight Arts" by the Congress of NASA Design Engineers**

A week before the launch, the colonists were driven in a bus to the liftoff site and sequestered for last-minute quarantine and preparation. The previous 36 hours had been a whirlwind of drills, most of which Pierre was thankful to have avoided through his house arrest. Each team member went through a series of final paperwork and video interviews, which unfortunately even Pierre could not avoid—training was optional it seems, but paperwork was not. And the actual morning of the launch was no different, replete with protocol.

It was 4am when the centralized alarm woke everyone. Pierre pulled the gray blanket aside and stood up. He walked out into the hallway in nothing but his underwear and an undershirt, covered loosely with a cornflower blue medical dressing gown. All his other clothing had been confiscated the night before. He walked across the smooth concrete floor as his body heat was being sucked out of the soles of his bare feet. There was nowhere to go other than the mess where they were corralled upon waking up.

As he entered with the others, he was given a small eight-ounce glass of liquid nutrition. They were prohibited from eating the night before and immediately prior to launch. The liquid nutrition was only meant to take the edge off their hunger and thirst and contained an anti-nausea drug to prevent vomiting during the flight.

Pierre grabbed the plastic cup and took a drink of the artificial orange having all the charm of dental fluoride. The concoction, gritty and drab, lacked the zing of true citrus. If he had known this would be the last taste of anything citrus, he would have availed himself of more real oranges. Regardless, it no longer mattered. This was his last earthbound meal, if he could call it that, and his next taste of solid food would be on an alien world.

Even though the team of twelve had assembled in the mess, nobody was talking. The tension and remorse in the room was palpable. The mess had large panel windows, and everyone could see the launch vehicle in the distance. Robots loaded large cargo crates into the launcher. Their last view of Earth was a never-ending field of asphalt fading to the horizon.

Everyone knew once the booster rockets fired the biggest worry would be mechanical failure. As with any rocket, the slightest physical flaw in materials or workmanship would be magnified by the extreme stress upon the vehicle.

Once orbit was achieved, machines would take over. A MegaAI, a sentient supercomputer orbiting the earth, directed all space-faring traffic. The launch vehicle from earth would automatically attach to an orbital docking station where the transport vessel loomed as a large, pointed needle within the metal frame of the shipyard. The transport vessel, a space liner capable of traveling at 70% the speed of light, was parked in the giant docking lattice of the station, waiting for its crew and cargo destined for Gliese. The transport had arrived a little over a week ago, and meanwhile heavy-duty class E structural repair robots and the smaller, nimbler class F maintenance droids scoured the ship, looking for every loose bolt and faulty system that needed to be replaced.

Once the launcher arrived at the docking station, robust class D service robots, resembling forklifts with legs, would move the cargo and pods with hibernating passengers into the transport ship. Then the onboard class A navigator, another sentient AI computer, would steer the liner's voyage to Gliese. Once arriving at the end of the voyage, the transport vessel would dock at the opposing orbital station, and a landing vehicle would place their fates into the hands of the humans on Gliese twenty-three years from now.

If tensions between the crew were not bad enough, the idea they were human cargo did not help. Having a mechanical AI in control of all navigation and the destinies of the crew vanquished any need for communication. Everything was automatic and nobody would even be aware of the trip except during reentry to the planet. If they were lucky, they wouldn't have to speak to each other again for the rest of the trip.

Pierre saw Commander Terry across the mess hall. He wore the same underwear and gown as everyone else, indignant and brooding in the corner. The lack of clothing or official uniform made him seem smaller and less imposing. But Pierre knew he would make up for it with posturing, bluster, and bullying.

The bronze-haired Tiffany entered the mess hall. She wore an official project jumpsuit and a surgical mask, more to isolate herself from the crew to prevent any chance of disease being transmitted to Gliese. She stood near the doorway to the complex with a clipboard in hand.

She cleared her throat and bellowed, "Here are your parting instructions. When I finish, you will exit out the anterior door." She pointed to the passage at the opposite end of the hall. "You will make your way down the hall to the launch clearance zone. There each of you will be placed in your assigned sleep pods. A medical technician will then connect you to the IV drip that will slow all your body functions to a minimal metabolic state. A second monitor will be attached, dosing your metabolic supplements over the trip. When you reach the orbital docking platform above Gliese, the monitors will restore your metabolic activity. Your pods will be loaded into a landing vehicle, and you will make the descent to Gliese.

"Once on the surface of Gliese, you will become subject to the laws of your Gliese colony and under the authority of the local governor notwithstanding any contractual obligation you may have with the European Space Agency. That is all. Proceed now to the sleep pods. Safe travels."

Tiffany returned to the command-and-control complex.

Pierre downed the final gulp of his liquid nutrition. The astringent orange powder abraded his teeth like sand. He stood up, rinsed his mouth with saliva, and walked out to the clearance zone. He arrived at his assigned sleep pod. A two-piece metallic silver environmental suit waited for him, hanging outside of the pod. The top, which only covered the head and torso, left his arms and trunk exposed. The suit served to supply oxygen and monitor vital signs. It was not designed to protect from the harsh conditions of outer space.

Pierre dropped the dressing gown and put the environmental suit over his head and pulled it over until it stopped around his diaphragm. He wriggled into the arm holes through the tight elastic belts, exposing his arms above the elbow. He hoped these pods were going to be heated as it would be unseemly to arrive with frostbitten fingers. He put on the accompanying set of pants that was held up by elastic cinches at the waist and ankles. The shiny, all-silver suit made him feel like a wrapped baking potato ready for the oven. The helmet of the suit was practical, not the oversized astronaut's balloon helmet, but a slender breathing apparatus with a port on the back which plugged into an air valve on the headrest.

He pushed some plastic sheets aside and crawled inside the pod. He eased back until he felt the vibration of the helmet snap into the air feed. Immediately, he realized his movements were restricted. His head was locked in place, and he was only going where the pod was taking him.

He could hear his pulse in his ears. Pierre played simple mental games to pass the time and suppress his heart rate. He would have loved to say all this worked, but that would have been lying to himself. If anything, these tricks caused his heart to pound more.

The medical technicians trotted their way down the line of pods. A faint rustle of plastic followed by the clopping of boots on concrete. The wait seemed to be forever, but the boots grew ever louder. His last memories of Earth were going to be from the inside of a modular plastic crate. But he realized, if someone wanted to put a couple of bullets into him and deliver a lifeless corpse to Gliese, there was nothing he could do about it. He was completely helpless within the pod and at the mercy of the operators.

The boots got loud. A pause for a moment, and the blurred shadow of a figure appeared through the plastic sheets covering the pod entrance. The plastic sheet rustled and was swept aside by a white figure, a man in a glaring white biohazard suit leaned into the pod. The man reflected all the light from the pod back into Pierre's face.

"Have you been exposed to any illness in the past thirty days?" said the man in the white.

"No," said Pierre somewhat startled. "How would I be? I haven't left the facility."

"Have to ask anyway. You may have met with family who could've been sick, and you might be ill now."

"I have no family or friends," Pierre said dryly.

"I'll forgo the rest of the questions then." The man clearly conceded to whom he was speaking and got directly to business. He withdrew the intravenous apparatus from the arm of the pod. "Okay, the way this works is this armband straps around your bicep. It has sixty needles. Each needle delivers the same feed. The number of needles mitigate against one needle failing or becoming blocked. This prevents you from starving to death mid-flight. However, this is going to hurt."

The technician grabbed Pierre's right arm and stretched it out. He slapped the arm band on and strapped it tight. The needles drove deep into his bicep. Pierre bit his lip as the needles dug into his arm. The pain seared, a thousand small hot pokers. The technician flipped a switch on the pod—anesthetic coursed into Pierre's veins.

"That should be better," said the technician. "The pod has been programmed to supply you with all your needs until you arrive at Gliese. Right now, you are receiving a sedative. After launch, the flow will deliver a drug that induces coma and a second drug that slows your metabolism. You'll also receive small amounts of nutrition to sustain you."

"I understand." Even though Pierre could feel the sedative flow into his veins, he could not overcome the claustrophobia gripping him. It was much smaller and more cramped than the tombs he was accustomed to.

"I thought you would," the tech said. He checked the pod to make sure everything was tight. "Okay, it looks like you're good to go. I wish you much fortune in a new world."

Pierre noted he was not wished *best of luck* or similar platitude. Luck was verboten. The agency had done its best to eliminate random factors so luck would be minimized. Yet, bad fortune was ever in the back of Pierre's mind after all he was still not clear why Gliese would want someone of his skills.

The technician disappeared behind the veil of plastic never to be seen again. Pierre could hear the commotion from other pods. As the technicians worked the line, the sounds grew more muffled. Two hours passed and the port had become almost silent, the silence of a graveyard, ominous and foreboding. The sedative distorted the passage of time, making the passage of his final minutes on earth a blur. Then movement.

Pierre braced himself. Not that he needed to since he was well-strapped into the pod. The pod was picked up. He rocked side to side as his pod jostled. A slight tremor and hum indicated this was a vehicle like a forklift but was probably a class D heavy loader robot. While having humans drive you around was always subject to accidents, robots made less errors although their errors had a higher risk of fatality. Robots like that were not permitted to be in contact with the civilian population, but the launch site was a joint project of Earth Central Command and the European Space Agency, which as a para-military installation allowed the use of mechanicals.

Minutes later the tremor in the capsule changed from the rough timbre of a reciprocating engine to a lower pitch hum of electric motors. He was no longer being moved in the forward direction by an operator but sideways to the left. A conveyor system of some kind was moving him. Humans were no longer involved in the process of his journey. Machines had taken over, and his last contact with true "earthlings" was with a nameless, faceless computer who did its job with parameterized care and efficiency.

Things moved quickly. He heard himself loaded into the launch vehicle, and his pod locked in place. A video screen opened inside his helmet. The resolution was not the best. But it did not have to be. It was meant for single use.

A vignette of images from planet Earth was on display. A rocky beach faded to a forest, fading into a waterfall, fading into a glacier with all the heart and soul of a discount airline promo video. The vignette was accompanied by oddly inappropriate soft music followed by a text message, "Farewell, from Mother Earth." The words trickled off with a distinct echo. This was followed by the soft melancholy of elevator music.

Pierre, being an Egyptologist, snorted at the message. In the Egyptian world view, earth was not female at all. The gender roles of earth and sky were reversed in ancient Egypt. The sky was represented by the goddess Nut while the earth was the male god Geb. It always blew student's minds when they were told not every culture considered the earth female, and the Egyptians were a notable exception to this rule.

Twenty minutes later all the moving around from the conveyor system stopped. A pressure door swung closed over the entrance of the pod. Pierre assumed he had been loaded into the launch vehicle. No return from this point. While the rest of the journey to Gliese was out of his control, accidents could still happen. The launch vehicle could explode. The interstellar transport ship could lose its atmosphere. The pod could malfunction. Any number of problems could spell disaster, and he would not even be aware he had died in the process.

The walls of the pod shuddered from the giant engines of the launch vehicle. Everything shook. Then a silence, followed by tremendous pressure forced him into his seat. The pressure on Pierre's frame went from pressing to oppressing, overwhelming him. Pierre found it difficult to breathe amid the g-forces. The respirator responded according to the pressure, and somehow he continued to breathe despite feeling all his ribs were crushed.

Nine minutes of discomfort gave way to release. He no longer felt as though he was under pressure. Now, the sensation was quite the opposite. If he had not been strapped in the pod, he would have floated away. The experience of weightlessness left him nauseous. However, not being allowed any solid food prior to liftoff, there was little risk of him messing up his pod. Pierre figured it would be about four hours before arriving at the transport vessel. At that point, the voyage to Gliese would begin in earnest.

Pierre yawned, and then the scent of roses. At first the smell was faint, but it grew stronger. He breathed in the fragrance realizing it was a kind of anesthetic and at the same time his intravenous starting pumping chemicals to slow down his metabolism. He did not have long to reflect upon this, however, as his eyes became heavy. And soon he could no longer force himself to remain conscious. His last lingering thought bothered him. When he woke up, what would he find?

* * *

A sudden rocking forced Pierre awake. Red light bathed his pod. A chubby redheaded woman, Alicia, swept aside the plastic covering. She reached inside and ripped off Pierre's armband. She grabbed him by the lapels and yanked him to his feet. His forehead hit the front of the environmental suit helmet. Pierre staggered out of the pod. The helmet he was wearing bounced on the floor. He was dizzy but found himself in a corridor of metal beams.

"Get your shit together," chided Alicia. "The transport is breaking up."

"How can that be?" said Pierre.

"There's been an explosion. The navigator has been destroyed. We can't enter the docking station."

"Where's Terry?"

"The asshole was the first to abandon ship."

"What? Why?" The gangway trembled beneath Pierre's feet. The girders groaned and creaked as they twisted from the torsional strain. A bang sounded from a breaking bolt.

"Why you think?" she said. "Time for us to go."

She grabbed the shoulder of Pierre's shiny flight suit and pushed him down the hallway. She moved him towards the escape capsule. Escape capsules were less ideal than proper landing vessels, but if you had to abandon the cargo and save human life, an escape capsule was better than flapping your arms in the vacuum of space.

"The others?" said Pierre. There were twelve of them.

"Gone." An electronic component let off a spark overhead. And even though it didn't touch her, she yelped. "Four dead. Six escaped."

"They left us for dead?"

Alicia looked side to side to ascertain situational awareness. Seconds mattered and making the wrong choice would cost both their lives. Pierre was delirious from the aftereffects of the metabolism inhibiting drugs. She must have been awake a lot longer than him and was in a better mental state.

"Pretty much sums it up," said Alicia. "Looks like Terry used this happy accident to rid himself of undesirables."

"I always hated that man," admitted Pierre.

"Not my fav either."

The two of them made it to a pressure door. Alicia pressed a button to unlock the door and cranked a lever to open it. She threw Pierre inside the reentry capsule. Pierre fell against the end of the capsule, landing seated on the floor in a crumpled mess. She took a deep breath and entered the capsule after him. She closed the pressure door then pushed the eject button.

Thrusters fired and the capsule heaved away from the transport. Within seconds, they found themselves weightless as the capsule drifted from the transport vessel. They watched as the transport broke up. Flaming plasma burst from the sections of the hull until the entire ship blew apart in a fiery conflagration of explosive decompression. A shock wave hit the capsule, and both occupants were unsettled for a moment.

Pierre was still blurry as the metabolism drugs wore off. But it dawned on him how close he was to biting it. He looked out the side portal window. The transport vessel sheered in half. The sections broke apart, bursts of fire shooting from the seams of the vessel. The great interstellar liner cracked and peeled apart like a boiled egg. Its skin sloughed off in sections blown off into distant space while the core of the vessel burned brightly. He felt his pulse slow to a normal rate.

"I'm grateful you got me to a capsule," he finally said. It was going to be five or six hours until they made planetfall. A long time for uncomfortable silence and awkward conversation.

"Don't take me saving you as a sign I'm attracted to you or anything," said Alicia with a stammer.

Where did that come from? Sure, Pierre expected awkward conversation. But that? Really?

"Never said you were." Sweat dripped down the side of Pierre's face. It was uncomfortably warm. He looked around for some kind of relief. Was it unreasonable to think people saved each other just on the grounds of human decency?

"Have you thought about the 22-month rule?" Alicia floated away to the back of the capsule into the darkest corner. Perspiration beaded on her ruddy skin. She was breathing heavily.

"Not really." Pierre had been so wrapped up in catching up for the mission he had given no thought to the future. "Two years seems like forever."

"A matter of perspective, I suppose. The 22-month rule is essential to being fully accepted as a member of the colony. Don't you want to be accepted by the colonists?"

Pierre shrugged. "Making babies is a duty of every colonist, at least that's what we're told." He rolled his eyes and scrunched up his face. Propaganda made his stomach churn even if for a noble reason.

"I figure there's no more than forty single people in the colony."

Pierre looked at the chronometer. It was going to be hours before they landed on the planet's surface. A lot of time for this conversation to grow ever more awkward.

"Is that a concern?" said Pierre.

"Native born are not subject to the 22-month rule."

"Afraid they have the advantage of time," Pierre smirked. "But your natural charm will carry you."

"I would never be interested in someone like you," she sneered.

Was that called for? Pierre looked away. He was not going to press the matter.

Alicia paused to think about what she said. "It's not personal."

"That sounded pretty damn personal."

"It's not your fault God didn't give you what is needed to please a woman."

That sounded even more personal. Pierre thought about what she said, and then the meaning occurred to him. "And if you don't find someone with the right stuff?"

"Then take one for the team. Perhaps, a sham marriage." Alicia did not seem bothered by the duplicity of her statement.

"Good luck with that," Pierre said. "Since I don't even know why I'm here, mating games are not even on my mind."

"Were you always so focused on your work?"

"People betray you but work never does." Pierre had spent many sleepless nights thinking about past relationships, and what went wrong. Events kept looping in his thoughts. Introspective and wasted energy, energy better used towards moving his research forward.

"Sounds like denial," said Alicia.

"Some deny, others drift from one relationship to the next, some crawl into a bottle, some work," said Pierre. "All of us find ways to deal with personal pain." It was all about forgetting or at least drifting into a fog where at least the pain became confused. Work at least came with the advantage of fatigue. And within fatigue, he could find sleep while the ghosts of his past went off to war. "Speaking of work, what was your assignment on Gliese supposed to be?"

Alicia chuckled at Pierre then grinned. "I am a physician."

"How does a physician get into the space program?"

"Even colonists need to be patched up from time to time."

"Is that it?" said Pierre probing deeper.

"I know how to patch wounds when the bullets are flying," said Alicia. "Basra doesn't have a physician."

Pierre eased back. Why did she save him? Why did she defy the mission commander when he winnowed out the undesirables?

"It looks like we're getting close to re-entry," said Pierre. He touched the port window with his finger. The icy cold of space crept through the plastoglass. If Terry tried to kill him up here, when would he try to finish the job?

Alicia floated towards him in the weightlessness of space and pointed out the portal down to the planet. "Terry ejected early so he could rendezvous with Basra. It looks like you and me are going to land near Arish. The two colonies are separated by half a planet."

"Will half a planet be enough to separate us?"

"If forgiveness extends from the east to the west, then it is enough." Alicia settled back into a seat in the pod. She strapped herself in readying for reentry. It was going to be a rough landing. However, this is what they had trained for.

The capsule shook violently as it kissed the atmosphere. Both passengers braced for penetration. Reentry was going to be a rough ride, but the ESA promised, if they followed their procedures, the capsule would get them to their destination. That said, it would not be without having them reflect upon the most distressing moments of their lives.

CHAPTER FIVE

Gliese 832 is a red dwarf star located in the constellation of Grus, approximately 16.16 light years from Earth. The star is orbited by one habitable exoplanet (Gliese 832 c). Gliese 832 c is an earth-type rocky planet of 5.4 earth masses. The orbit of the planet is 370 days. The planet has two moons. The first colony, Arish, was established in AD 2329. Analysts currently believe the Arish colony to have a population of about 300, and a fertility rate of 0.3 children per woman. The colony in its last survival assessment was categorized as CRITICALLY ENDANGERED. — **"The Exoplanet Factbook (2465 edition)" by the Central Intelligence Agency**

Crank, crank, crank and the door opened. A flash flooded the capsule with blinding white light. Strange air swept through the cabin. Pierre's head was still swirling from the hard landing. The escape pod had rolled down an embankment after it lost its footing at the crest of the hill.

Pierre breathed in and he could tell the gaseous mixture was different. The new atmosphere felt stifling, thinner than he was used to. The transport vessel had adapted his physiology to the new atmosphere, but his psychology desired having unlimited oxygen on demand.

An old man opened the door and peered in. His skin was like aged paper, wrinkled and fragile. He had a large handle-bar moustache, and his complexion was darkly tanned. He was mostly bald except for a crown of gray hair completely sun bleached. He was at least in his late seventies, possibly older.

"I'm James Gardiner," said the old man. "Governor of Arish. You have arrived on Gliese 832 c."

Gardiner reached into the capsule, grabbed Pierre's hand, and yanked him out. The old man had surprising grip strength, remarkably strong for a man of his age. Even though he was the governor, this was a man who didn't mind physical labor. Pierre's foot touched the planet's surface and immediately he fell forward and sprawled face first across the sand. His silver flight suit ripped at the knees.

Pierre took a few deep breaths and tried to orient himself to his new surroundings. He looked around and saw nothing but yellow sand dunes, indistinguishable from the myriad in Egypt, Libya, and Sudan. Wasn't this all supposed to be a terraformed forest?

After a moment to collect his breath, he stood up and turned around. Six colonists helped Alicia out of the capsule with more gentleness than they had shown him. Pierre looked beyond the capsule to the basin floor, parched and dry. A brisk wind picked up the reddish dust that whirled around and danced in the midday sun. Pierre looked up. The primary star illuminating the planet was about twice the size of Earth's sun, but redder and cooler. What Gliese's star lacked in heat, it made up for in size. But it still burned hot enough to make the heat of the day oppressive.

Once the colonists pulled Alicia out of the capsule, Gardiner turned to Pierre. "We need to get back to the colony. A rover is waiting for us at the top of the ridge." He turned and walked up the incline.

"What about the others?" asked Pierre.

"They touched down near Basra." Gardiner without effort trucked up the hill. "You will be inducted into Arish."

"I was assigned to Basra," protested Alicia.

"Not going to happen," said Gardiner. "We requested the services of Dr. Gulet, so he's staying put. We aren't about to trek 8,000 miles to relocate one person. Sorry, but Arish is going to be your new home."

Alicia looked around and sniffed. "What a home."

* * *

Gardiner drove the rover to his office. Pierre stepped out of the vehicle. His back was stiff from the drive. The office was little more than a destroyed transport vessel, the ruined vestiges of a post-apocalyptic nightmare. The salvaged wreckage of a two-hundred-year-old colony star liner repurposed into administrative offices.

When they reached the fuselage of the old spaceship, Gardiner opened the door and allowed Pierre and Alicia to step inside ahead of him. It was the manners of a bygone era. After the three were inside, Gardiner led them down a gangway and to an office, then closed the door behind him. He wrenched the latch on the door to seal it shut. The air outside was perfectly breathable, so the hatch must have served other purposes: security, protection, dust control. Everything was grimy, an inevitability of living on the cusp of a desert. Gardiner's office was covered in a thick film of iron oxide. Mildew was pungent in the air.

The room was two dozen feet in all directions. Hard to believe this was the room where the first twenty colonists lived for the first decade. Mining, manufacturing, and agricultural equipment had been hermetically sealed in crates. The job of the first colonists was to unpack the equipment sent years before and get it running. They were technicians, not scientists.

"Have a seat," said Gardiner. He walked behind his desk, finely crafted from native woods that once grew locally. The wood was stained and lacquered, which bloomed into a burnt umber patina. His desk was cluttered with broken components, souvenirs, and knickknacks, crowded and tipping over like ships falling off the edge of the world. The two colonists sat in a pair of musty old chrome and fabric chairs. The cushions blew plumes of dust out the sides.

The old man blew the dust out of three metal cups and wiped them with a dirty rag. He opened a drawer and pulled out a bottle of clear alcohol. He poured three cups. Vapor from the liquor overpowered the room. He grabbed the cups and glided around his desk so that he was between the two newbies and the front of his desk. He leaned against the desk as he offered the two a drink.

"I don't drink," said Alicia. She held her hand up.

"Start," said Gardiner. Her refusal brought a menacing quality out of the man. He was not going to tolerate complaints or wilting flowers. "Everyone drinks. The local whisky is all we make. And you won't last long if you don't drink."

Alicia reluctantly took the cup.

Pierre sipped from his cup. His mouth was on fire. High octane. He did everything in his power not to cough. He was a whisky drinker, but this stuff was strong. "56% alcohol by volume?"

Gardiner laughed and slammed his down in a single shot. "You've got a keen palette. 58%." He circled his desk and sat and poured another shot. "I'm going to be straight with you recruits. This tub I was expecting." He pointed at Pierre. "I have a dossier for him."

Gardiner continued, "But I don't have any paperwork for you. What are you useful for?" He glowered at Alicia.

She stammered for a moment, seemingly at a loss for words. "I am a physician, and I can fix things in a pinch."

"Oh, you can, can ya?" Gardiner leaned back in his chair. "I got a doc and fixers. I need special skills. Basra needs medics because they keep losing people. Here people stay alive. I plan on keeping it that way. Understood?"

"Yes, sir," Alicia and Pierre instantly replied. They both stood up and to attention, straight as boards.

"Miss Stripes, report to the mess hall. Mapes will find you something to do," ordered Gardiner. They set their cups on the desk. Pierre turned towards the door. "Pierre!"

Pierre froze in his tracks.

"Sit your ass back down! I'm not done with you."

Pierre swallowed hard. His mouth was dry, and he now regretted not finishing his drink. He turned back and sat back down.

Alicia looked over her shoulder at the two men, her face flushed red. Her smile fell, and she heaved a sigh. This was not what she was hoping for.

Alicia opened the latch and stepped out of the office. She caught a glimpse of Pierre, then closed the hatch and heard the latch lock from the other side.

Hiss!

She turned abruptly. Two feet away, on the raised walkway, a cobra reared—its hood flared and ready to strike. Alicia froze as the snake eyed her. Her heart thumped, trying to break free from her chest. If the cobra wanted to strike, Alicia could do little to stop it. It was fast, venomous, and way too close. Instead, it turned ninety degrees and struck into the shadows. It had a large rat in its mouth and slithered off the walkway, descending to its den underneath the bulkheads of the wreckage. She had not even noticed how rapidly her disappointment switched to terror.

"They don't care about you, you know?" A girl in a pink t-shirt and gray clam-diggers loitered by the gangway exit. She must have been around twelve years old and covered in dust and grime with long stringy brown hair and ocean blue eyes. "Cobras are more interested in rats. They're rat control."

Alicia stepped away from the office door, no longer feeling cornered, and approached the young girl. "So a bit like cats?"

"What's a cat?" The girl gave her a blank look. "I'm here to bring you to the mess hall. A wind's blowing out there. Not quite a storm, but not knowing the layout could get you lost."

"I'd appreciate that," said Alicia with some relief. "I'm Alicia. What's your name?"

"Melissa," she said. "Follow my lead." The little girl forcefully grabbed Alicia's hand and pulled her out of the wreckage into the blowing sand. Melissa stomped like a soldier, marching against the strength of the wind. Alicia covered her eyes to protect herself from the stinging grains of sand. Melissa made no attempt to cover her eyes but squinted instead. As they trudged through the wind, Alicia stumbled behind.

A shiny metal dome loomed over the rest of the colony. Melissa cranked open the latch and swung Alicia inside. The young girl followed and closed the hatch behind them. Alicia was covered in sand, and her red hair was blown into a tangled mess that stood over her. Melissa looked the same as she had before, the same dirty child.

The mess hall was a massive hut of communal tables and benches. Even though it held little more than three hundred people, the building was by far the largest on the planet. It was also the first building constructed on the colony, which allowed the colonists to move out of the lander module and into more spacious accommodations. Eventually, as private accommodations, labs, and offices were built, the dome was converted into a communal eating and meeting area. In the far corner, a small group of people were preparing food at a cooking station. The cooking station was a line of metal serving stations, cutting boards, and stoves, protected by plastoglass shields.

"Over there." Melissa took the lead to the cooking station.

Behind the counter was a chubby woman in her late fifties with salt and pepper gray hair tied up in a yellow cloth wrapped around her head. She wore basic blue work scrubs and a white chef's apron like she stepped out of a Vermeer painting then aged thirty years.

"How's the weather out there?" the older woman asked Melissa.

"A slight breeze," replied Melissa with a shrug.

"Are you Mapes?" Alicia was still a bit stunned by her trip through the camp.

"You must be the one Gardiner sent over. Wish he'd stop calling me Mapes. Miserable old goat. The name is Madi." She scowled, picked up an electronic pad, and checked the instant message. "Yes, you're Alicia Stripes. Gardiner sends me anyone he doesn't know what to do with like I'm some sort of employment counselor. For Love's sake, I'm trying to get dinner done before three hundred workers flood in and eat us out of house and home."

Madi took off her apron and laid it on the counter. She shouted at the young girl, "Melissa! Don't you have work to do?"

"Yes, ma'am," droned Melissa. She scurried away and headed to the back of the hut where connecting tunnels led to other parts of the complex.

Madi exited the cooking station and hobbled over to Alicia. She pressed into Alicia's personal space, peering into each of Alicia's eyes. Alicia did not flinch. The older women grabbed each of Alicia's hands, checked the backs, then turned them over to examine the palms. She let both palms go and stepped back.

"You're ex-military," declared Madi. Disappointment rang in her voice.

"Marine veteran," said Alicia. "Worked my way to Army Medical Corp battalion surgeon, O-3."

"Can you cook for an army?"

"No."

"Then what can you do?"

Alicia swallowed hard remembering how the last time she was asked that it did not go so well. "I am a physician, and I fix things."

"Okay, I think terraforming can use you. Have a seat, and Habib will be here shortly to collect you." Madi returned to the cooking station, typed a message in her electronic pad, put on her apron, and resumed cooking.

Twenty minutes later, a short Arabic man in a green jumpsuit arrived from the far side of the mess hall.

"Follow me," he said to Alicia. The two walked to a staircase, descending to an underground passage. The claustrophobic tunnels reminded Alicia of a rabbit warren. The passage branched towards the living spaces of Arish's complex. They arrived at a staircase and ascended it into a large mechanical shop.

Habib reached into a cubby hole and pulled out a fresh green jumpsuit. "Your new uniform. There's a secluded spot other side of that wall. You can get changed there."

Alicia accepted the uniform, went behind the wall to change, and in a few minutes returned wearing coveralls. "What do I do with the space suit?"

"Trash it," said Habib. "The environment is too harsh for space suits. Simply won't last."

Alicia shrugged and tossed the spacesuit into an open bin.

"Fine. In case you didn't already know, this is terraforming," said Habib. "We are responsible for turning Gliese into a verdant paradise."

Was he joking? She had just waded through a sandstorm.

"Yeah, I know." Habib sighed. "Something's gone wrong. The big-brained guys are trying to figure it out."

"What do you mean?"

"The scatterbugs are not working," said Habib.

"Scatterbugs?" Alicia raised an eyebrow.

He picked a brushed brass metal orb with eight spider-like mechanical legs. Habib handled the small robot from the rear like a crabber. The front two legs had long caliper shaped claws, and a big plastoglass lens covered the ocular sensor in the front. "This is a scatterbug. The technology used to terraform every colony world. At Basra, they managed to build a 1000 km^2 jungle using these technological marvels. But for some reason, our scatterbugs are no longer doing their job."

"How so?" said Alicia.

"They're broken. Wish we knew why." Habib shook his head in defeat. "We've traced every line of code, tested the contents of thousands of bioreactors. They worked for a century, and now they don't."

"So what are we doing about it?"

"We have been ordered to maintain the technology. So, when the level eight engineers figure out the problem, they can deploy it quickly. What is your technical rating?"

"Level five."

"Well, your job only requires level four."

"And what is the job?"

"Maintenance and repair of the terraforming equipment."

"I see."

"It sounds impressive, but we have only two jobs: maintaining the scatterbugs and keeping the mother machine running. We also fix anything else that breaks. When we arrived at Gliese, there was no life. No animals, no plants, no bacteria. The problem for plants from earth is there's no bacteria in the soil to fix nitrogen from the air.

"Scatterbugs are solar powered, autonomous robots that wander the surface and spread soil bacteria. They respond to simple commands, have a high-resolution imaging camera, and can relay information about what they encounter. They can seed about a half a kilometer per day."

"Doesn't seem much."

"We've produced enough scatterbugs to terraform 700 square kilometers," said Habib. He cleared his throat. "Each scatterbug has a built-in bioreactor. They rest at night to conserve energy and allow their bioreactors to recharge with bacteria. During the day, they power back up, seed the ground, and interact with other scatterbugs."

"Interact?"

"Scatterbugs coordinate so they don't cover the same territory. And they can detect a malfunctioning unit and call it in. When we get the call, we go out, pick up the broken bugs, and bring them back for servicing. Ninety percent of the work we do is bug servicing. It's boring, repetitive, and necessary."

"And the rest of the job?"

"The rest is feeding the mother machine with raw materials so that it continues making scatterbugs. Once a day, mother sends a report of her raw ingredient requirements, and we play fetch. Mostly refined metals and hydrocarbons from mineral processing. The internals of the mother are just a set of glorified class F robots, which process the raw components and assemble the bugs."

"What if we don't have a particular component?"

"Fortunately, the mother is capable of using a wide range of substitutes," said Habib. "The Gliesian soil is rich in silica, iron, and aluminum oxides. So that's become the principal components for our bugs. But if ever needed, it can create bugs out of plastic, ceramic, or even laminates made from seashells. The mother has many redundant systems and is capable of self-repair. If a part breaks, the mother manufactures a replacement and the discard is ejected from the machine, which we toss. Repair through replacement parts. Rarely, the mother might request a specialized part it cannot replicate. If that happens, the level eight engineers will take care of that. So all we need to do is feed the mother and scatterbug repair."

* * *

Pierre had not finished his whisky. Gardiner winced and reopened the bottle and refilled Pierre's glass, signaling him to resume drinking. The way Gardiner had dismissed Alicia left a sour taste in Pierre's mouth—abrupt and curt, a crime boss demeaning a subordinate. But Pierre picked up the glass and drank.

"Do you know the history of the Gliese colonies?" Gardiner corked the bottle—the rubber-like stopper squeaked.

Pierre shook his head. He was embarrassed that, as a historian, he had not even bothered to ask about the local history.

"I am its tenth governor." Gardiner sat and folded his arms. "The colony was founded 152 years ago. Do you know what we found on this planet when we first arrived?"

"Nothing?" guessed Pierre, cautiously recalling the mission briefings.

"Nothing," repeated Gardiner. He stretched an arm towards Pierre and pounded the desk with his fist. "Absolutely nothing. Not a bird. Not an insect. No animals. No plants. No fungus or even a single native bacterium. Not even any fossils. There has never been life on Gliese."

"Okay." Pierre acknowledged Gardiner's words. Agreement was another matter. He was all too aware of the tenuous value of sweeping claims based upon an absence of evidence. He reflexively raised a single eyebrow. Inferences from a lack of data could lead one to personal humiliation, but for the scholar eager to discredit the common knowledge of the day it remained a dangerous siren call ever beckoning the academic to crash into the shoals of remorseless facts. To claim something did not exist was a badge worn on the sleeves of academics worldly enough to see it all and sufficiently unwise to think one can know it all. Basing opinions only upon positive evidence was like navigating by the stars, a discipline requiring persistent and eternal vigilance.

Gardiner picked up a deactivated scatterbug from the corner of his desk and held it up. "You know what this is?"

Pierre looked at it for a moment. "A type-4 class V terraforming robot with what looks like a steel case."

"Essentially correct. We call them *scatterbugs*. We disperse scatterbugs to terraform a region and occasionally send out other bugs to update the existing bugs or to recall old ones needing retirement."

Pierre squinted. The sand dunes they drove past to arrive at the colony were unmistakably desert. "You're telling me what I saw outside is terraformed?"

"What you see out there is what this planet was like when we first arrived," said Gardiner. "The original colonists reported and filmed sandstorms, raging heat, and—God help us—the winters. Cold like you cannot possibly believe. 60 degrees below zero, and that's not even accounting for the wind chill. Sand so cold it sticks to your skin and burns with frostbite."

"That's cold." Despite the heat, Pierre shivered instinctively. He didn't like the cold. He was an Egyptologist. He liked desert, hot and dry. Cold was not doing it for him.

"What you've got to look forward to come February and March," said Gardiner. He poured another whisky and leaned back into the chair. "The first colonists arrived with type-1 terraforming equipment. Within a few weeks, they had the equipment up and running. The mother churned out bugs, and the bugs were set to work in the agricultural dome and then released out into the wild."

"And?"

Gardiner raised his eyebrows, sighed, and looked inside his cup. He shrugged. "Success." He took a sip of his drink. "The soil responded well to the scatterbugs. A few months later viable soil. A couple months after that, seeds from the genetic bank germinated. Every plant we tried was a success. Two years, the first saplings. Forty years later, the entire area around our colony was a lush jungle. Our colony was the paragon of terraforming success."

"Didn't see much jungle out there."

"We settled here eight decades before Basra and were leagues ahead of them in terraformation." Gardiner sighed and nodded. "Then about seventy years ago, the desert started reclaiming the jungle. We sent out more scatterbugs. Nothing helped. Nothing we did stopped the decline. Simply put, the scatterbugs stopped working."

The governor downed the rest of his drink and held the cup in his hand. He looked at the bottom of the empty cup, full of disappointment. The shiny metal reflected a mangled reflection back at him. Was he seeking hope in a distorted visage that would bless him with instant insight like a medium looking into tea leaves? "The colony is on the brink of collapse. Basra has more injuries and fatalities than we do, but we haven't had a live birth in the last five years. Now, the crops in the agricultural dome are dying off. We'll be out of food in eighteen months. People are going to get desperate and will start taking dangerous risks."

"If Basra is doing so much better, why don't we go there?" Pierre shrugged. The solution to him seemed obvious.

"Can't," said Gardiner. "Their governor has declared a quarantine. Until we locate the source of the die-off, no one is allowed near their colony. They have the green light to defend themselves from contagion. Earth is willing to lose one colony rather than risk both."

"Any guesses as to the source?" Pierre ground his teeth together. He was irked Earth knew about this and didn't tell him.

"Our best guess is the scatterbugs." Gardiner poured his fourth drink. "We've brought in agricultural specialists, meteorologists, chemists, biologists, microbiologists, physicists, physicians, and engineers. The experts have come up empty."

Gardiner continued. "When you meet them, don't let them deter you from your mission. They claim they're researching the problem, but we don't have another decade to let them putter. Speed is of the essence; otherwise, hundreds will die."

"You must have been thinking ahead to request someone like me forty years ago."

"The key to running a colony is forward thinking," said Gardiner, "If you have a crisis, you don't only order what you think you need, but what you think you might need when you exhaust every avenue. However, to be honest, I never expected everyone else to fail before you."

Pierre deflated as the implications of that settled in. It's never a good feeling to be the option of last resort. "Sounds like you have all the experts you could need. Many more qualified for this than me. If they couldn't find the cause, I don't know what I could do."

"I've left out a detail," admitted Gardiner. "About forty years ago, a type-3 scatterbug returned with something. The bug's reset and return function allowed it to come back with a sample. This is what made me think to call in an ancient Near Eastern specialist." Gardiner opened a safe under his desk and pulled out a small opaque sample box. He slid it across the desk towards Pierre. "Open it."

Pierre reached forward and pulled the box towards him. The dust ground against the surface of the desk like sandpaper. He picked up the box and opened the cover with a pop. A small object was inside wrapped in cotton insulation. Pierre pulled the insulation aside to expose a thin ceramic shard. The shard was about four by seven centimeters. The porcelain surface was ivory with a deep black writing. The ceramic was surprisingly thin like the broken glass shard of a Christmas tree bauble. He noted some symbols that could have been recognizable as Egyptian.

Pierre grimaced. "It's not Egyptian," he said matter of fact.

"We figured that," said Gardiner. "But it seems like a pictographic language. Who better to help us than an Egyptologist or perhaps one familiar with Mayan or Luwian?"

Pierre realized at that moment he was not dealing with a fool. Gardiner clearly did his homework.

"I will need to have a look at where this was found." Pierre put the lid back on the sample box. He placed the object gently back onto the desk.

"That's going to be a problem," said Gardiner. "The geolocation data got scrambled. When we found the bug, it was delirious but was holding the shard in a climbing claw. That's our only clue."

"Strange," said Pierre. "How do we know it's not someone fooling around?"

Gardiner squinted. "I have zero tolerance for time wasters and dead weight. Those who don't pull their own soon find themselves outside." On a planet like Gliese, with no native plants or animals, life outside of the protection of the collective would be hard, nasty, and short.

"You haven't given me much to go on," said Pierre.

"Earth Central Command said you were up to the task," said Gardiner. "I hope they weren't exaggerating."

On earth Pierre had been a washout. His excavations at Naqada had been a complete disaster. Evidently, Earth had neglected to tell Gardiner about his professional reputation just as they had neglected to tell him about the blight. A double-blind wall. And Pierre could not be completely honest with them—not during a time of crisis. The colonists were only a heartbeat from turning into homicidal maniacs.

"The only lead I have for the shard is the scatterbugs," said Pierre. "Who knows the most about the bugs?"

"Brian Johnson, our level 8 engineer, knows the mother and the overall network architecture. But no one knows the bugs better than Habib."

"That's where I will start," said Pierre. He stood up eager to begin the hunt.

"One small matter," said Gardiner. "Most of the colonists believe we are alone on this planet. I want it to stay that way unless there's solid evidence to the contrary. Keep any half-baked theories and wild rumors under wraps."

"What do I tell them if they ask what I'm doing?"

"Tell them you are investigating the blight, and any further questions need to be directed to me. That should deter needless curiosity."

* * *

After meeting with Gardiner, Pierre secured a change of clothing, opting for the regulation BDUs, and went to the colony mess. He was hungry and wanted his first square meal in what felt like days but was in reality over two decades. He had not been conscious during his flight from Earth, but that didn't make him any less hungry right now. It was 2pm local time, and the commissary was gearing down from lunch. Most of the trays only contained scraps, but he was happy for anything. Madi and Melissa leaned over their prep stations, their backs turned to him.

"Can I get something to eat?" said Pierre to Madi. Melissa perked up.

"I'll take care of this," said Madi to Melissa. "Get back to your prep." The young girl resumed her focus upon the cutting board in front of her. Madi ambled up to the serving station. She was covered head to toe in flour even though she wore an apron and held a rolling pin in her hand. "Melissa might be young, but like everyone here, she's capable."

"I can see," said Pierre.

"What can I do for you? Or are you here to waste my time?"

Pierre did not like Madi's tone. He was in for a cold welcome. "I'd like a meal, please."

"Mess hours are from 6am to 9am, 11am to 2pm, and 4pm to 7pm."

"It's 2:05pm."

"You're late, and rules are rules."

"Hey," said Pierre, "I spent my morning with Gardiner. It's not my fault I couldn't work you into his schedule."

"Should've thought about that before someone like you volunteered for a place like this." Madi set the rolling pin on the counter of the serving station. Then she proceeded to pick up every food tray and dump it into the trash in front of Pierre. She even shook the waste bin to rub it in he was not going to get any food from her.

"I didn't volunteer," said Pierre. "I was drafted exactly because I have skills none of you have." He turned around, nearly colliding into three large men who stood behind him.

"What's this?" said the man in the middle. He was a giant bronze statue of a man that stepped off a plinth in front of a civic building. His massive frame towered over Pierre. "Dead weight I see."

"Care to explain?" Pierre's heart sank. But, if he was going to find the answer to the problems here on Gliese, he needed to navigate precarious social situations just like this.

"Dead weight are the useless people Earth sends us," said the large man. "Military advisors, social scientists, liberal arts majors... archaeologists."

"Oh?" His vocal pitch inflected up.

"You have no skills, and you come here expecting special treatment. Needless weight better served by extra cargo. A useless mouth to feed."

"Interesting. Because I thought I was here to save your helpless skins." Pierre stared his opponent in the face. Pierre saw the flash of the fist. A shovel-punch walloped Pierre on the head. Pierre spun around clockwise, crashing into the serving station. He was half-blind from the impact of the punch, and he groped for anything he could get his hands on. He felt the handle of something and completed the circle of the turn and struck the other man in the head with what was in hand. The Goliath of a man collapsed to the floor like a rag doll. Pierre panted for a moment. Blood ran down the left side of his face and in his hand a rolling pin. Pierre looked at the rolling pin and said, "And that's why grandpa feared grandma."

The other two men went white in shock over the speed of what happened. One ran away, leaving the other one alone with Pierre looking crazed and ready to snap. The second man held up his hands and stepped back slowly. Pierre grabbed him by the collar and raised the rolling pin.

"Who was that?" Pierre nodded towards the blubbering mess on the floor, crumpled up like last week's dirty laundry.

"That's Luke Bronson." The second man was terrified by Pierre's demeanor. Pierre grabbed his collar and raised the rolling pin ready to strike. "An agricultural scientist... from Ohio. Arrived about four years ago."

"And you?" said Pierre.

"Hans Poul." The man was a rugged Scandinavian in his forties with aqua aura blue eyes, blonde hair, and a cleft chin covered in a four-day stubble. Hans trembled before Pierre even though he was two inches taller.

"What do you do?" asked Pierre.

"Engineer, sir."

"What kind of engineer?"

"Environmental."

"Do you know computer programming?"

Hans nodded rapidly. Pierre released him.

"You owe me for not caving in your skull," said Pierre, pointing the rolling pin at Hans. "And I will collect that favor." He had heard that in a movie he couldn't recall, but he was going to need a programmer. Already a plan was coming together in his punch-drunk mind, but he also knew sometimes those were the best plans.

Hans scurried away in the same direction the other guy had gone. Luke was out cold on the floor. Pierre could see he was still breathing, so he did not bother calling for help. He looked over at the food prep station. Madi and Melissa were motionless, staring at him.

"I'm still hungry!" yelled Pierre. "I'm very, very grumpy when... I ... am ... hungry!"

The two women turned about and scrambled around the kitchen, looking for something to prepare. Pierre grabbed a clump of paper napkins from a dispenser and sat on one of the mess hall benches. He straddled the bench so one leg was on one side of the bench under the table and the other was outside. A large cut oozed blood from his forehead. He wiped his face with the napkins. The wound probably wouldn't require stitches, but it was marginal. He soaked six napkins with his own blood by the time Madi arrived with a plate of hot synthesized protein cordon blue and a side of baked beans—she even supplied a bottle of ketchup.

"Thank you," said Pierre. He picked up a fork and knife and began tearing into the food. He was not fooled for a moment he was eating anything other than simulated animal protein, a crime against the culinary arts. The food had the mouth feel of mashed cardboard, and it was doubtful he was going to finish the meal. But the mouthfuls provided some badly needed sustenance.

Luke moaned beside his foot. Pierre kicked Luke hard in the head. He was going to eat his first meal on Gliese in peace without having to deal with local politics.

This was a good lesson for him. The colony had serious problems that had accumulated over decades, problems more cultural than scientific or technological. They needed him over all the scientists, engineers, and experts since the real problem with Arish was not the terraforming blight.

Yes, terraforming was a problem but a symptom of a bigger problem. The colonists could no longer engage problems with any other approach than what they were comfortable using. And problems like these were best solved by *out-of-the-box* thinking.

CHAPTER SIX

Since the 20th Century, the world has endured a repetitive cycle of global war. With each world war, mankind has looked in hindsight and been horrified by the destruction leveled by the hands of men. Some technologies and practices were so evil and inhumane they would never again be used on the battlefield or in acts of terror. WWI saw the end of poison gas, WWII forever vilified genocide and eugenics, WWIII finally brought an end to nuclear weapons, and WWIV banned the use of androids and cybernetic organisms in warfare and in civil society. — **"Articles of the Armistice: A Commentary"**

Pierre knocked on the door of Brian's office. There was no answer. But Pierre knew Brian was inside, so he let himself in. Brian was looking at blueprints printed on translucent plastic sheets and technical specs on electronic pads. The office was festooned with the layout for every complex system on the colony.

"I didn't say you could come in." Brian said in the driest, most unwelcoming tone he could manage. He did not meet Pierre's eye contact. Brian was a large white guy in his early fifties, showing all the classic signs of middle age: thinning hairline, a pot belly, and a double chin. Back on earth he would have been middle management, padding a nest towards an early retirement with a golden parachute. He wore a gray explorer's collared shirt akin to casual colonist wear and BDU pants with the draw string untied. Despite his size, his shirt hung loosely as if he had recently lost about ten pounds.

"And I didn't ask," said Pierre. "I need information on planetary surveys."

"I need a hot bath, a real filet mignon, and a bottle of Champagne."

"I wasn't dragged here 16 light years to cater to your wants," said Pierre. Brian fidgeted at his desk. "How about getting me those planetary surveys?"

"If I had a mainframe server, I could tell you where to find that. But we don't."

"Why don't you have a centralized server?" said Pierre.

"It broke," Brian said, shrugging his shoulders.

"What do you mean it broke?"

"What didn't you understand? We didn't get it replaced."

"Does that mean you have no planetary surveys from the satellites?"

"No," said Brian. "Everything on Arish is stored on computers scattered around the facility. But no one has ordered us a data librarian because they're sending us dead weight archaeologists."

"So you have satellite surveys but can't find them?" Pierre slumped his head and sighed out loud. "That sounds like dereliction."

"Anything else?" Brian looked at Pierre with glassy eyes.

"Yeah, ground penetrating radar."

"What about it?"

Pierre huffed, annoyed at Brian's obstruction. "Do you have any GPR surveys?"

"No."

"Isn't GPR standard equipment on any mission to an exoplanet?"

"It died 80 years ago," said Brian.

"What?" said Pierre incredulously.

"You heard me right. Our unit malfunctioned 80 years ago, and we never requisitioned a replacement."

"Going to blame that on dead weight too?"

"Do you know how often parts fail?"

"Do you?" Pierre sensed this was more than a failure to replace. Dereliction of duty was becoming a common theme.

"Enough to know we can't waste valuable shipping space on secondary equipment. Have you any idea how many water bypass valves we need to replace in a year? I'd rather earth ship us the replacement valves to maintain the supply in life-giving water than to replace a GPR we'll never use or even a useless archaeologist."

"Thankfully, I don't need to prove my worth to you." Pierre glowered at Brian.

"Colonies run on practical skills and the ability to get along."

"And you're *getting along* all the way to your utter destruction."

Brian blanched white for a moment. He could not say anything for a few seconds.

Pierre sucked in a long breath. "You haven't been told, have you?"

"Told what? If things go belly-up here, there's always Basra."

Pierre's eyes dilated into saucers. He blinked. He couldn't believe what he was hearing. "Okay… got to go." With that, Pierre hurried out of Brian's office. The problems were systemic with the organization, but no one person could deal with them alone. This had to be addressed from the top on down, which meant he needed a come-to-Jesus meeting with Gardiner himself.

* * *

"Thank you for seeing me," said Pierre. The Geiger counter was still on Gardiner's desk, clicking away at the elevated background radiation.

"What is it?" Gardiner shuffled the papers before him.

Pierre put both hands on Gardiner's desk. Gardiner stopped and looked up at Pierre.

"Excellent," said Pierre. "I've got your attention. You're not a fool, so I'm not going to treat you like a fool. And I would appreciate it if you don't waste my time."

"Time is of the essence," said Gardiner.

"Too bad no one around here seems to know that."

Gardiner sucked a breath in and remained silent.

"My last 24 hours have been a rude awakening of denial, professional hedge protection, physical violence, and if I may quote 'that's the way we've always done it,'" said Pierre. "Sir, the terraforming issues of this colony pale in comparison to the internal systemic problems. And I regret to say these problems point to derelict management at the top."

"How dare you?" Gardiner slammed his fists on the desk. He was on his feet, ready for a fight.

"How dare you drag people this far from home to fix what could be solved by a change in management?" Pierre paused. "But the situation is not unsalvageable. I am here to help, and to help you specifically, *if you will listen.*"

Gardiner eased back behind his desk, swallowing his pent-up rage. He sat in his chair and poured a drink. The whisky splashed onto his desk as he poured from the bottle.

"You called me here to fix your problems," said Pierre. "You thought your problems were entirely external. But the internal problems are far more serious to the long-term survival of the colony. You may think this colony had 18 months by way of food. But if you don't address the cultural problems, this colony may have no more than 9 months. I've seen a breakdown in unit cohesion and infighting, and the formation of factions and gangs. Your team has lost its way." Pierre pointed to the still fresh wound on his forehead.

"One of my men?" said Gardiner.

"Did I have that when you pulled me out of the escape pod?" Pierre looked Gardiner cold in the eye. "You were there. You should know."

"Who?"

"Is it not more important to ask *what did it*?"

"Not following." Gardiner took a sip of his drink.

"Better to ask what caused an incident than who was responsible," said Pierre.

"What does that mean?"

"No one except you and me has a complete picture of what's happening. Complacency is rife because everyone thinks Basra is our backup plan. They don't know about their hostility towards us. Moreover, since this colony is stacked with science and engineering types, elitism and scientism have become entrenched. In other words, I can't work in this environment because I am facing intense resistance to my presence."

"I see." Gardiner slumped in his chair. "A few others know the situation. Madi knows as does Pavel Urbanovich."

"Oh great, so your cook and your gardener know. I know you don't want to incite panic. But if you don't make the real situation public knowledge now, you will not only have panic, but you will have riots, gang violence, and civil war."

Gardiner leaned forward and placed both elbows on his desk. He stroked his handlebar moustache. "I can only tell them if there is a beacon of hope. Are you that hope? Do you have a plan?"

"I do," said Pierre. "It's a plan with a good methodology. But I cannot guarantee the plan will succeed. If it doesn't, this colony will have probably run out of options at that point."

"So… they will hang us together." Gardiner laughed at the prospect of being lynched. Pierre was less amused at being lynched. He was, however, satisfied by the thought that anyone who lynched him would soon starve to death.

"I would rather it not come to that. But let's say I believe that our external problems can be narrowed down, identified, and may be eliminated through a methodical systematic approach. That is, if I have access to the facilities, information, and *cooperation* of the colony's personnel."

"Okay," said Gardiner. "I will call a staff meeting tomorrow morning to handle this."

* * *

True to his words, Gardiner called an early morning staff meeting. It was 5am, and the room was packed with senior staff. While Pierre was a morning person, many in the crowd were not. Some were noticeably groggy.

There were more people than chairs, and those who had not arrived early stood at the edge of the room. Among them was Pierre who, to his knowledge, was not senior staff but was invited anyway. Pierre could feel eyes all over the room glaring at him: Brian, the chief engineer; Madi, head of food services; Luke, agricultural scientist whose head was wrapped in bandages. He also caught a glimpse of an Arabic man he assumed was Habib.

Brian got up out of his seat and walked to Pierre. No one dared take his empty seat. Everyone watched as he approached Pierre.

"This meeting is for senior staff," said Brian. Pierre had not noticed until now how much bigger Brian was to him, outweighing him by at least a hundred pounds. Brian's gray explorer shirt was stained with yellow mustard from last night's dinner.

"So?" Pierre shrugged his shoulders. Meetings were a waste of time. If he had not been told to be present, he would be happily off doing something more productive.

Brian looked to both sides. "I see *only* senior staff here."

"Why don't you take it up with Gardiner? That would be fun to watch."

Brian scowled and nodded his head. He spat on Pierre. Pierre brushed off his lapel with the back of his hand. "After you've been spit on by a camel, no one can insult you with saliva although a camel has better breath."

Brian pursed his lips and bobbed his head. He walked back to his seat. Brian grinned and looked to his comrades. Those sitting beside him laughed and patted him on the shoulders.

Gardiner walked into the room. A couple of military police followed in after him, securing the door behind him. He marched to the front of the room. Gardiner curled his moustache between his fingers, taking a moment to scan the room. He laid out some papers on the lectern. He raised his chin and waited until the room grew silent.

"Distressing matters have come to my attention," said Gardiner. "Do I have your attention?"

"Yes, Governor," everyone shouted in perfect military sync. A colony governor had the absolute power of life and death, and everyone knew it.

"Straight up!" said the Governor. He frowned and looked over the crowd again. "We are eighteen months away from colony collapse. The greenhouse crops will feed us for the next twelve months, but that's if we eat all the seed. Based on current projections, mass fatalities from starvation will take place in twenty months."

A deathly hush settled over the group.

"And you can forget any aid from Basra. They have orders to shoot us on sight. Let me be emphatic, *no help is coming from Basra.*"

Disquiet swept across the senior staff. Gardiner hit his fist on the lectern, bringing the group back to silence. Below his eye, his cheek trembled. He squinted and stared at the staff like a wild tiger.

"We've fucked about for fifty years!" Gardiner yelled at the crowd. "Bandaged it by bringing in scientists of every kind. Time's up. Your solutions, where are they? Anyone holding out?"

Gardiner waited for a second to see if anyone would respond to his challenge. No one did. "And that is the least of our problems. Reports of hazing and factionalism have crossed my desk… even incidents of violence. Do none of you understand? We're on our own. No help from Earth. No help from Basra.

"Reductionist scientific thinking was never going to solve our problem." A murmur washed over the crowd. "Most of you were trained as scientists, mathematicians, engineers. And I recognize your contribution to the colony. But our problem transcends reductionist thinking."

Gardiner looked into the eyes of each person. They turned their glance away from him. At the back of the room, Pierre looked right back at him. Gardiner had bet the farm on him. He was down to his last chip, rolling the dice, and snake eyes meant death for the colony.

"In World War Two, ancient Near Eastern specialists were enlisted as intelligence agents to vet high altitude photographs," said Gardiner. He did everything to prevent his voice from wavering, but even so some cracking could not be avoided. "They identified the first V2 rockets from nothing more than shadows on the ground of launch pads. Scientists, engineers, and military officers were unable to see what those men saw."

Gardiner was getting into it. "Five centuries of the humanities taking a back seat to the STEM fields has been to our detriment. But when push comes to shove, we must marshal those greater faculties of our humanity to save us. Reductionist thinking has brought us to the brink of disaster. That is why, forty years ago, I personally requested a non-scientist, a man learned in lateral thinking to navigate the crisis. Dr. Pierre Gulet is an expert in his field, and I am appointing him Deputy Governor of the Crisis."

Gardiner paused. This decision was not going to be popular even though the position had no real power according to the colony charter. But Gardiner no longer had the luxury of playing to popularity. Colony survival was on the line. The unease from the crowd was palpable. They hated Pierre. Rumors of Pierre had spread through the colony like a disease, months before Pierre ever touched down on Gliese.

"Make no mistake. If I need to, I will invoke martial law. If any man or women gets between Gulet and his mission to fix this crisis, I will not hesitate to exercise my authority. Clear?" The colony charter gave the governor practically unlimited power to ensure the colony's survival; however, any position below that was taken far less seriously. And truth be told, while the title of deputy governor sounded impressive, it was a gesture, a vote of confidence, but effectively a figurehead role.

"Yes governor, sir!" shouted everyone in the room.

Gardiner gathered his papers and walked down the aisle. Before exiting, he turned to Pierre. He worked his way to Pierre. He took his hand and shook it. He hugged Pierre and whispered in his ear: "Bring results or you'll be the first I lynch."

* * *

Pierre opened the door to the agriculture domes. A wall of humidity hit him in the face. He stepped into a hallway leading to work rooms and greenhouses. He closed the door behind him. Computer banks and sensor units, a botany lab, and a selection of gardening tools were inside rooms, forking off from the entry hall. A long table of seedlings in propagation trays divided the hall down the center. Pierre exited the hallway and entered the farming tracts. The greenhouses, arranged in rows, spanned acres. Agricultural workers lingered in the distance.

Pierre looked at the plants at his feet. He kneeled and held a leaf in his hand. The plant was some sort of bean. The stalk was little more than six inches tall with yellow, sickly leaves. He was no gardener, but he recognized the plant was underperforming.

Pierre stood up, and one of the men in the distance walked towards him.

"This area is *off* limits," said the man with a strong Russian accent. He was dressed in a white biohazard suit. Even his boots were covered in white fabric. Eyes dark and recessed glowered with disapproval. His concrete jaw was covered with a tightly trimmed beard. His bristle hair and sandpaper skin were abrasive enough to scrub pots.

"Pavel Urbanovich?" said Pierre.

The stout Russian man leaned back to eye Pierre. "Deputy… governor."

"I have some questions."

"You would. This area is *off* limits to regular colony personnel."

"Your bean plants, are they all that bad?"

Pavel winced. "Afraid so."

"Was it always like this?"

"According to the logs, the greenhouses were the first ground to be terraformed," said the Russian. "Where you are standing used to be an orangery."

"1.0 version scatterbugs?"

"Yes, we still have 1.0 scatterbugs in the greenhouses." Pavel paused for a moment. "You wouldn't know it now. Outside the domes used to be trees, grasslands, crops. You can still see the occasional stump out there. The desert… the desert clawed it all back. And now the blight is here… in our greenhouses."

"If scatterbugs made the soil fertile, shouldn't it stay fertile as long as you supplement it with nutrients and fertilizers?" said Pierre. "I can see you are growing nitrogen-fixing plants. That should help."

"It should. No one can explain why we can't keep the soil fertile." Pavel pointed at the plants at his feet. "Look at these plants. It's as if they are completely malnourished."

"They're not?" One hardly needed to be a gardener to see these plants were on death's doorstep.

"It's not for lack of synthetic fertilizers, seeded ground bacteria, or nitrogen fixing crops. The plants can't pick up nutrients, and we don't know why."

Pierre stooped and grabbed a handful of soil. He pressed the soil between his fingers. The lumps of soil were held together by chains of earth-sourced bacteria. The dirt crumbled between his fingers. Something was working, but something else was going badly wrong.

"Is the soil in the greenhouse isolated from the outside?"

"The dome only covers and maintains temperature, humidity, and atmosphere. The soil is the same we find elsewhere on Gliese." Pavel cocked his head. "But it's not as if this soil hasn't been fertile in the past. We know the soil is capable of supporting life."

"Don't take this the wrong way. I'm just trying to collect the facts," said Pierre. "The walls don't isolate the soil?"

"Colony infrastructure is only designed to keep the humans comfortable. No need to isolate the soil since Gliese has no native life. The native soil was completely sterile prior to our arrival."

"So do you plant directly into soil? Or do you start plants in a nursery first?" Pierre recalled the seedlings he saw in the hallway.

"We nursery first."

"And how do the nursery plants do?"

"Fine. The soil we use for planting and the nursery is the same."

"Is it the same?"

"I just said it was." Pavel shuffled uncomfortably. "Dirt is dirt. Take soil. Put it in a pot. Grow a seed. Take the seedlings and plant them into the native soil from which I took the soil to germinate the seedling."

"I'm afraid you're missing the point." Pierre stood up and looked out across the greenhouse. "You grew the seedlings in small pots continuously washed top-down with water. Most of their nutrients came from the seed cotyledons. Isn't that more akin to hydroponic growing?"

"Aren't you an Egyptologist?" Pavel showed annoyance at the questions.

"Just asking questions." Pierre realized that he had to press harder to get the information he needed. "Once you replant the seedlings, they are no longer isolated. They are part of the planet's biozone, including whatever is inhibiting the growth of the crops."

"Look, we have tested the soil many times." Pavel sputtered. "Nothing in the soil kills plants. No viruses, toxins, fungi, or bacterial contagions."

"You mean nothing in the soil is deadly to plants *that you can detect*. Because you haven't detected a problem, doesn't mean a problem is not there. That's fallacious reasoning."

"Get out," said Pavel.

"This won't be our last conversation," said Pierre. "I would suggest you isolate the soil you're planting in from the rest of the soil. Perhaps planting pots in the soil." Pierre left the agricultural domes. He now knew who he needed to talk to next.

* * *

Pierre entered the maintenance bay. The scatterbug mother churned out new scatterbugs into a bin. The smooth round orbs seemed dormant, but they only needed to be cast out into the world to be activated. Pierre saw Habib working on his bench.

93

"Habib," said Pierre.

Habib picked up a large wrench and wildly swung. He clipped Pierre's shoulder. Pierre reeled back, falling against a trash can. The trash can fell over, and Pierre collapsed to the ground.

Alicia stepped from the shadows and grabbed Habib's arm. Her strength overpowered Habib.

"What the fuck are you're doing?" Alicia said to Habib.

"He's going to kill us all," said Habib.

"What the fuck are you talking about?" screamed Alicia. "Stand down!"

"No, I'm going to finish him." Habib raised the wrench over his head.

"Stand down. Now!" Alicia was red in the face.

Pierre scrambled back to his feet and fell back still dazed from the assault.

Habib puffed and dropped the wrench. The tool clanked against the floor with a loud ring. The Arabic man threw up his arms and walked back to the work bench. Alicia walked over to Pierre. She put his arm over her shoulder and helped him to his feet.

"What are you doing here?" said Alicia.

"My job," said Pierre.

"What?"

"Didn't Habib tell you? He was at the staff meeting."

"Tell me what?" Alicia stepped aside once Pierre was steady on his feet.

"None of your concern," said Habib. His fingers curled against the counter of the work bench.

She looked at Pierre.

"Why not tell her the entire colony is about to collapse?" said Pierre. "And everyone is about to die?"

"Shut up," said Habib.

"Why the secrets when the information is already public?" said Pierre.

Alicia picked up the wrench and marched towards Habib. She raised the wrench ready to clobber Habib from behind. Pierre grabbed her and restrained her. "Whoa! Whoa! Whoa! You don't want to do that," said Pierre.

She threw the wrench at Habib. It missed his head. Pierre grabbed her and swung her aside. Alicia screamed and sulked off. Pierre took a deep breath to calm down and turned to Habib.

"Habib, I need your help." Pierre spoke in a soft methodical tone. "I'd prefer if you were cooperative."

"What you need?" Habib hunched over his workbench, turning his back to Pierre, and shook his head.

"I want to talk scatterbugs."

"What about scatterbugs?"

"I need a survey of the area the scatterbugs have tried to terraform," said Pierre. "Any historical data would be helpful."

"We don't keep historical data," said Habib. "Scatterbugs are autonomous. They don't need centralized computer support to do their jobs. We haven't tracked their movements for decades."

"But you used to? I need that data."

"You might be able to get data going forward," said Habib. "Scatterbugs are programmed to check in once daily. But don't know if we're still receiving any of those signals with the orbital docking station damaged."

"That's better than nothing. But if we don't have a central mainframe, do we have the computing power to do this?"

"Sure, the computing power needed isn't significant," said Habib. "The problem is you need an interface program to collect and organize the encoded messages."

"I know someone who can help," said Pierre. "That reminds me. How many active scatterbugs are in service?"

"Don't know. About a million."

"Is that a million made or a million still running?"

"Not sure."

"No matter," said Pierre. "The incoming scatterbug data will tell us more." Alicia still sulked in the corner of the room. He turned back to Habib. "Can I borrow Alicia?"

"I suppose. Why?" said Habib.

"I need an assistant."

"What about all these broken scatterbugs?" Habib picked up a broken scatterbug whose legs hung limply from its husk.

"As you said, scatterbugs are autonomous. They don't need human operators. But I need Alicia." Pierre walked over to the completion bin next to the scatterbug mother. He grabbed a brand-new type-4 scatterbug. "I'm also going to need one of these. *Shukran.*"

* * *

The tunnel between the maintenance unit and the central colony hub was lit with metal halide bulbs that had not been changed in over a decade. The lights were dim and flickered on and off. Pierre and Alicia walked the long tunnel back to the hub.

"Why me as your assistant?" said Alicia.

"You haven't tried to kill me," said Pierre. "That's the first qualification for the job."

"You remember, I'm an army doctor?" she said.

"Considering how many times I've been beaten up in the past thirty-six hours, a person with medical knowledge might be good to have on hand."

"You're kidding, right?"

He pointed to the large healing wound on his forehead.

"I guess not." Alicia looked at the wound. She had hazel-gray eyes, not adaptive to low light conditions.

Pierre led the way through the dark tunnel. Their footsteps echoed down the subterranean corridor. It was the ideal spot for an ambush. Rafters creaked above him. He was anxious to get out of there as quickly as possible, not because it was dark, but because confined tunnels often gave their denizens an advantage.

"The situation is not as bad as you said back there, right?" said Alicia.

Pierre stopped and looked Alicia in the eyes. He said nothing.

"It's not as bad, right?" she offered weakly.

A shadowy figure stepped from a nook in the tunnel. Its eyes stared at them for a few seconds. It sauntered on down the tunnel away from them, remaining in the shadows. Probably just some guy looking for a moment of privacy, waiting for an illicit sexual rendezvous, or perhaps trying to find momentary relief from the cacophony of the dome's public areas. Either way, it showed them no interest.

"It's not safe to talk here." Pierre looked about. He felt like they were being watched. Like the walls had eyes. "Let's get back to the hub and go to my office. We'll talk there."

Pierre turned and picked up the pace, wary about his surroundings. Alicia had difficulty keeping up.

Once they got up to the surface, Pierre and Alicia grabbed a quick breakfast from the commissary and took it with them to Pierre's office. He took his ID card and flashed it to the reader. It failed with a buzz and a red light. He presented it a second time. It failed again.

"Are you sure this is *your* office?" said Alicia.

"This my first time here," said Pierre. "Of course I'm not sure." He flashed it a third time, the lock beeped with a green light and opened the lock. "Perhaps I got lucky."

"Perhaps the lock is broken."

He opened the door and let them both in. He closed the door behind them.

The office was cold and dank. Yellowed papers littered a pair of old sheet metal desks. The desks seemed to have no apparent place in the room having been moved away from the walls. It was more of a storage room than a place for serious work. Opposite the door was a large plastoglass window. The view outdoors was a fog of reddish-orange sand that whistled and whipped. Where was the verdant terraformed jungle of seventy years ago?

Sandstorms were nothing new for Pierre. When he worked in Egypt, he had seen many sandstorms. Walking into a sandstorm was to pass through a wall of blindness where every grain bites your face. Visibility reduced to mere inches, and the force could strip paint off a vehicle.

Pierre pushed one desk against the wall between the door and a whiteboard size NextCompZ terminal. "That's going to be your desk."

"I get a desk?" said Alicia.

"Don't flatter yourself," said Pierre, followed by a laugh. "You will grow to resent it if you have any sense at all." He turned around and pushed the other desk against the far side of the room. "That's my desk."

He opened the drawers of his desk. The metal hinges slid open roughly. Poorly oiled metal on metal rasped and scraped. Pierre dropped the dormant scatterbug into an empty drawer and shut it.

"Okay," said Alicia. "Now what?"

"Now, we eat breakfast and talk." Pierre opened his takeaway container, a sad mix of simulated eggs, simulated protein cakes, and beans. "I hope you like beans."

"Not particularly," said Alicia.

"That's unfortunate," said Pierre. "Our gardener-in-chief is riding on the notion that beans will solve the agricultural collapse."

"Is that so unwise? Beans are a good staple crop. High in protein, moderate in carbohydrates, a good source of iron, calcium, magnesium, and phosphorus."

"As long as the beans last," said Pierre. "I saw Pavel's bean plants. I wouldn't count on them feeding us the next six minutes let alone Gardiner's projected eighteen months."

"What do you mean?" she said.

"The greenhouse is full of failing and dying plants."

"Does the Governor know?"

"Gardiner is trying to prevent panic." Pierre took a bite of his breakfast and ate it while contemplating the situation. "He's treading a tightrope. If he tells everyone how truly serious things are, civil unrest will result. He will be forced to kill large numbers of people. That has the unintended consequence of extending the colony's survival but will make him look weak, losing the colony's confidence. And you get a civil unrest positive feedback loop. The more he tells, the weaker he appears—the more unrest and killing will ensue.

"On the other hand," Pierre continued. "If Gardiner says little or nothing, the internal problems in the colony will fester and continue as the status quo. Then one day the food will run out, then the colony will fracture into factions all fighting over food scraps. Things will get desperate fast. Some will try to encroach Basra, getting shot in the process. Some will steal food by force. Some will resort to cannibalism."

"I guess it is that bad." Alicia sighed and looked at her breakfast.

"Well, at least, I now know why my little cannibalism joke didn't go over so well at the ESA."

"You think they knew?" She stopped eating. "I'm not so hungry anymore."

"Don't," said Pierre. "You know how scarce food is going to be. Every calorie is precious. Force yourself to eat because you don't know if or when you're going to get your next meal. Understood?"

"I wish the ESA would have told me the situation before I volunteered." Alicia poked at her food with her fork.

"Knowing would not have changed much for me." Pierre wolfed his breakfast but was unable to stomach it. "That said, the problem we have before us is fascinating."

"I don't see anything fascinating about our situation."

"Not the situation," said Pierre. "But the curious mind does see a strange and intractable problem. The Earth's best minds have tried to discover the cause of the blight, which has thrown a monkey-wrench into our terraforming efforts. And I have already found something all those minds have missed."

"What's that?" said Alicia.

"Our bean plants do worse when planted in the ground than when kept in pots."

"That's not much of a clue."

"It's the only one we've got." Pierre tossed the food container with half its contents on the stacks of paper covering his desk. He stepped over to the whiteboard terminal, which was a computerized workstation with a 60-inch touch screen.

Pierre pressed a button and waited for the whiteboard terminal to boot up. Several software updates were installed on the device—the computer clearly had not been powered up in a while. Once the terminal was ready, Pierre proceeded to initiate the device.

"Computer: State ID," said Pierre.

"Acknowledged, I am Stacy597," replied the computer. Pierre feared these computers were named after someone's long-dead sweetheart, but IT naming conventions mattered not to him right now.

"Stacy597: New primary user with admin rights."

"Acknowledged, network authorization required."

"Pierre Gulet, deputy governor, Arish."

"Acknowledged, checking voice authorization against security access server…" While Pierre had not undergone any security induction process when he arrived, basic biometric data had been supplied to the colony prior to his arrival. The cursor blinked a few more minutes, then responded, "Voice identification accepted. Resetting authorizations. Primary user accepted for this terminal. New desktop set up. Terminal ready for use."

"Okay," said Pierre, "We are getting somewhere."

"If you say so," said Alicia.

"You're not a computer user?"

"Not at this level," she said. "But I'm more than happy to play a video game if you got one."

"These NextCompZ terminals are kind of an antique," said Pierre. "The great, great, grandchild of the old POSIX operating systems like Linux. A throwback when you think about it, but they're cheap, rugged, reliable, and eminently practical. Perfect for colony living, but not state of the art."

"Why do they have these antiques?" said Alicia.

"It takes 23 years to make the journey from Earth to Gliese," said Pierre. "Any of the best computers here are going to be decades behind Earth's best technology. And I think this terminal is probably another twenty years old on top of that."

"So you're saying the computer we are using is about forty years old."

"If we are being optimistic, but I'm still hoping it's going to be fit for purpose."

"What purpose is that?"

"We need to do a survey."

"A survey of what?"

"Of scatterbug terraforming activities."

"Will that work?"

"Let's see," said Pierre. "Stacy597: Open GIS map of the area surrounding Arish with a topographic overlay and all current data of scatterbug positions."

"Processing," said the computer. A moment later, the computer returned a topographical map of the area surrounding the colony. An outline of the colony was traced in faint blue. A single red dot was placed near the center of the map.

"What's that?" Alicia pointed to the red dot.

"A single scatterbug," said Pierre. "The computer didn't know what to do with my request, so it took the only data it had and applied it to my GIS request. This is pretty much what I expected."

"What do you mean?"

"We need a programmer who knows how to pipe scatterbug data into a repository where our terminal can integrate it into the GIS program. Fortunately, I happen to know such a person who can help. The downside is he will need some persuading."

* * *

Pierre and Alicia arrived at the door of one of the outer huts reserved for families. It was past dark, and the sand was blowing hard. Each grain of sand stung against their exposed skin. "Is this the place?" said Pierre.

"Seems so," said Alicia. She covered her face to keep the sand out of her nose and wore goggles to protect her eyes. Pierre was quite used to the elements and used neither goggles nor facial protection. He reached out and banged on the door.

Hans Poul cracked the door open, "It's the middle of the night." The blonde man was dressed only in a pair of BDU pants. He looked Alicia up and down from head to foot.

"Mr. Poul," said Pierre.

"You?" said Hans. He stepped outside, closing the door behind him.

"I told you I'd come to collect." Pierre squinted to make himself more menacing.

"Don't need any trouble. My family doesn't need trouble."

Pierre handed him a letter. "Tomorrow. 6am in the commissary. Be there." He turned abruptly and walked away from the hut. Alicia paused for a few moments, looking Hans in the eye. When Hans returned the look, she nodded then followed Pierre. Hans took the envelope and stepped back inside.

"Was that necessary?" said Alicia after they put some distance from the hut.

"We have his attention," said Pierre. They arrived at the door to the main dome of the colony. Pierre opened the latch and held the door open for Alicia. They stepped inside. He closed the outer door after them, and they shook the sand off. "Things are going to get bad. The colonists won't act rationally as soon as hunger becomes their number one motivation. We need their help while they're still useful."

"You're wrong," said Alicia. She pulled off a boot and shook a small pile of sand onto the floor. "People have a sense of duty. We shouldn't be threatening anyone."

"Haven't you noticed it?" said Pierre. "The colonists are on edge… and have been even before Gardiner's big reveal. Brian is craving a real filet mignon. He has also recently lost some weight. Pavel acted hostile when he missed something seemingly insignificant. Do you think Habib flipping out was normal?"

"Threats are unnecessary and cruel."

"You're missing the point. Rationing has already begun. Adding small amounts of inert filler to each meal. Reduce everyone's daily intake by two hundred calories. Doesn't seem like much, but that stretches nine months of meals into ten. They're buying time, but our bodies aren't fooled. Judging how everyone is behaving, food services has already been doing that for some time."

"Does it help to provoke Hans?" said Alicia.

"Hans needs to do work neither of us is capable of." Pierre checked his tablet. It was well past midnight. "You should probably head to the barracks and get some sleep. I need you at tomorrow's meeting. I can't stress this enough. Without his help, we're all dead."

* * *

The next morning the commissary was packed with people for the breakfast rush. Alicia and Hans sat together on a bench. They had already eaten and were engaged in small talk. Hans side-looked a leggy brunette, who responded with a coquettish smile. Alicia licked her lips.

"Morning." Pierre interrupted their conversation. He arrived a few minutes late. A short stack of folders was tucked under his arm.

Hans refused to say anything. Pierre could tell Hans was going to be difficult.

"Hans, I'm not going to waste your time," said Pierre. "The colony needs your programming skills."

"You came to my home in the middle of the night," said Hans. Pierre perceived that as a firm *no*.

Pierre pulled a file out of his stack and opened it up. He paused at the first page. He licked his finger and flipped to the next page. Then he carefully read the second page. He repeated the pattern onto the third page. He slowly flipped through the pages.

"What is that?" said Hans.

"It's your personnel jacket," said Pierre. "Hans Pieter Poul, 46, blonde, blue eyes; born in Oslo, Norway; occupation, computer engineer. You are mate-bonded to Arianna O'Connell, 36, brown hair, green eyes, Gliesian-born. You have two daughters: Melissa, 13 and Serena, 10. Both with light brown hair and blue eyes."

Hans broke out in a cold sweat. "You wouldn't...." His fingers tapped nervously on the tabletop. "You wouldn't...."

"Wouldn't what?" said Pierre.

"My family."

"Everyone here has family," said Pierre. He flipped to the fourth page. "What makes your family so special?"

"Long service? I've been here nearly 20 years."

Pierre flipped the folder closed, folded his arms, and leaned back. "Where do you think you are? There's no tenure here. No preferential treatment for long service. Weren't you brought in to solve the failure of the terraforming project?"

"You can't understand the difficulties of...."

"Excuses are a waste of time," said Pierre. "You know better than most what's coming. And it's coming quickly."

"But my family." Hans' face flushed and his cheeks puffed out. "You can't let my family starve."

"Can't I?" said Pierre. "You said some people here are dead weight, not worth feeding. What do you contribute?"

"I recommend better seed breeds."

"Breeds that aren't growing or producing food. Failure!"

"I improved the irrigation system."

"You irrigate where nothing grows. Failure!"

"I have—"

"Failure! Why should your family eat when every other family is going to starve because of your failures?"

The veins on Hans' forearms bulged as he clenched his fist. His torso trembled. Pierre darted a glance at Alicia. She glowered at Pierre. The bridge of her nose crinkled.

"Hans, you're going to get a chance to redeem yourself," said Pierre. "And if the work is good, I cannot see you or your family being left out in the cold."

"What do you need?" said Hans. His voice was icy.

"We need you to help us find out what's wrong with the scatterbugs. Terraforming has failed." Pierre sat back. Was he going to be able to break past Hans' resistance? "I don't need much from you. What I am asking is a trifling for someone of your talents. I feel embarrassed even asking you for something so simple."

Hans squirmed and nodded his head.

"Scatterbugs once a day send their position data by microwave to the receiver on the docking station in orbit. The station then retransmits the scatterbug position data to the colony receiver. I need you to pipe that data into a GIS map. I need to map the position of every scatterbug." Pierre picked up another folder. He opened the folder and pulled out a specifications sheet. He handed the sheet to Hans. "That wouldn't be that hard, would it?"

Hans took the spec sheet and read it. "I suppose not."

"How long would it take to get it done?"

"A week," said Hans.

"You have four days," said Pierre.

"Four days?"

"If you cannot do it, I'm sure some other programmer with a family would be eager to secure their place as part of the team."

Hans stood up, his hands rigid at his side. "I'll get it done."

"Never doubted it," said Pierre. Hans marched away from the table and left the commissary.

Pierre stood up. Alicia grabbed his wrist and pulled him back to the cafeteria bench. "That was despicable," she whispered. "Threatening a man's family."

"You heard him. Do you think he cares if other people's families starve?" said Pierre. "Besides, I didn't threaten him or his family."

"You let him believe you were threatening his family."

"Would it be better to let everyone die?"

"I didn't say that."

"So, as long as you don't make people feel uncomfortable, if a few people die, that's okay?"

"Not saying that." Alicia spoke through her bottom row of teeth. "But is this the best way to incentivize people?"

"That might work for army medics but look around you." Pierre glanced around him. "We are surrounded by scientists, engineers, technicians. Elitists who think some people are special and worth saving and others like miners, janitors, cooks, and dead weight should be sacrificed for the greater good. We need them to understand that no one is special, and everyone is dead weight."

CHAPTER SEVEN

The class V terraforming robot is better known among colonists as the scatterbug. A scatterbug is essentially a wandering bioreactor that seeds bacteria and fungus and even vascular plants for the propagation of new life. The typical scatterbug is designed as a single cephalothorax with six walking legs and two forelimbs having clamps for climbing and sample retrieval. They are equipped with a low-light-sensitive monocular eye. They can receive and pass along programmed instructions from a central distribution point. And they are equipped to call in their status using satellite relay, as well as a large selection of legacy standards, e.g., WiFi, Infrared, and LoRa. — "Class V Scatterbugs: A Field Service Manual"

"That is wild!" said Pierre, a big grin crossed his face. Melissa sat across from him in the cafeteria. As Alicia walked by carrying a tray with lunch, Pierre called out to her.

"You've got to hear this," said Pierre. Alicia sat at the table beside Pierre. He turned back to Melissa, "Tell Alicia what you told me."

"The solar year is 370 and roughly a third days," said the young girl with dirty hair. "The year is divided into 10 months of 35 days."

"And the months are called?"

"January, February, March, April, May, June, September, October, November, and December. And at the end of the year is a short month called Intercalarus, which is normally 20 days."

"Why are July and August left out?"

"Because they are named after earth men," Melissa explained. "If we ever decide to name a month, we will do so from the stories of our own heroes."

"Yes," said Pierre. "Those months were named after Julius Caesar and Augustus Caesar, both Roman emperors. Interestingly, the Old Roman Republic calendar had a short month called *mensis intercalaris*, placed between February and March."

"That's so cool," said Melissa.

"And the leap year?" said Pierre.

"The year is actually 370.3011 days. So we calculate the leap year in years that we can divide by 3 and skip the leap year if we can divide the year by 10."

"So, this year, GE 153, would be a leap year?" asked Pierre.

"Yes, this year Intercalarus has 21 days." Melissa beamed from being asked so many questions. She smiled widely and laughed. Her massive grin exposed way too many teeth. Her cheeks were red, and her lake blue eyes sparkled. "Oh… and January 1 is always on a Monday, every year."

"Interesting," said Pierre. "Leap years have a number of days that divide evenly into 7, but what about regular years?"

"Isn't it obvious?" Melissa laughed. "Saturday Intercalarus 20th is followed by Monday January 1st."

"Clever," said Pierre. "So, when we landed on Gliese seven days ago and since today is Wednesday September 3rd, we arrived on the planet on…"

"That's simple. June 32nd." Melissa said proud of herself.

"You didn't know any of that?" said Alicia.

Hans stepped up behind Melissa. "Melissa, darling. You have duties. Go help Madi."

"Yes daddy," said Melissa. The perpetually dirty young girl wiped her hands on her BDU jumpsuit, got up, and ran over to the food prep station. She proceeded to wash her hands.

Hans sat in her place.

"She's a bright girl," said Pierre. "You have every reason to be proud of her."

"I am proud enough of her," said Hans. "You, I don't trust."

Pierre clammed up, sucking in a deep breath.

"Stay away from my daughter." Hans tried to be as threatening as possible given his weak position.

"Have you got something for me?" Pierre squinted at Hans but understood his point of view. Best to get right to business.

"Bad news." Hans dropped a folder on the table.

"Give me the synopsis." Pierre picked up the folder and thumbed through it.

"The receiver dish on the orbital docking station was badly damaged," said Hans. "When your transport ship broke up last week, fragments from the ship tore through the station including the receiver dish."

"Are we cut off from Earth?"

"They should still be able to receive our transmissions, but we'll have difficulties receiving any message they send. The receiver dish on the docking station was more than a receiver. It amplified signals before relaying the message to us."

"Was the black box from our escape pod ever recovered?" said Pierre.

"The black box was completely scrambled."

"What about the other pods?"

"They landed near Basra." Hans shook his head. "They refuse to share any data with us or even acknowledge our transmissions."

"There goes my ebook collection. Has this been going on long?"

"Close to fifteen years now," said Hans. He pushed a hand through his blonde hair. "A lot of people have uneasy feelings about what's happening at Basra. They seem to be militarizing."

"That may be." At the ESA launch site, there seemed to be an imbalance of military veterans being sent to Basra, particularly hot heads like Terry. "What does the damage to the receiver dish mean for collecting scatterbug data?"

"The receiver dish barely functions. It is too damaged to pick up most of the microwave transmissions. I ran some tests from the data collector. I only got a couple hundred signals."

"That's too few," said Pierre. "We'll never get a proper ground survey with that."

"There could be a silver lining," said Hans. "A MegaAI is coming within a few light months of the Gliese system."

"What's a MegaAI?"

"They are massive transport ships piloted by a SuperAI computer and crewed by androids. They're deep explorer ships, but they swing by colony worlds to render assistance and do repairs on satellites and equipment in orbit. While in orbit, the MegaAI allows colonists to use its AI functions. We've sent a signal to the MegaAI. If they agree to help, they could arrive in about seven months."

"Seven months might be too little, too late." Pierre thought for a moment. "We need an alternative to satellite communication."

* * *

Later that afternoon, Pierre was in the boardroom. Across the table from him sat Peter Chin and Dutch Haring.

"Let's begin the meeting," said Pierre. He picked up a stack of papers and laid them out in front of him. "I am having these small meetings with all department heads. The purpose of these meetings is to learn what you guys have discovered about the blight."

Peter was a Taiwanese man in his early fifties with salt and pepper gray hair. He arrived on Gliese twenty years ago, in the same cohort as Hans. "I'm Harvard Professor Peter Chin," he said. "Head of the biology department."

"Everyone here is smart," said Pierre. "I'm not interested in your vocational pedigree. I want to know what you've discovered about the blight."

"Right, do you have questions?" said Chin.

Pierre was put off by Chin's imperious manner. He had employment jackets for both Chin and Haring. Chin had done his entire education at Harvard but lacked publications. Pierre was unimpressed by Chin's social gameplaying and his attempt to establish a pecking order.

"Why are the plants in our greenhouses dying?" said Pierre.

"Isn't that what you're here to tell us?" said Chin.

"Yes, but you've had twenty years to answer that question," said Pierre with a smirk. "I just arrived."

"Obviously, because they're unable to uptake nutrients," replied Chin.

"What is causing the plants to not uptake nutrients?" Pierre squinted at Chin. He recognized the deflection instantly.

"Inhibiting factors."

"What factors?" said Pierre. Chin was being evasive.

"I could explain it to you, but the biological mechanism is complex."

"Humor me. Are those factors biological, chemical, microbiological?"

"Multivariate. It's difficult to isolate it to a single cause."

"Sounds like you don't know."

"We've been working diligently on the problem," said Chin.

"So you know that *something* is inhibiting the uptake of nutrients by our food crops, but you have failed to identify a cause," said Pierre. Chin gritted his teeth. Pierre turned to Dutch. "What about the department of chemistry? What've you discovered?"

Dutch stammered for a moment. He looked to Chin who only offered an icy stare in return. Pierre noticed that there was no lost love between them. Dutch was slightly older than Chin. He had short, cropped hair, grayed at the temples. Dutch was not as polished as Chin at answering tough questions, but he was no less competent than the other staff members.

"We've done several chemical analyses of the soil," said Dutch with a faint Plattdeutsch accent. "Nothing significant found. We looked for heavy metals, toxins, herbicides, and antibiotic compounds. I can't find a reason for why our plants are dying."

"How is your lab set up?" said Pierre.

"Mass spectrometers, biochemical analyzers, centrifuges, titration apparatus, all the standard industry equipment." Dutch listed off his inventory of equipment. "Most of what we have in the lab is relatively new. Only about 30 years old. For a place like this, that's new. If there was something in the soil, we should have found it."

"Any explanation for why, with all your equipment, you haven't found the cause of the failed terraforming?"

"No," admitted Dutch.

Pierre did not detect any dissembling from Dutch. "Gentlemen, we are all constrained by our means and methods. I can work with researchers who are honest." Pierre wrote some notes down. "Chin?"

"Yes," said Chin. His back stiffened.

"You don't have the mental flexibility I need," said Pierre. He made another note. "I am going to recommend that you be transferred to the agricultural greenhouse where you can study plant biology. Hopefully, you can make a meaningful contribution as a sole contributor."

Chin scowled at Pierre.

"Dutch, I want a tour of your lab. We might need your services at a moment's notice. Are you up to the challenge?"

* * *

Alicia opened the door to the office and walked inside. A spider-like creature eight inches across skittered across the floor towards her. The click-clack of spiky metal feet clattered towards Alicia. It stopped in front of her, balanced on six legs, extended its front two climbing legs, and snipped its claws like fine calipers. She shrieked and grabbed a heavy textbook off the shelf ready to clobber the bug.

"Whoa, whoa!" said Pierre from across the room. He placed both hands out to try to calm her down.

"What's that?" Alicia was red in the face and ready to kill.

"A scatterbug." Pierre approached her, stepping over the small robot on the floor.

112

"I know it's a scatterbug. What's it doing here?" She clutched the textbook tighter.

"It's being observed," said Pierre.

The scatterbug tilted and looked up. A large violet glass camera eye focused on Alicia. Its lens shutter blinked. Alicia looked down and frowned at the small robot. The scatterbug turned around and retreated towards Pierre. The eight spiked metal feet tattered across the particulite floor.

"Observing?" said Alicia. She raised an eyebrow and leaned against her desk.

Pierre huffed. "Okay, it's more like a pet."

"Scatterbugs are not pets."

"It's better than a goldfish." Pierre bobbed his head side to side. "Cleaner than a cat. Not as good as a bunny. As far as pets go, scatterbugs aren't bad pets."

"How can you say that? Scatterbugs are nothing but robotic tools."

"They're super easy to care for." Pierre pointed to a small green plastic tray in the corner with some dirt in it.

"A litter box?" Alicia's jaw dropped. "Are you kidding me? I am not about to change a litter box for a robot."

"It's not a litter box. It's a sandbox." Pierre picked up the tray and set it down on the desk to show Alicia. "All we have in here is soil from outside that I've rinsed thoroughly and sterilized by baking it in a kiln. I then sprayed the sand with some water. The scatterbug nestles into the sand taking up minerals and water for its bioreactor."

The scatterbug stopped walking for a moment. A small mist was discharged from its belly.

"Did it pee on the floor?" said Alicia. Her face flushed with anger.

"No." Pierre picked up the scatterbug and held it in his arms. He kneeled. "Look, there's not even a puddle. And no, it's not urine. It was a soil bacteria spray. That's how it terraforms. It seeds soil bacteria and microrrhiza fungus spores as it wanders the landscape. It's harmless and completely sanitary."

"But why, of all things, a scatterbug… as a pet?"

"Scatterbugs are a culmination of centuries of technological innovation. They have gone through generations of development and programming. They have storage space for additional programs and even a small neural processor acting almost like an artificial cerebral cortex." Pierre sat at his desk then placed the scatterbug on the desktop. The scatterbug explored the surface of the desk. The robot returned to Pierre. It beeped at Pierre.

"You see," said Pierre, touching the scatterbug above its ocular camera. "Scatterbug programming contains billions of lines of code. They have adaptive behavior protocols and can learn. And they can pass learned behaviors to other scatterbugs. They are a technological masterpiece, but they're also complex."

"I don't see how," said Alicia. "If they were programmed by humans, surely we already understand everything about them."

"We understand the factory settings." Pierre peered into the standard 70 mm plastoglass lens covering the camera of the scatterbug eye. "But look at this one. It has the good sense not to jump off the desk onto a hard floor. Yet, if it were in the wild, it would tuck its legs in and roll down an embankment in anticipation of being safe at the bottom of an elevated height."

"Are you saying they can be domesticated?"

"I'm saying, if they can learn, they can be taught. If they can be taught, all I need to do is find what incentivizes them."

"What could possibly incentivize a machine?"

"I don't know," Pierre admitted. "But that's why I need to study them."

"They're fucking robots." Alicia threw up her arms and shook her head, as if she was dealing with a mad man. "They have no needs. No need, no incentive."

"That's an excellent point." Pierre ignored his adjutant's frustration. A dichotomy of needs and wants might be a completely wrong approach. The scatterbug programmers made it so the little robots have no real needs. If they get water and minerals, their bioreactor requirements are satisfied. But if they don't, they have an unlimited supply of solar energy to pick up and seek out raw materials. He took his index finger and rubbed the scatterbug over its brow. The robot settled down, crouched, and mewed with a purr of appreciation. "Perhaps, I'm viewing this all wrong."

"You? Wrong?" said Alicia. "How could *you* possibly be wrong?" Pierre ignored the tone of sarcasm.

"We've treated scatterbugs as mindless automatons for generations and have forgotten what they are capable of." As Pierre stroked his pet robot, the iris of the scatterbug rotated. Pierre smiled as he played with the small machine. Remarkable how much the scatterbug behaved like an animal. "Maybe, I am not the first person to adopt a scatterbug as a pet. Look at how readily this scatterbug takes to being treated like a pet. It's almost as if someone has done this before, and all we're doing is introducing a fish to water."

"What are you saying?"

"Maybe, these machines have a long genetic memory. Who knows the name of the first researcher that made a scatterbug a pet? But the work he or she did is now being replicated into the active memory of this little robot. Scatterbugs carry a huge repository of unused programming code like the genetic complement of so-called junk DNA. And when the applicable situation arises, they copy portions of that code into volatile memory and edit them into new code variants. Those edits are saved back into its data bank. We are building upon all that cumulative work."

"That sounds like a complex system," said Alicia. "I'm no expert but how can you study something you cannot nail down? That's like trying to understand the thinking process of a SuperAI—the system is so complex, but somehow the entire supercomputing apparatus works in a way no one entirely understands."

"You can't understand every single behavior of a complex system," said Pierre, still stroking the scatterbug. "You need an etic approach to behavioral observation. It's not much different from the discipline of anthropology. You observe and take note." He gave it a few more rubs and then sat back. "Maybe I should cover him in faux fur. Would that help him socialize? You know I named him."

"You did what?" she said aghast.

"I named him Maat. It means *order* in ancient Egyptian."

"Why?" Alicia flicked her hands. As she said that, the terminal screen flickered on, followed by the ring tone of an antique telephone.

Pierre jumped up out of his chair. He stepped over and faced the terminal. Pierre spoke to the terminal, "Stacy597: who's calling?"

The computer replied in a vaguely feminine voice, "Hans Poul, environmental engineer."

"Stacy597: accept call."

The face of Hans appeared on the terminal screen.

"What is it?" said Pierre.

"I have a solution to our satellite problem."

"I'm listening."

"It's so obvious. LoRa."

"LoRa?"

"Yes, LoRa is a long range, low energy radio protocol," said Hans. "It's what the scatterbugs use to communicate with each other. Why can't we use that to transmit position data back to base?"

"What's the range for LoRa?"

"About 6 miles."

"How exactly does that help?"

Hans grinned widely. "Almost every scatterbug is within that range of another scatterbug. We get the bugs to pass each other's position data back to home base."

"What would that take?"

"In theory, uploading a small program to the local bugs that pass the same program onto the other bugs."

"So a kind of computer virus."

"The difference between a virus and an update is a matter of owner intent," said Hans. "Regardless, this program would take the GPS position of the bug, calculate the next closest peer to home base, then sends its ID, position, and environmental conditions to the peer, which passes that report on to the next closest peer until the message arrives at the LoRa receiver we are going to set up on the transmission tower."

"Sounds simple and brilliant. How long before we start getting results?"

"We are talking about an estimated million scatterbugs out there." Hans punched calculations into his terminal. "It looks like the program will be fully propagated in about two weeks."

"It's already mid-September," whined Pierre.

"Plus, three days of programming time."

"You're killing me, Hans," said Pierre. "I can't do anything without that survey. Get it done fast." Pierre turned off the communications link to Hans.

"That was rude," said Alicia.

"Three more weeks, after two weeks of delay." Pierre eased back into his chair. Maat skittered up to the edge of the desk. Pierre reached out and rubbed the side of the scatterbug's metallic shell. "Dates on the calendar are closer than they appear. We've only just started running out of time."

* * *

A throbbing buzz woke Pierre in his barracks. The barracks were shared bunks for the single men and women. There were only about forty beds in the barracks because of the mandate to couple up within two years or face exile. He checked his tablet—October 3rd, 4am in the damn morning. An alert indicated an influx of data had been dumped to his office terminal.

He threw the covers of his bunk aside. His mouth was full of mucus, like he had been drinking glue. He scratched the back of his head and stood up. He tightened the draw cord on the pants he had slept in and threw on a jacket but did not bother buttoning it up. He left the barracks and ventured into the hallway. His naked feet went frigid against the unheated metal floors. He went to the bathroom and gathered a cup of hot water, then went to his office.

He entered his office and turned on the lights. Maat was resting in its dirt tray. The sand had turned a mottled green, covered with algae patches growing in symbiosis with moss and lichen. The scatterbug woke up, dusted itself off, and shuffled around the perimeter of its tray. It seemed groggy like it had not had enough time to fully recharge. Pierre stepped over to his terminal and woke it out of hibernation state. The giant computer screen illuminated with white light, a NextCompZ logo appeared, then diagnostic text messages scrolled down.

As Pierre waited for the terminal to boot up, he looked out the window. The month-long sandstorm finally stopped. The reddish hue of the sand fog was replaced by a dull gray lunar landscape. He could now see out the window for miles. Extended visibility was quite common after a sandstorm. The crisp quality of the air enhanced the transmission of the pre-dawn light. Tree stumps littered the landscape, the tops sheared off by decades of cutting wind and sand. Not a blade of grass thrived out there and not a single green leaf.

"Stacy597 ready," said the computer after booting up.

Pierre turned his attention from the outdoors to the terminal. He spoke "Stacy597: open GIS schema and ingest data dump of scatterbug location and tracking data."

"Processing," said the computer in its feminine monotone. A reticle on the screen began to turn as a sign the computer was working on the data. "Data acquisition complete."

"Stacy597: display data on a topographic map. Update data real-time." Pierre sat at his desk and watched the screen. He took his cup of water and added a packet of insta-caff, stirring it with his finger. He sucked his finger dry. The room was frigid, and he folded his arms to keep warm. The coffee substitute was only lukewarm but still better than nothing.

The computer displayed a blank map of the colony. The reticle stopped and a single red dot appeared on the screen. Pierre recognized the position. It was his own office. The terminal displayed the geographic position from one—only one—scatterbug. And that bug was his pet, Maat.

"Well, at least I know they were able to get you working." Pierre reached over and touched his pet scatterbug on the back and rocked it gently side to side. "I hope that data alert didn't wake me up just to tell me my pet was in my office." Pierre snickered. "It would be like a mindless terminal to do something like that."

The reticle reappeared on the screen followed by a text message: "Update in progress…"

A couple hundred more red dots appeared.

"That's better," said Pierre to himself. "Still not enough but better."

More and more dots appeared.

"Stacy597: add a counter for the number of unique scatterbug data instances that have reported in over the most recent 24-hour period cycle." Pierre perched on the edge of his seat anticipating more data.

A counter appeared on the screen and numbers incremented as the dots appeared. Hours passed and the counter slowed as it reached six hundred and ninety-eight thousand. The bulk of the data had arrived.

"Stacy597: how many scatterbugs have been issued?" Pierre asked the computer for the total count of scatterbugs.

The computer processed the information and replied. "1,026,728 units deployed. 186,253 reclaimed."

"Reclaimed? What does *reclaimed* mean?" Pierre scratched his head.

"It means returned to base and damaged beyond repair," said Alicia from the office door.

"I didn't hear you come in," said Pierre.

"I saw you were engrossed in what you were doing." Alicia stepped up to Pierre who was still seated. "What's with the smear of red?"

"We finally got position data from the scatterbugs." Pierre zoomed out the view. "There is a problem."

"What's that?"

"Only about 83% of the units have reported in. Where are the rest of them?"

Alicia stepped over to Pierre and looked over his shoulder at the data counter. "I agree. That's way too low."

"What would cause them not to report in?"

"The most likely cause is accidental damage," she said.

"Aren't they supposed to be able to take a tumble down a hill and get back up?"

"Sure." Alicia leaned in, looking at the screen. The terminal made a dull clicking noise as it processed new data points. "But if a bug fell into a lake or a deep shaft or was completely buried by an avalanche, that could spell the end to it. They aren't indestructible."

Pierre took a closer look at the map. He zoomed way in. Small blue arrows marked the general vector for each scatterbug's direction of travel. "I think we can rule out the lake scenario. And avalanches wouldn't account for losing one hundred, forty-six thousand units." He pursed his lips and thought about the problem. "That's a lot of lost bugs."

"Exiles?" offered Alicia.

"Who?" Pierre raised his eyebrow.

"They're outcasts: criminals, mentally ill, those who refuse to mate."

"Why would exiles want to destroy scatterbugs?"

"It's the camera." Alicia pointed at Maat. "That big ocular eye. Exiles are not permitted within the perimeter of the colony. The perimeter is defined as the outer limits of the scatterbug range. Exiles encroach a colony because the best food sources are nearby. If exiles get too close, the scatterbugs could send photos back of an intruder. Easier to smash a scatterbug rather than to deal with an armed party."

"Still, I don't think a few exiles could destroy hundreds of thousands of scatterbugs," said Pierre. "There has to be something else going on."

Pierre zoomed out the map. The red dots blurred out into a round circular shape.

"It looks like a cookie with a bite out of it," said Alicia.

Once she said it, Pierre could not unsee it. She was right. The map when zoomed out did look like a cookie with a bite out of the top right corner. The bottom of the cookie was colored green as if the cookie had been dipped in milk. "What's this strip south of the colony?"

"That's the Southern Crescent," said Alicia. "It's the last green zone the desert hasn't reclaimed."

"I think we need to check that out," said Pierre. "Grab some rebreathers and a variety of sterile sample containers and requisition a rover. The weather is clement out there for a change. And bring a rifle in case we run into some… exiles. We are going to take a trip to Gliese's vacation destination."

* * *

The rover bounced across the desert terrain. The wide wheels with large treads glided easily over the loose sand. Alicia drove while Pierre sat in the passenger seat. Both wore rebreathers. While short trips outside were safe without a rebreather, the thin atmosphere required breathing assistance when trips got more physical. A rebreather was nothing more than a small air pump, pressurizing the air to make the oxygen easier to breathe and stripping out some carbon dioxide, a simple and effective device.

In the distance they could see the green zone. A stand of trees rose up ahead of them. He recognized the fast-growing species used for terraforming. Savannah grasses gave way to eucalyptus and acacia trees. As they crossed into damper soils, the yellow grasses became increasingly green. A canopy of kapok and rubber trees came into sight. Bamboo and alder grew in the underbrush. The growth on the floor was covered in detritus and lush green moss salted with mushroom caps.

Alicia parked the rover near the forest edge. Pierre grabbed the rifle out of the back, while Alicia grabbed a backpack containing the sample containers. Pierre slung the rifle over his shoulder, swinging the muzzle dangerously close to Alicia's face.

"Whoa, there!" said Alicia. "Have you ever fired a rifle?"

"No," said Pierre. "How hard could it be? Point and pull the trigger."

"Okay." Alicia threw the backpack into Pierre's chest. "You collect the samples. I'll take the rifle." She took the rifle off Pierre's shoulder. She opened the breach, felt that it was empty, and loaded a round into the barrel. "Can't have you shooting yourself. Or worse, shooting me."

Pierre nodded his head. "Okay, I'll do the samples."

"That's sensible." Alicia led the way into the forest.

"Where does the water come from to sustain the green zone?" said Pierre.

"Ground water," said Alicia. "This area sits above a large aquifer with a high water table. It's why this site was chosen for colonization… easily obtainable water."

Pierre found it reassuring at least there was no risk of running out of water. Running out of food would be bad, but running out water would have been so much worse.

As they entered the woods, Pierre listened carefully. Insects buzzed, but the woods were exceptionally quiet. It was unsettlingly quiet. "This is weird. It looks like a perfect forest, but something feels missing."

"No birds," said Alicia.

"That's it, isn't it? No bird chirps."

"Birds have to be brought in by hibernating eggs. It can be done, but it's expensive and difficult. So it's usually the last step in the terraforming process." Alicia trudged ahead of Pierre. She pushed the underbrush aside as they moved deeper into the forest. "After the scatterbugs plant bacteria and condition the soil, microrrhiza is established, then mosses, lichens, grasses, bushes, trees, then insects and animals. Birds don't survive the hibernation process all that well."

"There are animals out here."

"Some." Alicia pushed some of the brush aside as she moved from fallen log to fallen log. "All the animals are introduced from earth. There are worms and nematodes, dung beetles, ants, and spiders. If pools of water develop, then amphibians and frogs may be introduced. In drier conditions, snakes including king snakes and Egyptian cobras. Then finally small mammals are introduced. Bats, hares, and fallow deer are introduced to small steads like this." Alicia scanned the underbrush and stopped at a fallen log. "We've arrived. Get your samples, and let's get out of here. I would rather not encounter an exile if I can avoid it."

Pierre knelt on the moss. He pulled a small shovel out of the backpack. He cut into the moss with the blade of the shovel. Beneath the moss was rich black soil. Pierre put on a pair of nitrile gloves. He grabbed a handful of the soil, soft, moist, and full of loam. The fresh dirt smell permeated the air. It was so unlike all the sand surrounding the colony. He let the dirt fall apart through his fingers. Pierre reached back into his bag and pulled out sample containers. He filled a dozen small vials with soil and two five-liter bags with black dirt. As he filled the second bag, a scatterbug climbed onto the log beside him and walked along to the top of the log. The bug had a more squashed appearance, a type-3 scatterbug. He packed his bag and stood up.

"Ready to go back?" he said.

"We are not alone." Alicia stepped backwards towards him. The rifle pointed into the forest.

"Let's get out of here," said Pierre. "If it's a two-legged animal, perhaps they aren't interested in a fight today."

They backed their way out of the forest. Twigs snapped in the direction they were facing. As soon as they got back into the rover, Alicia cranked the throttle, and the vehicle lurched towards the colony. Pierre looked into the side mirror as they sped away. A fallow deer fawn peered out from the edge of the forest cover. Pierre sighed in relief.

* * *

Back at the colony, Pierre took the soil samples and brought the vials to Dutch Haring in the chemistry lab. He found Haring working on a set of flasks. As soon as he stepped into the lab, Haring spoke.

"You've got something for me?" said Dutch. He wore a pair of wire frame reading glasses and a white lab coat. His vision had evidently deteriorated since he left Earth despite having gone through corrective eye surgery.

"Soil samples," said Pierre. He put six of the samples on the counter.

"What exactly do you want me to do with these?"

"I want a differential analysis. I want these samples compared to the soil found in the agricultural domes."

Dutch rattled off all the potential testing procedures from rote memory. He had done them so many times. "A panel of minerals and heavy metals. Panel of organics. Fixed nitrogen, phosphorus, and potash. Trace minerals, including calcium, sulfur, magnesium, zinc, boron, and copper. That about it?"

"That would be great, thank you."

"I don't think you'll find anything." Dutch wrote the request in his notebook. "You think we haven't done this before?"

"Humor me," said Pierre.

"I am," said Dutch. "You will have the results in three days. Now, get out of my lab."

CHAPTER EIGHT

NextCompZ Corporation was founded in AD 2175 as an alternative to the highly complicated operating systems of the late 22nd Century. While other companies sought to produce feature-rich systems that acted like personal assistants indistinguishable from human personality models (HPMs), NextCompZ produced simple, powerful, reliable terminals that retained a high resale value. Their motto was "a terminal that serves you for fifty years will serve your children for the next twenty-five." After the cybernetic wars, when HPMs were restricted, most OS vendors found themselves virtually out of business. NextCompZ Corporation with its simple non-HPM interface overnight became the de facto computing standard globally. — **"NextCompZ Corporation: A History"**

Pierre was mesmerized by the terminal in his office. He reviewed still-footage from the scatterbugs. The sand box on the floor was lush with grass, natural weeds like plantain, purslane, and clover, and a micro-orchid sprouted in the corner. Maat was exploring the far dark extremes of the office floor. Alicia entered with a report in her hand. She dropped the stack of paper on Pierre's desk. Oblivious to Alicia's presence, Pierre advanced through every photograph from the bugs.

"The results you asked for," said Alicia. "No elevated heavy metals. Trace nutrients are good. Organics are higher in the green zone sample as expected. No appreciable difference between the greenhouse soil and the green zone." She sighed and put her hand on the desk beside him, making certain she was in his field of vision. "It's the fifteenth report you've asked Dutch for. Are you going to keep repeating the same tests?"

"I'm missing something." Pierre hissed as he exhaled. "And I can't put my finger on it." He picked up the report and dumped it into the trash.

"It's been nearly three months." She picked up her hand and folded her arms. "Visiting each cluster of bug activity is not working. And everyone is impatient with you, especially Gardiner."

"I know." He leaned back in the chair.

"Did you ask the terminal to find photos with anomalies? Use the terminal's built-in AI."

"All that gets you is an endless stream of rat photos and the occasional cobra," said Pierre. "The only two critters thriving on this shitty rock."

"Have you learned anything new about the Southern Crescent?"

"Yes." He scratched the side of his cheek. He had not shaved for four days. The dirty blonde whiskers were itchy but getting soft and velvety. "The green zone is moving further south. In the last three months, it has moved about 150 meters. Like the jungle is crawling away from us."

"Strange." Alicia looked over Pierre's shoulder. "Can you see that on the maps?"

"Here's the first map with all the scatterbugs." On the terminal, Pierre exited the photo view and returned to the GIS view.

"It still looks like a cookie with a bite out of it to me." Alicia snorted.

He flipped to the second map from a month ago, and then the latest map.

"Did you see that?" said Pierre. He leaned into the terminal, looking closer at the map.

"You're right the green zone is moving further south."

"No not that," he said. "The circle of scatterbug activity has grown."

"That's what scatterbugs are supposed to do. Scatter out and terraform the land. They are supposed to spread out."

Pierre flipped back and forth between the first and last maps. He stopped again on the first map and used his finger to draw an orange line around the area of the bite. "The bite in the cookie is also growing."

"What do you mean?"

"It looks like the Bite is growing faster than the rate at which the bugs are spreading out. Scatterbugs are supposed to spread out in a uniform distribution. Why are they retreating from the Bite?"

Alicia shrugged her shoulders.

Pierre stroked his chin. He glanced at the sand tray near his feet and stared at it for a moment. He marveled at the lush green plants in the tray. It occurred to him. "We've assumed that something is wrong with the scatterbugs. The experts have told us the problem rests with the bugs ability to terraform. What if that's wrong?"

"What do you mean?"

Pierre reached down, grabbed the sandbox from the floor, picked it up, and set it on the desk. "Look at this. Does this look like the scatterbugs are not working?" Pierre ran his hand through the grass. He plucked a broad leaf off a plantain. He held up the leaf to show Alicia. He then curled up the leaf and popped it in his mouth, chewed, and swallowed it. "Ew, grassy."

"So the scatterbugs are working. What does that prove?"

"What if scatterbugs avoid the Bite *because they're functioning as programmed* and something is driving them off? What if the problem lies somewhere in the Bite, and we should investigate not where the scatterbugs have gone, but where they're avoiding? Do we know if anything would cause scatterbugs to avoid an area?"

"If bugs get multiple distress signals, other bugs might construe the area as having a hazard to avoid," said Alicia.

Pierre zoomed the map into the area of the Bite. "Do we know what's there?"

"Some foothills. Nothing but an empty wasteland."

"Should be an ideal place to terraform." Pierre magnified the map even further. He saw a line running up through the area of the cookie. "What's that line?"

Alicia looked at the terminal monitor. She squinted as she looked at the map. "That's Varney Ridge. It's an escarpment."

"What do we know about Varney Ridge?"

"A natural limestone formation. There's a cliff face that has been eroded from an ancient flood plain. Nobody has any reason to go there."

"Well, now we do." Pierre set the sandbox back on the ground. "You know the drill. Grab some sample bags, a couple of recording tablets, a rifle, and a rover. We're off to check out Varney Ridge."

* * *

Alicia parked the rover. Pierre hopped out as soon as the vehicle was motionless. It was starting out as a hot day, unseasonable for the month of December. With the most recent sandstorm over, temperatures rose quickly. But as soon as night fell, the temperature would drop again to sub-freezing.

Pierre put on a floppy cotton hat and polarized sunglasses to protect him from the sun. They were both wearing drab green military uniforms without camouflage and rebreathers. Alicia's fatigues were perfectly tied and trimmed, even the leg closure drawstrings were tied over her army boots. On the other hand, Pierre wore his jacket fully open with a white undershirt exposed and his leg closures were wide open—he wore what looked like tan suede slippers.

"Are you wearing slippers?" said Alicia. "You do realize we are going to be hiking twenty miles?"

"They're sandshoes." Pierre looked at his feet. "Okay, actually gym shoes, but essentially they're the same."

"And you're going to hike in those?"

"Yup." He grabbed the backpack holding the sample containers from the back of the rover. He also opened an equipment storage trunk in the back of the rover and grabbed binoculars, a first aid kit, a small flashlight, a hand-held multi-spectrum radio, a water canteen, and a flare gun. He stuffed the aid kit and flare gun in the backpack, hung the binoculars over his neck, attached the canteen to his belt, and jammed the radio and flashlight into the pockets of his jacket. Finally, he strapped on the backpack.

"Why are we walking along the ridge?" Alicia squirmed in her combat boots. It had been a long time since she did a substantial hike. Even though she had passed basic training, that had been a decade ago. She kept passing her physicals by strenuous weight-lifting and minimal cardio. With her stocky frame, she considered herself more built for strength than speed or endurance. She grabbed the rifle, checked the chamber, and put it over her shoulder.

"We are doing site proofing." Pierre grabbed the binoculars and looked through them. He looked up at the escarpment of the ridge. He estimated the cliff face was about two hundred feet from the plateau above to the sand basin below. He turned his view out to the rest of the basin. Beyond the ridge to the north and to the west, he could see the foothills. There was nothing out there that interested him. He had seen a lot of terrain like this before. Most of it wasn't promising.

Back on earth in Egypt, finding things was easy. He would walk the foothills near King's Valley and make small finds indicative of human activity: flint blades, potshards, and once even the ball joint of a human femur. Being bipedal meant you could access out-of-reach places and find strange loose items. If it is strange, it is important. And if it is important, there is nuance and context waiting to be discovered.

But he also knew the best finds were surrounded by evidence of intentional human activity. Most of the time, activity took place where there were transitions in terrain: a defensible mountain, a cavern underneath a mesa, or along a ridge in the middle of nowhere. Those are the places to find things both natural and unnatural, whether an underground tomb or a mineral deposit such as a vein of sea-green emeralds.

But Gliese 832 c had no history of civilization, no life, and pretty crystals would have no interest other than as a mineral oddity. Finding anything that could help solve the terraforming problem was a shot in the dark at best, and at worst a complete waste of valuable time better spent poring over more data. But Pierre remembered his professor who said to him towards the end of his doctoral studies: *While it's best to spend most of your time in the library, at some point you have to get your shoes sandy.*

"What is site proofing?" said Alicia.

"It's where you walk and look at what's on the ground."

"Why can't we take the rover and drive along the ridge and look from the comfort of a four-wheel drive?"

"The reason is because we are looking for things that are small." Pierre took the binoculars from his eyes and walked along the bottom of the cliff face. Alicia shook her head and reluctantly followed. Pierre stopped and picked up a fist-sized rock. He handed it to her. "What is that?"

"It's a rock?" she said.

"Yes, what's it made of?"

"I don't know. Limestone?"

"Yes. Is it naturally or unnaturally caused?"

"Looks natural."

Pierre took the rock back. "Exactly." He chucked the rock away. "It's not what we are looking for. But we can't know that riding at forty miles per hour."

He turned away and continued to walk along the escarpment. Every so often, he picked up a rock, checked it, and tossed it aside. Alicia struggled to keep up. She raised her eyebrows as Pierre deftly moved from sand patch to sand patch like a dancer. Like a leopard naturally born to the desert, he knew his way around the terrain.

"What do you think we will find out here?" said Alicia.

"Cobras, rats, beetles, perhaps the occasional falling rock." Pierre kept looking at his feet.

"Are we wasting our time out here?"

"Quite likely." Pierre paused and looked again through the binoculars. It all still looked grim. The same dreary yellow scenery. "You know. If you spend enough time in the desert, you start to crave any other color than yellow. Everything out in the desert is yellow. There's no reds, greens, or blues. You get color starved." He dropped the binoculars, and they swung over his chest. He grabbed his canteen and took a sip.

"You don't say." Alicia signaled him for the canteen. He handed her the canteen. She took a sip of water and handed it back to Pierre.

"It's the null hypothesis. If we find nothing out here, what will we know that we didn't know before?"

"We would learn that the Bite in the cookie is nothing but a coincidence. The scatterbugs avoided this area by random chance."

"That's one possibility. What's another?"

"The cause is where we can't see it."

"Indeed, what's another?"

"We didn't find the cause?"

"Absence of evidence is not evidence of absence," Pierre finally said. "So, if we find nothing out here, what have we learned?"

"Absolutely nothing."

Pierre raised his eyebrows, smiled, and nodded his head. "Exactly, that's why we're looking. We need to find… something. We need to find the cause of the terraforming failure. Or we need to find evidence the answer is not out here because of some other factor, indicating something else is happening."

"How do we do that?"

"It's not as hard as it sounds. Let's say we travel another mile and find scatterbugs all happily doing their jobs exactly as designed. That would be evidence that the LoRa protocol is simply not working correctly out here, and the Bite is nothing more than a geographic feature that's inhibiting LoRa transmissions."

"Is that likely?"

"I don't know. But right now, we don't have any positive evidence to say anything one way or the other, which is why we need to finish the site proofing." Pierre hooked the canteen back onto his belt and pressed forward.

An hour had passed, and they were still walking along the ridge line. It was a little after noon, and the sun was directly overhead. The shadow from the cliff face sunk back into the rock. Nowhere to hide from the sun's intense rays. Their progress slowed with the increased heat.

"I need to rest," said Alicia. Pierre put his hands on his hips and agreed with a nod of his head. A few large boulders had fallen close to the face of the escarpment. She found herself a convenient boulder and plunked herself down. Sweat poured off her forehead. She was sunburnt, and her face matched her striking red hair. Her Irish ancestry was making navigating the desert difficult. But truth be told, he also needed rest.

Pierre selected a boulder opposite her and sat down. His shoes kicked up some sand. A small flat stone was beside the toe of his shoe. He nudged it a bit and flipped it over with his foot. Bending down, he picked up the stone and dusted it off.

The stone, about the size of a business card, was white with a slight gray tint. One side of stone felt waxy and smooth beneath his thumbs. The material was fine-grained limestone. He had seen this type of stone many times. He'd wager every rocky planet would have some stone like this. Any planet that once had oceans and enough calcite and dolomite could produce limestone of this fine granularity. Billions of years ago, this area had been an ancient ocean and flood plain. So such a rock here would not be unexpected. Along the short end was a round groove, and over the back surface were small square marks. Pierre could not do much other than stare at the rock.

Alicia stood up. She had enough of sitting and wanted to move on. "Shall we?" she said finally. Pierre, still sitting, handed the rock to Alicia. She accepted the rock. "More limestone?"

"Natural or unnatural?"

"Natural," she said.

"Wrong." Pierre bounced up to his feet, turned around, and put the binoculars to his eyes. He scanned the cliff face looking for anomalies.

"What?"

"The long rectangular groves are chisel marks. And the round groove is where a wedge chisel was placed to pop the shard off a rock face." Pierre pointed to a nook about 20 feet up the embankment.

"Outside of the rock cut tombs at the Valley of the Kings, you can find thousands of rock shards that look just like this one. Limestone fragments cut from a tomb and discarded outside."

She looked again at the rock. "I would've missed it."

"There's a small recess up there. I'm going to go up to see if that's where this fragment came from." Pierre dropped his backpack. He took off as much weight as he could. While the embankment was not a straight drop, it was still steep and covered with loose stones and sand. He climbed up the embankment. Stones gave way under his grasp, tumbling to the desert floor below. He double-stepped to keep up with the sand giving way beneath his feet.

This could be what he was looking for. Several of the Dead Sea Scrolls were found in little more than four-foot-deep nooks in the rock. Even artifacts from the Bar Kochba Revolt had been found in recesses like this, as desperate Jewish rebels unsuccessfully hid from the wrath of the Roman invaders.

Pierre made it up to the nook. He grabbed onto a rock with one hand and pulled himself up so he could see inside the nook. He pulled the flashlight out of his jacket pocket and turned it on. No light. Pierre looked at the flashlight, tried the button again, shook the body of the flashlight. Still no light.

The rock let go. Pierre was thrown out of the nook. He tumbled down the slope of the embankment until he came to rest facing the bottom. Alicia ran over to him, and she pulled him up off the sand. She eased him back. Pierre coughed up dust he inhaled during his tumble down the slope.

"Are you alright?" said Alicia.

"No," said Pierre. He spat sand out of his mouth. "That's not the cave we're looking for."

"I mean are you physically hurt?"

"That hurt more." Pierre hoisted himself up. "That nook was caused by erosion. It's not what we are looking for. Do you still have the rock we found?"

"Yes."

"Bag it. It's evidence." Pierre looked at the escarpment. His face was covered in dirt and fresh abrasions. Nothing seemed to indicate the source of the unnatural rock. "Rocks in the desert can move by natural forces, so finding the source could take some work. But what's worse is that some idiot forgot to charge the flashlight. The battery is completely dead."

"Pretty serious." Alicia shook her head. "All rover equipment is supposed to be logged, replaced, and recharged upon return for the next users. It's a matter of life or death."

"Do you have your tablet on you?"

"Of course."

"Take a photograph of the cave so we can keep track of where we've been in case we need to come back."

Alicia reached into her pocket and pulled out her tablet. She pressed the side button repeatedly. "Strange. It's not turning on. Out of power too?"

"I'm not so sure," said Pierre. He walked over to his backpack and pulled out the spare tablet. It too failed to power up. He reached into his pocket and pulled out the hand-held radio. It too was dead. "What are the odds that four powered devices would fail all at once?"

"Small to none."

"I agree, and that too is evidence," said Pierre. "Thank your lucky tea leaves we left the rover on the edge of the Bite and walked in on foot. Otherwise, we might have been stranded here."

Alicia turned a sickly pale. Pierre pulled out a folded piece of paper that was in his pocket. He drew a crude line down the middle of the paper.

"What are you doing?" she said.

"Doing it old school," said Pierre. He marked a spot on the paper. "I'm making a crude map. Okay, we need to walk the rest of the ridge and pick up any of these shards."

* * *

The next day Pierre called an early morning meeting of the senior technical staff. He had spent the night preparing his presentation. They were in a dimly lit conference room with a long table. The terminal glowed bright with more illumination than the overhead lights.

Pierre lingered near the terminal with two shoe boxes on the table. He recognized some of the faces: Peter Chin, Pavel Urbanovich, Dutch Haring, Brian Johnson, Hans Poul, Luke Bronson, and at the head of the table opposite the video terminal was Governor Gardiner slumped in his seat. Others in the room, he recognized but never met personally. Across the table from Peter and Hans sat Vladomyr Golenishchev, colony physicist.

Vladomyr brooded silently, fingers tented and pressed to his full lips. His full head of black hair, straight and glossy, parted over a heavy-set brow that shaded his eyes, slate black and penetrating. Behind Gardiner in the left corner stood a large Nigerian in full battle fatigues— Pierre deduced this was Okeli Negedu, the security chief.

"Do you think we can begin?" offered Pierre.

"The floor is yours," said Gardiner. "Let's see what you have."

"I have not yet found the cause of the terraforming failure—"

"Isn't that what you're supposed to be doing?" Chin pointed into the tabletop.

"Yeah!" shouted Luke, who then eased back and smirked. Hans chuckled along with the other sycophants.

Pierre stopped speaking.

"Gentlemen," said Gardiner angrily. After pausing for a few seconds, he spoke with slow cadence. "We are here to find out what Pierre has found. You need to let him reveal his findings first. Then, you can dump on him. Pierre… please… continue." Pierre resented how Gardiner pitted his people against each other.

Pierre turned to the computer terminal and pulled up the area map on the screen. "Here is the local area of the colony." Pierre pointed out the spot in the center of the map where the colony was located. He then showed the data with the scatterbug activity. "The red area is our scatterbug activity. Our attention turned to the northeast portion where there is no activity. We call this area *the Bite.*"

"The Bite?" asked Gardiner.

"Yes," said Pierre. "My assistant named it. Think about this as a giant cookie and this area like a Bite out of the cookie." Everyone in the room laughed. At that moment, Pierre realized he had lost some respect in the room. "That was our first clue. So we did site proofing of Varney Ridge."

Pierre picked up the top shoebox and dumped the contents. The two tablets, hand-held radio, and flashlight spilled onto the table. "All these electronics died while on the survey."

"Died as in out of power?" asked Vladomyr with a pronounced Ukrainian accent. He picked up the flashlight, unscrewed the focusing lens, and looked inside. "Sloppy equipment handling isn't unknown."

"No, died as in fried." Pierre shook his head and smiled. "I had Habib look at these. He says the electronics are all dead. Not a power supply problem."

Vladomyr pursed his lips and nodded.

"What can kill all these electronics at once?" Chin blew off dust that coated one of the tablets. "I think Pierre broke these intentionally to keep his little scam going."

"Never heard of an electromagnetic pulse, have you?" said Vladomyr.

"A flashlight too?" said Chin incredulously. "An electronic? Seriously?"

"This is an LED flashlight," said Vladomyr. He shook the handle at Chin. "It uses an integrated circuit as a driver and is as much an electronic device as any tablet or radio."

"Brian, is that true?" said Chin, calling on the chief engineer's opinion.

"I'm finding it hard to believe too," said Brian. His pot belly folded over the edge of the conference table.

Vladomyr turned to Brian seated two chairs from him. "Oh, you would side with that scientific ignoramus. You need to crawl out of his ass and stop tickling his spleen."

Pierre's eyebrows rose. "I'm not done." He whispered hoping to grab attention from the arguing men.

"Sorry," said Valdomyr. "Go on."

"Thank you," said Pierre. He opened the lid of the second box. He pushed the box across the table. "The last sandstorm seems to have uncovered these."

"What's this?" said Chin. He reached in and pulled out a stone shard. "A rock."

"The limestone is local to Varney Ridge," said Pierre. "We found twenty-seven of these fragments. Each of these limestone shards has at least one chisel mark."

"Do you realize what you are saying?" said Valdomyr.

"Yes," said Pierre. "Someone has been building on our doorstep, and they don't want us to find it."

The tension in the room changed suddenly. The group murmured to each other. Pierre could not make out what they were saying.

Okeli stepped up to the table by Gardiner's side. "We have a security concern here."

"Basra?" said Gardiner.

"Yes, sir."

"I'll take it under advisement."

"Vladomyr," said Gardiner. "Do we have EMP meters?"

"Yes," said the Ukrainian.

"Are they shielded?"

"They wouldn't be much use if they weren't."

"Can't say I'm happy to receive your report," said Gardiner.

"A small team is needed to survey Varney Ridge to narrow where the digging was done." Pierre then said, "We would advise anyone entering the Bite to do so only on foot." Their label, *the Bite*, no longer seemed funny and perhaps a little too ironic. No one was laughing.

"You'll have it." The governor stood up. "I'm also assigning you an armed security detail for whenever you go to the ridge. And we'll need extra security patrols around our perimeter. Dismissed gentlemen." Gardiner walked out of the room, followed immediately by Okeli. The lights brightened, and the meeting broke up.

"What happened here?" Pierre asked Vladomyr.

"World War Five," he answered.

CHAPTER NINE

Insta-caff is an instant enjoyable beverage containing many of the essential stimulants for peak performance. Combine with 250ml hot or cold water to deliver a smooth 80mg dose of caffeine for keen alertness and 2g of taurine neurotransmitters for heightened awareness, blended with delightful artificial coffee flavors. Use in moderation. Side-effects include increased heart rate and blood pressure, disturbed sleep, anxiety, weight gain, elevated blood sugar, coma, and death. — **"Packaging on the side of an insta-caff packet"**

Vladomyr slammed the shot of white whisky and pounded the empty glass onto the desk.

"Another?" said Pierre. He held up a half-empty bottle. Vladomyr held up his hand, refusing a second.

"I like that stuff way too much, and it's way too early in the morning." Vladomyr laughed. He touched his brow with the back of his hand. "I don't like doing my heavy drinking until at least 8am. However, I presume I'm here because you need my help."

Pierre put the bottle back in the drawer of his desk and closed it shut. "I want to locate where the digging was being done in the Bite. But electronics get fried anytime we get near the area. So GPS readers are out of the question as are laser rangefinders."

"You're fortunate," said Vladomyr.

"How so?"

"The sand basin is level, and visibility is excellent." Vladomyr grabbed a paper and pen and drew on the back. "Set up three surveyors outside of the Bite. Use them as spotters. Two people enter the Bite with

EMP meters, walking in from opposite directions along the ridge. One spotter is stationary at a far corner; he doesn't move. The other two spotters stay on the same longitude as the stationary surveyor but follow the two inside the Bite along the latitude. The rest is simple geometry."

"Then what?"

"Have them at certain times raise a flag. The surveyors record the reader's positions, and the readers take EMP readings. The EMP readings should pinpoint the source of the EMP at least within about a few hundred meters. That should narrow things down."

"Sounds like a plan," said Pierre. "I'd like to get started today by noon."

"I think we can do that," said Vladomyr.

"That's assuming the construction is tied to EMPs." The Frenchman paused for a moment and downed his own drink. "Can I ask you something?"

"You just did."

"What's between you and Chin?"

"You noticed?" Vladomyr gave a short laugh. It was hard to miss. "There are two types of academics: those obsessed with research and those obsessed with prestige, awards, and respect. Peter was a university professor who was politically astute but incompetent. He plagiarized dozens of journal articles and faked results. Talk to him and you soon find out he knows nothing."

"How'd he get sent here as a biology expert?"

"Great recommendations," said Vladomyr with a snort. "It's called *decruitment*. His university wanted to get rid of him, so they provided great recommendations to encourage him to move on. And he moved on into the space program."

"Sounds familiar," said Pierre, recalling his own decruitment experience. However, while anyone could have a bad run of luck or be misunderstood, chronic academic dishonesty was less easy to overlook. Pierre hoped he had learned from his own past competence issues.

Vladomyr sniggered. "Don't let what they say get to you."

Pierre now was wondering what *they* were saying. He figured he was being called *dead weight*. Was there more to the rumors?

"In the end, results are going to matter," said Vladomyr.

"It won't matter much if I cannot find the source of the blight."

Vladomyr stood up and walked to the door of the office. "Just a piece of friendly advice. Don't waste a second. Time is your enemy. If you fail, death will be swift."

* * *

An olive-green tent served as the survey home base. There were three tables and a whiteboard set up. Computer terminals were on the tables, and on the whiteboard hung an oversized map of the Bite. A radio linked the tent to the surveyors. Alicia sat at the radio wearing a headset.

"Pierre," she said. "The EMP readers are in place and about to begin. We have one positioned in the north intersection of the Bite and ridge and the other to the south. Any last-minute instructions before they enter the Bite and are out of radio contact?"

He thought for a moment and answered, "About three hours to cross the Bite. Take a reading every 20 minutes. That should give us enough samples to make our calculations." Pierre picked up a piece of paper, as Alicia gave the instructions. "Remind them about the semaphores."

Alicia nodded and spoke into the radio. "Readers, the surveyors will be keeping track of you. Pay close attention to the built-in clocks on your EMP meters. Also, remember your flags. Red flag, take the position and reading. Blue flag, cannot take reading, returning to the rover. Green flag, emergency and shoot flare gun for emergency assistance." Alicia covered her microphone and whispered to Pierre. "Why the green flag for an emergency? Wouldn't red or yellow make more sense?"

"Yellow flags are camouflaged in the desert," said Pierre. "The surveyors need to key off the flags, so they need the flag that is easiest to see. Hence, the red for the readings. That leaves blue or green. The choice between the two is arbitrary. Frankly, if a surveyor gets in trouble out there, the flare is what's going to alert us. All the flag does is help us locate them, and that shouldn't even be necessary since two of the three surveyors should always have eyes on them anyway."

Alicia repeated the flag instructions to the readers and surveyors. She then gave the readers the command to begin.

"Can I get you a coffee?" said Pierre to Alicia. She replied with an appreciative nod. Everyone had something to do except him. So he went to the coffee machine and poured a mug of instant caffeinated coffee substitute. He brought it back to Alicia who was still operating the radio. He set the mug beside her. She picked up the mug, took a sip, and winced.

"Tastes like shit," she said. "I've never gotten used to insta-caff."

Pierre paced while looking at the clock. The first twenty minutes went by. He heard a crackle and a voice bleed from Alicia's headphones.

"Spotters report first position readings," she said.

Pierre sighed with relief. He thought at least one reading had been taken. Twenty minutes later, a second position reading. Then two more readings. An hour, twenty minutes pass, then another report.

Alicia pulled off her headset. "Bad news. The northern reader sent up a blue flag."

"Damn, equipment malfunction," said Pierre. "Get the coordinates from the surveyors." Alicia wrote the coordinates from the spotters. Pierre marked the positions on the map. "Have both readers return to their rovers."

After the readers got back to their rovers, they radioed to home base. Pierre grabbed the headset. He put on the headset and adjusted the mouthpiece. "Hey, guys," he said. "What happened out there?"

"Marcus, here," said the Northern reader. Marcus was part of the security detail, but he was also good with repetitive technical tasks. "I got a little more than four kilometers, and the EMP reader burned out."

"Thanks," said Pierre. "Do you have a spare EMP reader in the rover?"

"Yeah," said Marcus.

"Excellent," said Pierre. "What about you, Hans?"

"My EMP meter is still working. I got decent readings but only when I got six kilometers in. The EMP readings are highly variable in strength."

"We might not have what we need," said Pierre. "It's half past one o'clock. We still have time to repeat the survey before dark. It's unlikely the source of the pulses is in the southern third of the ridge. This time, give Hans an hour head start. Everyone understand?"

"Yes," said both readers in unison.

* * *

Pierre looked up at the clock on his terminal. It was 9pm, and he was back in the office. When the readers got out of the Bite, it was a little after 4pm, which gave them time to tear down the base camp and return to the colony. Before him on his desk was the stack of notes. Position data and the EMP strengths at least until the meters conked out. He now had to place the data into the GIS system and see what the results would be.

Alicia entered the office. She slammed the door behind her to grab his attention. "You weren't at the mess hall."

"No, I wasn't." Pierre looked at the stack of papers in front of him. He had never been good with paperwork, and data entry was his least favorite task. "I forgot about the time."

"I see you have the notes from today."

"Yes, I have to enter them in before I go to bed."

"I can see you are making good progress." She poked him. Pierre looked up at her. His eyes were bloodshot with dark circles. He had been doing a lot of all-nighters. "Why don't you pack it in? I'll enter the notes into the terminal."

143

"I need to input the data."

"Nonsense." Alicia swiveled Pierre around in his chair. "You're getting nothing done. Go! Crash! Sleep. And the results will magically appear on your terminal in the morning." She dragged Pierre to his feet. Her strength overwhelmed him. She pushed him out of the office and locked the door behind him.

Pierre stood momentarily in the wide hallway outside his office. The hallway was more like a bunker than an office building. He saw a rover driving down the hallway. The driver parked in front of Pierre.

"You okay?" said Harvey, an elderly bald man wearing gray coveralls. He was doing his night janitorial duties. A used copy of *Engineering Times* was rolled up and stuffed in the dashboard.

"Can I bum a ride back to the barracks?" said Pierre.

"Are you drunk?"

"I wish." Pierre snorted.

Harvey smiled. "Hop on board."

* * *

In the morning, Pierre returned to his office. He found a note on his desk. "All done. Sleep well?" He smiled then turned on the terminal. When the computer had finished its boot cycle, he pulled up the GIS program. "Stacy597: Add EMP signal data to GIS map."

"Working," said the computer. The blue reticle turned periodically. Then sixteen glowing orange circles appeared inside the Bite. He zoomed into the area where a plurality of circles intersected.

Alicia bounced into the office with two trays. "Morning," she said cheerfully.

"Yup," said Pierre. He turned his head to her. "What's that?"

"Breakfast. You might have heard of it."

"I'm from Paris. Of course, I've never heard of breakfast." He turned back to the screen. "Thank you for inputting the data."

"Only took twenty minutes," she said proudly. Alicia put one of the breakfast boxes in front of him. "You! Eat!"

"Says who?"

"Says me," she said. "You didn't eat dinner last night. Your lunch yesterday was six cups of insta-caff, and I'm not even aware if you have had anything to eat before that. I'm confident you haven't eaten for at least 24 hours."

Pierre opened the tray. Three breakfast sausages and simulated scrambled eggs made of plant protein. He shook his head. The ESA could export baby cobras to control rats, fawns for terraforming, but not a single chicken for eggs? A waste to turn plants into protein substitutes when chickens were much more capable and efficient at turning plants into real animal protein.

"Have you noticed all the protein substitutes taste like cardboard?" Pierre picked up the fork inside of the tray. He stabbed a sausage and ate half of it.

"Everything here tastes like garbage." Alicia devoured her food. "Worse than MREs. Never thought I would say that. If the ESA had fed us what we were going to be eating, I would have quit and taken my chances with the snipers."

Pierre chuckled. "It was false advertising."

"No shit."

He put down the fork and turned back to the terminal. "Any problems inputting the data?"

"No," she said. Her mouth was full of food as she spoke. "The notes were quite clear."

"I noticed that the EMP signal strengths are not all intersecting in the same place. Any thoughts?"

"EMP strength fluctuated. And the readers being a couple of seconds off here and there could account for variations in the readings."

"Makes sense." Pierre measured the area. "It looks like the measurements have narrowed the area to about sixty thousand square meters, about a 440-foot section of Varney Ridge."

"So about 1.2 football fields. We should plant two flags outside the Bite using GPS and go in by compass."

"That would seem prudent." Pierre sent a copy of the map vignette to the print center. Printing at the colony was centralized. The print center manager scrutinized the use of printing like every resource of the colony was scrutinized. Waste was discouraged. Frivolous printouts were reported.

"I'll saddle up the horses and request a posse," said Alicia. "We walked by that section of the ridge, and I don't recall seeing anything conspicuous there. Nothing I recall resembling a cave or tunnel."

"Make sure there are enough shovels for the posse," said Pierre. "At least the ones who aren't part of the security detail."

"I'll see what we can do."

"Let's head out by 11am."

* * *

The search party parked a pair of rovers on the north side of the Bite. This made the security detachment nervous. If there was an incident from Basra or even exiles, it would come from the north. A couple of guards watched the rovers while the rest of the party did the hour-long hike to the EMP hot zone.

When the six of them arrived, Pierre looked over the stretch of the escarpment with binoculars. He looked for signs of construction: caves, nooks, tunnels. Nothing obvious. He turned to the other five and gave them their instructions.

"We are here to find the source of the EMP pulses," said Pierre. "It could be located anywhere north or south of where we are now in an approximately plus or minus 225-foot range. We are going to spread out. Each of you is going to get a 75-foot section, which Alicia will mark off with neon green spray paint. I want you guys to go through the scree."

Melissa raised her hand. "What's a *scree*?"

Pierre smirked and said, "A scree is a slope of small loose stones covering the base of a cliff or mountain."

146

"Learned a new word."

"Awesome!" Pierre smiled at Melissa. He might have been happy as a high school teacher and regretted never having the opportunity to teach. Maybe, when this is all over and they survive this, being a social studies teacher wouldn't be so bad after all. "As you dig, look for anything out of the ordinary."

Hans raised his hand. "What would be out of the ordinary?"

"Limestone shards like the ones we showed you. Caves, tunnels, or any strange geological features. Anything that looks manmade. Old containers. Trash. Whatever can help us zero in on what we are looking for."

"Here's to finding trash," said Marcus, a Hispanic man in his thirties. He was accompanied by his wife of ten years, Jasmine, a tall, slender woman of Indian descent. Unlike Marcus, Jasmine was born on Gliese and had never been to earth. Marcus was infamous for telling his wife recollections of earth; however, Jasmine had little conception of things such as high school, the subway, or even mysterious animals like dogs. "My first job out of high school was picking up trash," continued Marcus. "The ESA told me this would be the adventure of a lifetime."

Everyone laughed.

"Let's hope we find some trash. Our lives might depend on it," said Pierre. "Okay, I've numbered the sections from 1 to 6. Hans, I've assigned you to the southmost section, that's number 1. Melissa, section 2, we don't want you far from your father. Alicia, you get 3. I'll take 4. Jasmine, 5. And Marcus gets the north section, number 6. Any questions?"

"What if we don't find anything?" said Hans.

"Then start digging. That's why you all have shovels. Anything else?" He waited a moment for questions, but none were forthcoming. "Okay, proceed to your assigned sections. Happy hunting."

The six of them separated and went to their assigned sections. Alicia went to the first section and marked off the boundaries with spray paint. She made sure that each member of the party knew their section boundaries. When she finished marking off the final section, she returned to her own section to begin her search.

At 3pm, the searchers stopped for a break and an update. It was a cool day. It felt like fall even though it was December 10ᵗʰ. Christmas was coming, but no one had even a glimmer of festivity. The workers took out pocket-sized lunches and had something to eat while they rested. When they saw Pierre had no food, Marcus offered part of his lunch burrito.

"Not hungry," said Pierre. "Has anything been found? Any limestone shards?"

"I found one," said Jasmine. She pulled it out of her pocket and showed Pierre.

Pierre took it and looked at it. "Nice. This one has distinct chisel marks. That's a good start."

"I wish I found something," said Melissa. The thirteen-year-old girl frowned and slumped her head.

"I found trash," said Marcus. He handed Pierre a sliver of metal.

Pierre saw that it had three joints. "A scatterbug leg. Curious."

"What's so curious about that?"

"How did it get here with all the EMPs?"

"I can guess," said Hans. "The scatterbugs have a metal shell. They have their own Faraday cage. A scatterbug could sustain only minor damage as it travelled through the Bite. However, it would be like a human being exposed to radiation: the longer the exposure, the greater the damage."

"Interesting," said Pierre. "Okay, let's get back to work."

They worked another two hours. About an hour before quitting, Pierre visited each section. Marcus and Jasmine found more shards as did Alicia and Hans. When Pierre visited Melissa's section, he found her digging sand away at a furious pace. For a wiry young lady, she took to digging. Unlike the Earthers, she did not need a rebreather. She was born into this world and completely adapted to its conditions.

"Find anything?" said Pierre.

She did not stop digging. "Nope."

"Whoa there!" said Pierre.

Melissa stopped digging. She turned to face Pierre. She was panting. Her face and hair were covered in dirt. She wore loose fatigues without a hat and kept her hair long and loose.

"You're not just shoveling sand," said Pierre. "As you shovel, you must look through the sand. Otherwise, you might be throwing away something important."

Melissa looked at her feet. She bent and picked up a piece of what looked like a white stone. She stood back up and dusted it off.

"You mean like this?" she said.

"Let's see what you got?" Pierre took the object from her. The surface was smooth and glossy like glass, but it was ceramic. He looked at the surface. There was writing like the piece that Gardiner had.

"Is it something?"

Pierre turned to the left and shouted to Alicia in the next section. "Everyone to section 2! I want everyone digging right here for the rest of the shift!" He turned back to Melissa. "You might have made the most important discovery of the day." Pierre climbed to the top of the scree and began digging alongside Melissa. Melissa also resumed digging. As the others came over, everyone joined in. They formed a train of shovels and buckets to quickly move sand to a fill pile twenty feet away.

An hour later, a rock ledge appeared from beneath the sand.

"Clear the sand around the ledge," said Pierre. They were onto something. The sun was starting to set. He looked in his binoculars. The guards around the rovers were getting anxious. They held up red flags indicating time was up. Pierre held up a checkered flag indicating he needed another hour. It would still be twilight by the time they got back to the rovers—the advantage of a 28 earth-hour day. The guards acknowledged the signal. "Okay guys, one more hour, then we're heading back."

The others huddled around the ledge, clearing the sand away. They carried away bucket after bucket of sand. Pierre looked at the sand pile. The sand pile could go through dry sifting later if they found nothing more. Dry sifting could produce more white ceramic fragments.

An eight-inch space appeared underneath the rock ledge. Time was nearly up. It wouldn't be safe after dark.

"Okay, everyone! Stop work!" shouted Pierre. Everyone stopped and scaled down the scree away from the ledge.

"We need to go," said Alicia.

"I need your spray paint." Pierre took the spray paint and marched up the scree to the ledge. Alicia followed. He marked three large Xs over the ledge well above the sand meniscus. "If there is a sandstorm tonight, at least we won't lose where we were digging."

Pierre handed the paint can back to his assistant. He laid down by the ledge and stuck his arm into the space under the ledge.

"What are you doing?" yelled Alicia. "There might be a cobra in there."

"Don't be silly," said Pierre. "This crevice has been buried for ages. No way a cobra would've gotten in there while you were digging. Besides, I'm not going to come back tomorrow and stick my arm in there when a cobra could sneak in and call it home."

Pierre felt around inside the dark hole. The sand under his touch was cool and dry.

"Discover anything?" said Alicia.

"I'm feeling sand," said Pierre. He groped in the dark without seeing where his hand was. Under his forearm, he swept sand aside until his fingers touched a hard object. He brushed the sand away as best as he could. The object was long, slender, and light to the touch with a pronounced grain like fossilized wood. It was not limestone or ceramic. He grabbed the object and pulled. Stuck. He shook it until it came free.

Pierre pulled his arm out of the hole, holding the object. "I'm going to need a specimen bag."

"What is it?" said Alicia.

"A bone." Pierre held in hand a humerus from a biped.

CHAPTER TEN

Edible synthetic protein has become a mainstay of the colony worlds. This technology was patented in AD 2034 by KönigsAgra Corporation during the veganism craze among the North American upper classes. Protein is extracted from nitrogen-fixing plants: beans, peas, lentils. The protein is washed with solvents to remove all traces of flavor. Collagen is combined with the extract and polymerized to form a gelatin-like paste that can be colored, flavored, and molded to imitate many kinds of animal products, e.g., eggs and shrimp. During the 21st Century, synthetic protein was a commercial failure. However, after the patent expired, struggling colony worlds adopted synthetic protein as a food staple. — **"What We Eat in Space" by Noam Chompkin**

All the lights came on. Gardiner met Pierre in the biology lab. Pierre was uncomfortable with the new setting. A stack of boxes waited for him on an examination table.

"Chin is not going to like this," said Pierre. This had been Peter Chin's lab.

"I've reassigned him to the botany lab," said Gardiner, carefully stroking his handlebar moustache.

"That's about half the size. He's going to blame me for this."

"I'm still governor here," said Gardiner. "And it is my prerogative to prioritize the use of space. Maybe some real results will come out of one of these labs."

On a large steel work bench, Pierre laid out the bone and the ceramic ostracon. Beside them, he placed two boxes of limestone shards.

"What do we know about the bone?" said Gardiner.

"Still too early to say much," said Pierre.

"How old is it?" Gardiner pressed for more information.

"We don't have a carbon-14 profile for this planet. Testing directly for age will be difficult." Pierre picked up the bone. "The bone is completely clean. This means the flesh had to rot off with the assistance of bacteria and fungi. I was told that there was no life at all on this planet prior to colonization. When there is no bacteria or fungi and in desert conditions, flesh doesn't decay. It mummifies like in Egyptian pan graves."

"Pan graves… sounds promising. What's that?" said the old man.

"People too poor for a proper burial were thrown into sand pits. The dry sand turned them into natural mummies." Pierre looked closely at the bone. "But this limb underwent normal decomposition."

Gardiner tapped his fingers on the bench. "Any guesses?"

* * *

Later that morning at Varney Ridge, the workers gathered for another day. They found the three green Xs from the day before. Pierre began the day with a team meeting.

"I know there's been a lot of talk about the bone we found yesterday. And we might find more. The colony is on edge already. They don't need to overhear us talk about bones in the cafeteria. So, from now on, we are going to call them bananas."

Melissa giggled. "What's a banana?"

"A long curved yellow fruit." Hans chuckled.

"I know you still have a lot of questions about who this was. Did you know him or her? We don't have answers yet." Pierre shuffled towards the scree. "To get the answers, we need to proceed more carefully. We need to dig the rock and sand away but don't dig into the cave itself. Clear the entrance as best we can. Any questions?"

Jasmine raised her hand. "What if sand falls out of the cave as we dig?"

"That's fine. Clearing will help us figure out how big the cave is. Other questions?"

He waited until it was clear no more questions would be coming.

"We have enough limestone shards. Unless there's writing on them, any shard can go into the fill pile. All right, let's get digging."

As soon as the scrum was done, the team organized into a line to move the sand and rocks away. Each digger had a sense of what to do and fell into their role.

By midafternoon, the cave entrance had been cleared away. A path had been cut into the scree with an eight-foot wall of sand and rock to each side. Sand packed the mouth of the cave, but the entrance was clear. The opening appeared natural and unfinished, about seven feet tall and about eight feet wide. The mouth was slightly widened at the base but not enough to account for all the limestone shards they found.

"Okay, good enough." Pierre called the diggers back.

"What now, boss?" said Marcus.

"Now, I see what we got." Pierre picked up a hand whisk broom and stepped up to the entrance. Similar to a Renaissance master painter, he swept the sand away with swift gentle strokes. The sand flew aside out of the entrance, falling to the ground. He started from the top and worked his way down. Pierre removed the front layer of sand. He stepped back from the entrance and observed his handiwork. The weathered gray of cured bone appeared, stuffed into the cave from the floor to within inches of the ceiling.

Alicia stepped up to Pierre's side. "What does it mean?" said Alicia.

"It means we need more sample bags." Pierre put a hand in his pocket.

"How many skeletons do you think there are?"

"Depends how deep the cave is." He shrugged his shoulders. "Could be a couple dozen or a lot more."

"A cemetery?"

"Perhaps. But whose cemetery?"

"Basra's?"

"Basra is 8000 miles away," said Pierre. "It's practically on the other side of the planet. Coming here is not practical for a cemetery. It'd make more sense if this was one of our cemeteries."

"But Arish's cemetery is south of the colony." Alicia looked at the bones in the cave. "As far as I know, no burials are way out here."

"Can't be exiles, too many of them," said Pierre. "Children of exiles?"

"Hate to suggest this," said Alicia. "But could this be a mass grave from a war crime?"

"Let's not jump to conclusions." Pierre wiped his forehead with the back of his sleeve.

Alicia looked at Pierre expectantly.

"Hans!" Pierre called out. "I need you to take a rover back to the colony and bring back specimen boxes. They look like shoeboxes for boots. Bring back the flattened ones."

"How many?" said Hans.

"Start with a thirty pack," said Pierre. "That will be only the beginning. But probably all we'll get done today." Pierre called the rest of the workers together. "We need to categorize the skeletons and keep the assemblies together. Can anyone here draw?"

Jasmine raised her hand.

"Excellent. Digital cameras won't work out here. So I need you to record everything as we work. First, take a quick sketch of the cave entrance. Then we will start excavating the skeletons." Pierre handed Jasmine a notepad and a pencil. She quickly sketched what she saw. Pierre looked over her shoulder as she drew. She drew with a strong line, accurate detail, and precise shading. A technical artist. "You just became the dig artist."

One of the guards walked up to Pierre. "Sir?"

"What is it?" said Pierre.

"Gardiner wants you back at the colony to give him an update on your progress," said the man holding a rifle.

"Can't this wait until I return?"

"He said it's urgent."

"If I must…" He then turned his attention back to the team. He held up specimen bags in his hand for everyone to see. "Seems I won't be here to excavate the skeletons myself. I'm going to trust you with it. Work on only one skeleton at a time. Clear as much dirt as you can from it. Before you bag a skeleton, have Jasmine draw a sketch of it. Don't work on the skeleton beneath until you bag everything from the skeleton above. Think in layers. Top layers first and work your way down.

"On each bag, write your name, the date, and assign a number for each skeleton, and the number of bags if more than one is used. A complete skeleton won't fit in one bag. Put all the small bones like hands and feet into one bag, vertebrae in another, and other small bones as best fits in the bags until Hans returns with the boxes. Keep the bones of each skeleton separate. When a skeleton is complete, collect the bags and put them into a box. Put arm and leg bones as well as the skull and pelvis in the box without bagging them. Never put multiple skeletons in the same box. Everyone understand?"

"I'll make sure it stays organized," said Alicia.

"Thanks, I'll see you all back at the colony."

* * *

When Pierre got back to the colony, he went directly to Gardiner's office. He knocked on the door, and Gardiner called him in. Pierre entered the office and closed the hatch behind him. The door closed with a boom of impacting metal—it was robust earth technology, built like a battleship, and made all the same strange noises.

"Have a seat," said Gardiner. He stood behind his desk reading a printout. "I need an update."

Did he not get an update this morning? "Couldn't this have waited until I got back?" Pierre sat in the chair in front of Gardiner's desk.

"No, it couldn't."

"How many exiles have there been? "

"Right now?"

"In the history of the colony?"

"About a dozen."

"Well, that rules out exiles," said Pierre. "Probably over sixty skeletons in that cave."

"Where did they come from?" said Gardiner

"I'd be trying to figure that out if I wasn't here giving you another update." Pierre's nostrils flared. A lot of things he could be doing that would be a better use of his time than sitting in Gardiner's office. "Are you absolutely sure our colony has never used the cave as a cemetery?"

"Yes," said Gardiner. "Vital statistics have always been fastidiously done in the colonies. Colonies live and die by their birth and death records. We know who comes and who goes and where everyone is buried."

"Doubt they're from our colony anyway." Pierre tented his fingers. "This is damn strange, but we are getting closer to some sort of truth."

"Glad to hear that."

"We thought there was one body. Now, we know it's many."

"Not good news, but progress." Gardiner picked up the printout and skimmed it again. "While I appreciate the report, that wasn't the reason I called you back. We've received a text message from NASA."

"NASA? That's strange. Gliese is part of the ESA program."

"Bad news, I fear. A nuclear device was detonated at the Cagliari launch center. The whole place was destroyed."

Pierre's face went white. "We only received it now?"

"Yes, that means that the news is about 16 years old. So about 7 years after you left." Gardiner handed Pierre the printout. "They took out our relief transport. NASA said they will provide temporary communications support to ESA colonies until alternative facilities are constructed."

"That's bad." Pierre flipped through the printout, which provided a gratuitous amount of detail including casualty numbers, blast yield and radius, and the source of the nuclear material, the failed Pakistani state. He felt like someone just walked over his grave.

"It's worse than that," said Gardiner. "Without the orbital docking station, transport vessels intended for us will be redirected to other colonies. This will interrupt our relief supplies."

"What about the MegaAI?"

"That would save our bacon." Gardiner nodded his head. "However, we have not heard back from it. Frankly, it's a long shot. They could be near but still unable to alter their course to assist us."

"I see."

"It's also bad because Basra will have received the message."

"They wouldn't attack our colony, would they?"

"Anything to prevent it?" Gardiner raised his eyebrows.

"Who else knows?"

"Just Okeli," said Gardiner. "He's got a martial law plan ready in the event of the worst. So it's imperative that you discover what's causing the blight. Because we are not getting any more food shipments from earth."

* * *

Pierre was exhausted, but he could not sleep either. He still remembered Cagliari and the ESA launch center. What happened to all the people there? Were Tiffany and Roger still alive? Did they get incinerated in the blast? Did they face a long agonizing death of radiation sickness? Roger might have escaped being long-retired, but Tiffany would have been mid-career. How has this act of terror changed the world he once knew? While state actors had long given up nuclear weapons, a few prohibited weapons always seemed to "go missing" prior to being destroyed. Nevertheless, this shattered any illusion that Pierre still knew the earth he left. If he ever returned, he would be an alien, disconnected from a world he no longer recognized.

No sense going to bed, so he puttered about the biology lab. All the techs had gone for the night. In front of him were twenty-one bone boxes. He glanced through the drawings of the skeletons Jasmine had made. The cave was more densely packed than he realized. Prior to sunset, the team had not even dug into the first four feet of the cave. How far back did the cave extend? He was exhausted and in no mood to reconstruct skeletons.

A soft knock on the door of the biology lab.

Pierre stood up and walked over to the door. He unlocked and opened it. Melissa was standing outside. She was wearing her filthy fatigues from earlier in the day. Her sweat soured the air from five feet away.

"It's after 10pm," said Pierre. "What are you doing here?"

"Alicia told me you are putting together skeletons." She tried looking past him.

"Bananas." He corrected her.

"Ah yes, bananas," she said.

"Your dad wouldn't want you here by yourself," said Pierre. "Go home."

"Hans knows I'm here." Her curiosity was getting the better of her.

"I'm tired. Not up to entertaining guests."

"Please… please…" She drew out each word.

"You better not be lying to me."

Melissa shook her head.

"If I let you in, you must follow three rules. (1) These are remains of the dead and are to be treated with respect, (2) don't put your feet on the banana boxes, and (3) you can look but you can't touch any of the bananas. Alright?"

"Okay," said Melissa. Pierre let her in.

"You can sit on that stool over there." Pierre pointed to a stool beside the examination table. "Did you want some cookies?"

Melissa perked up. "Sure."

Pierre reached into a drawer and pulled out a plastic wrapped package. He tore off the plastic wrap, opened the box, and handed it to her. "They're some sort of frosting filled biscuit cookie."

She gleefully took the box and shoveled the cookies into her mouth.

"You can have the whole box if you want. They probably belonged to Peter Chin. But this is my lab now. And they were in my lab, so they are mine." Pierre laughed at the irony. "Just don't let Peter catch you with those in the hall."

She giggled and nodded her head.

"Okay, that's the important stuff. Now, let's work with some bones."

"Bananas," Melissa corrected him.

"Of course. We're not where anyone can hear us, so it's fine to call them bones inside the lab." Pierre strolled over to the stack of boxes. "Okay, box number 2."

"Why box number 2?"

He grabbed the box and put it on the examination table. "Remember that bone we found two days ago? It's part of this skeleton and should go in this box. But first, we are going to reconstruct the skeleton."

Melissa kept munching on the cookies.

Pierre lifted the top off the box and pulled specimen bags out of it.

"Why separate bags?" asked Melissa.

"Bones are separated out by category." Pierre laid out the bags on the examination table, one by one. He kept the loose bones in the box until he was ready for them.

"I like to begin with the spine and the major bones," said Pierre.

"Why don't you start with the skull?" asked Melissa.

"Some people do," said Pierre. "Reconstructing a skeleton is an art. Everyone does it in a slightly different way. The skull is the most interesting part of the skeleton. I'm more motivated to complete a skeleton if I leave the skull till the end."

"I'll say skulls are interesting," said Melissa. Crumbs flew from her mouth as she talked.

Pierre raised an eyebrow. An odd statement coming from a young girl.

He selected the first and second bags and emptied their contents on the table. He lined up the vertebrae into a straight line. He arranged the collar bones and scapulae, and the arm bones. He picked up the mandible. The teeth looked sharp and pointed, and the chin was recessed. After examining the bone, he gently placed the mandible above the top vertebra.

A skeleton slowly took shape. He removed the leg bones and hips from the box and put them in place. He looked at the hips. Something was not quite right. The hips were missing the coccyx and most of the sacrum, which were normally fused to the hips.

He emptied the third bag onto a free space on the table. Small bones spilled into a pile. "Once you have the major bones in place, next hands and feet. You need to separate out the carpels from the tarsals. It's a common student mistake to get them mixed up."

"They look similar," said Melissa.

"While I sort the small bones, why don't you tell me the real reason you wanted to be here as I put this jigsaw together?" Pierre squinted at the bones. He lifted one of the small bones that did not look right. He set it aside. The more he sorted, the more it became clear there were too many bones for hands and feet.

"Reasons," she said. "I'm curious."

"That all?"

"Wondering if I would get squeamish around so many bones."

"And are you?"

"No."

Pierre looked at his piles of bones. "Are all these really the bones from skeleton 2?"

"That's all there was." Melissa furrowed her brow.

"Damn strange," said Pierre. He shook his head. Nothing seemed the right size. "What kind of mutant was this guy?"

Melissa flashed a smirk. Pierre reconstructed the hands and feet. Each foot had four long tarsals with four elongated toes. Each hand had four carpels with four long fingers; each finger had three joints. And he still had a small pile of fine bones that were neither fingers nor toes.

"What are these?" The bones could easily fit with each other. They looked like small vertebrae, but they were not vertebrae. He counted the spine vertebrae. Thirty-five. Two too many. He looked at the hips, and it occurred to him. He matched the small bones to the sacrum.

"It's a tail." Pierre exhaled. All the wind went out of him. What the hell? He turned to the box and pulled out the skull. His pupils dilated. The skull was unlike any he had seen before: eye sockets larger and wider than a normal human's, sharp needle teeth, and a sagittal crest. "What's this?"

"The skull from skeleton #2," said Melissa. She swung her feet back and forth.

"You knew about this?"

"You didn't?" she said.

"No," admitted Pierre. He could not tell her what had happened and why Gardiner had kept him away from today's dig.

"All the skulls are weird. Dad completely freaked out. You freaked?"

"Honestly, yeah."

"I was wondering how you would react." Melissa instantly lost interest in the reconstruction.

"You don't seem freaked."

Melissa smiled. "Never seen a skull before. Didn't surprise me cause I didn't know what to expect." The right side of her mouth arched into a weird smile. "Perhaps, you should take a look inside the other boxes."

"Okay, that's enough for tonight." Pierre showed Melissa the door. "Time for you to go home."

"Ah…"

"What are you complaining about? You got a free box of cookies." Pierre opened the door of the lab for her. "You might want to save some of those cookies. It might be a long time before you get another box."

After she left, he locked the door. He went to the stack of boxes. He opened the top box and looked at the skull inside. Sure enough, this skull was different than the one for skeleton #2. This skull was broad and heavy. It had no sagittal crest and thick cheek bones. The skull had a full set of molars twice the size of any human tooth, no canines, and four cold chisel incisors, not designed to be sharp, but strong.

* * *

Pierre was eating breakfast in the cafeteria. Alicia sat across from him. She hovered over her tray, a felon guarding her food from the other inmates.

"What are those bodies?" said Alicia. "I'm a little rusty on my anatomy. But I've seen nothing like that, not in ten years of medical practice."

"Nobody has," whispered Pierre. He stabbed his simulated protein eggs with his fork. He looked over to the left. Chin and Luke were watching them. They probably already knew about what was found. "How is the team doing?"

"They have no idea what to think," Alicia whispered. "I don't know what to think."

Luke stood up and walked over to Pierre and Alicia. He put his hand on the table.

"Aren't you supposed to be doing something?" said Luke. "Like fixing our terraforming?" Chin and those at his table laughed.

Pierre pointed at Luke and said to Alicia. "That's what happens when space programs go cruelty free and send failed captains of the football teams into space instead of their betters."

"Are you talking about me?" said Luke. He curled his hand into a fist.

Pierre stood up and sniffed at Luke. "You don't bathe enough to keep kissing Chin's ass."

Luke scowled and turned red with fury. Pierre walked over to Chin. "You want to talk to me? You come yourself. Don't send your flunky."

"Terry says *hello*," said Chin. "He was surprised you survived."

"That almost sounds like the transport accident wasn't an accident." Pierre blanched like all life had drained from his face.

Chin hummed.

Pierre clenched his fists then relaxed. "I found your hidden stash of cookies, and they were delicious." Pierre strutted off smirking. Chin snarled and clenched his jaw.

* * *

In the conference room, the senior staff was once again gathered. Pierre dreaded this meeting. Vladomyr, Chin, Dutch, and Hans were present. Gardiner marched in and took his seat. He motioned to start the meeting even though not everyone had arrived.

"I want this one... brief," said Gardiner who clearly had a lot on his mind. The security chief, who was almost always attached to Gardiner's hip, was not in attendance.

"I'll get straight to the point," said Pierre. "As of last night, we have recovered the skeletal remains of twenty-one individuals."

"You said individuals," said Vladomyr. "You didn't say humans."

"You're right." Pierre put a slide on the monitor. The picture showed two different skulls side by side: the skull with the sagittal crest on the left, and the heavy one with the big teeth on the right. There was a hush in the room.

"Is this some kind of sick joke?" Chin stood up and shook his fist. "You think you can fool us with this fraud?"

"Sit down," said Vladomyr.

"Of the twenty-one skeletons, four were of the type on the left. We call that a Species 1 skeleton. Five were like the one on the right, Species 2."

"That's doesn't add up to twenty-one," said Vladomyr.

"Correct, the remaining skeletons are too fragmentary to identify," said Pierre. "Before we assign a Latin genus name, it is better that we assign them provisional numbers as we get a better understanding of their taxonomy."

Hans raised his hand. His blue eyes pierced the darkness. He sputtered and then said, "Are you saying these are two alien species?"

"I am saying two kinds of bipeds were discovered among those excavated. And that those bipeds do not appear human." Pierre dodged a half-full mug of insta-caff thrown at him. His shirt absorbed splatters of the caffeine substitute. Gardiner grinned like a child, successful in getting ants in a jar to fight.

"Don't be ridiculous," said Chin. "There are forty-eight human colony worlds. Not one of those planets has ever reported a shred of evidence for life. No civilizations, no fungi, no bacteria, not even complex proteins. Nothing. Alien life does not exist."

"Forty-eight worlds?" said Pierre. "Given how many exoplanets are in the galaxy, that's like an ant climbing his mound and declaring 'New York City does not exist.'"

"And you happened to find it on your first trip out?" said Chin. "Nonsense."

"That's a fallacy of invincible ignorance."

"Your results are fake."

"I don't know," said Hans. "I was there when the skulls were unearthed. How much time and manpower would it take to plant hundreds of fake bones? And then bury them under tons of loose rock and sand?"

"Maybe, you're in on it," said Chin.

"Watch yourself, Peter." Hans got up to his feet.

"Gentlemen, behave yourselves!" Gardiner banged on the table. "If this is true, it changes nothing."

"Except our status and place in the universe," said Vladomyr dryly.

"Vlad!" barked Gardiner, red in the face. He took a deep breath. "There are still a lot of unanswered questions."

Dutch raised his hand. "I have a question."

When the room quieted down, Gardiner motioned him to go ahead.

"Assuming you're telling us the truth, why would anyone bury bodies like this in a cave?" Dutch spoke softly and with intentionality.

"Who says they were buried?" said Pierre.

"Come on," said Dutch. "The bodies are obviously stacked in there like cord wood."

"Yes, stacked. But that doesn't mean *buried*." Pierre pulled up the slide of Jasmine's illustration of the partially excavated site. "When one encounters mass burials, they tend to follow one of two patterns. You have cemetery burials where the dead are laid out on their backs or on their sides in a fetal position, a layer of dirt is placed over the bodies, and the next layer of dead are buried on top. The other mass burial is a kind of disposal. This often is done when there is a plague or war crimes when less care is given to the dead. In that case, we would expect the bodies to be a random mix of positions."

"So which is it?"

"Neither," said Pierre. "The bodies were not piled into the cave. They are all face down and are at an angle to the south-east corner to the cave."

"What are you saying?"

"Looks like these people—if I can use that term—piled onto each other and died there."

"Why would anyone do that?"

"Don't know." Pierre shrugged his shoulders.

"I've got my own question," said Vladomyr. "We've been on this world for 150 years. Why is this the first evidence we've found of any life on this planet? Shouldn't there be other signs of civilization or traces of biological life?"

Pierre shot a glance at Gardiner. Gardiner shuffled uncomfortably in his chair. The ceramic shard discovered forty years ago was a secret and remained as such. Pierre could expect no help from Gardiner since the coverup would erode his authority.

"Ever heard of the Silurian hypothesis?" said Pierre, thinking on his feet.

"Isn't that a conspiracy theory?" said Vladomyr.

"It became a conspiracy theory, but it was originally a serious thought experiment. Let's assume there was a race of intelligent reptiles that briefly lived on Earth during the Silurian Period. How would we recognize that such a race ever existed? What would be their footprint? What would happen to their technology? After 400 million years, would anything they did survive the harsh environment? We know the survival of a civilization's footprint is directly proportional to how close they are to our own time."

"How old are these … bipeds?" said Vladomyr.

"Possibly hundreds of millions of years old."

"All this is fascinating," said Gardiner. "But we need to find the source of the blight and the EMPs so we can deactivate them."

"We still don't know if that's the problem."

"It's not helping," said Gardiner. He stood up to leave. "Get it done. Meeting adjourned."

* * *

Pierre returned to the cave. Stacks of boxes piled up at the bottom of the scree. The diggers hurriedly emptied the cave.

"What's going on here?" said Pierre to Alicia.

"Okeli came by," she said. "He ordered us to clear out the cave. Governor's orders, he said."

"Damn it! How am I supposed to find the answers when he keeps meddling in the dig?" Pierre kicked some sand in frustration. "How many boxes?"

"About fifty," she said. "All the skeletons are packed up and out of the cave. We found a few more ceramic fragments on the floor. And the back of the cave is a smooth stone wall with writing on it."

Pierre looked up into the sky. There was an angry overcast. He looked to the west. The sky glowed a resplendent orange red. A cool breeze whipped through the camp.

"We have a bigger problem," said Pierre. "Sandstorm is coming. We need to get everyone out of here right now. Carry as many boxes as you can back to rovers. Any boxes we cannot load onto the rovers need to go back into the cave."

By the time they got back to the colony, the storm was in full pitch. The dig team rushed to move the boxes inside. The blowing wind and sand carried the tops off the boxes and blew them into the desert. When the last box was inside, they shut the hatch.

"Eighteen boxes," said Pierre. "Okay, let's get them to the biology lab. Once we store them in the lab, you can call it a night."

"Are we digging tomorrow?" asked Melissa.

"I doubt it. Going to depend on the storm." Pierre took a breath and exhaled. "A few days at least. I guess we get to study more bananas."

Melissa nodded.

* * *

A knock on the door. Then a louder knock. Pierre groaned and sat up on the side of his bed. He checked the time. It was 7am. He had overslept. A third knock.

"Coming," said Pierre. He was half-dressed, wearing only pants. He opened the door to his barracks. Alicia stood there waiting.

"We have a problem," she said. "Get dressed."

Pierre grabbed a shirt and put on some shoes. "What is it?"

"The biology lab."

When they got to the lab, the door was hanging limply from a single hinge. Inside the lab, Melissa sat and cried. Her face was a mess with tear-smeared dirt running down her face. Papers were scattered all over the floor, and missing were the stacks of boxes.

"What happened?" said Pierre. "Where are the bones?"

"Gone," said Alicia. "Melissa came early to see if you were working and found the lab in this state. She called me immediately."

"Chin," said Pierre.

It did not take long to find Chin in the cafeteria laughing it up with his boys. As soon as he saw Pierre, he called to him, "Where's your evidence now?"

"Return it."

"No can do," said Chin. "I had your little fraud mulched and disposed of."

"Okeli doing your dirty work too? Vladomyr is right. You are a stupid man."

"Right clever enough to sus out your cave and get rid of the rest of your fakes. Good job marking it so anyone could find it... even in a sandstorm. I sent my own report of your conduct back to earth. You'll be disgraced forever."

Pierre grabbed Chin by the collar and punched him in the face. Alicia pulled Pierre back while Luke rushed to Chin's defense. Blood flowed out of Chin's broken nose.

"Don't you dare defend Chin, you stupid bag of rocks!" Pierre spit at Luke. "That weasel may have killed us all."

"Going to pay for that," said Chin.

"We're all going to end up paying for what you've done." Pierre pushed Alicia away and returned to his office, slamming the door behind him.

CHAPTER ELEVEN

Material science has transformed space travel. Plastoglass and alumasteel are resilient, inexpensive materials highly resistant to radiation, micro-meteorite impacts, and atomic oxygen. With the right equipment, both materials can be shaped and milled into practically any form. Plastoglass can endure higher internal pressures than alumasteel, making it ideal for high-pressure tubing and liquid gas applications; however, plastoglass can experience increased brittleness when used for these applications, which can cause the exterior to fracture when exposed to a high-pressure shock wave differential. — **"IEEE Colloquium on New Materials and Exoplanet Exploration"**

Pierre sat at his desk, shoulders slumped, gazing out the window. The wind whipped and whistled. Chin had reduced the first physical evidence of extraterrestrial life to a memory. Maat nestled in its sandbox, which now had knee-high grasses, young ferns, and a poplar tree seedling.

A knock resounded from the door. Pierre did not answer and didn't really care.

Vladomyr let himself in. "Heard what Chin did. Real class act that guy."

Pierre shrugged.

"You can't let that stop you." Vladomyr sat in Alicia's chair. "You've been brooding for a week."

"The storm is still raging," said Pierre.

"Not what I mean."

"Chin reported I faked evidence. He was a Harvard professor. His word carries weight. There'll forever be doubts about anything I discover."

"Are you a paleontologist or a xenobiologist?"

"No."

"Then why do you care?"

"I care about my integrity."

"Looks to me you never lost that."

"Slander never ends well even if you're innocent."

"Did you finish investigating the cave?"

"Chin cleaned it out."

"But did you investigate the final stages of the cave's excavation yourself?" said Vladomyr.

"No," admitted Pierre.

"I used to hear about archaeologists going back to a site after it was robbed and still find important things. Any truth to those stories?"

"Sure, it's done all the time. Fill piles sifted. Small finds missed in the hurry."

"Chin cleared the cave during a sandstorm... in the morning darkness. I bet he missed something. After all, he is a sloppy fuck."

Pierre smirked with a weak laugh. "You may have a point."

"When the storm lets up, take a couple of people you trust and go back to the cave. Do it quietly." Vladomyr stood up out of the chair, ready to leave. "In the meantime, have a better door put on the lab. I recommend all alumasteel this time. You don't want to make it easy for Chin's thugs and one other thing... leave Hans at home."

* * *

"Hey Harvey, has the door to the biology lab been upgraded?" said Pierre. Alicia was eating lunch at her desk. Harvey was changing the lock on the door of his office. There had not been a break-in into his office, but he did not trust the lock.

"This afternoon," said the bald maintenance man. He installed the new lock and bolted it into place.

"Will it be secure?"

"I'm not just replacing the door but the outer wall and door frame with reinforced alumasteel." Harvey tightened the entire lock and tested it to ensure everything worked.

"I'm amazed you can do all that in an afternoon."

"Colony dome walls are modular panels. Particulite panels there right now—you can break through'em with a fire axe. Replacing them with alumasteel panels not even a hydrogen torch can breech." Harvey laughed. "By the time I'm done with the biology lab, it will be a fortress you can hole up in."

"Sounds great. Really appreciate it."

"My pleasure, Pierre." Harvey continued, "I'll also make sure the lab is hermetically sealed like the chemistry lab."

"It's not already?"

"Never been a need." Harvey shrugged. "Then again, never been a need to replace the walls either. But if we are replacing the walls, might as well go all in and seal the lab too."

"Well, I appreciate it," said Pierre. "And while I think of it, only Alicia and I are to have access."

"Just so you know. The Governor and the Security Chief can access all locks."

"While I'm not so fond of that, I understand." Pierre was still suspicious. How much of Okeli's orders to his team were in collusion with Chin? He couldn't rule out that Okeli had been manipulated by Chin.

"All done," said Harvey.

"Thanks Harvey, your whisky is in the mail," said Pierre. Harvey left, closing the door behind him.

"Alicia," said Pierre. Alicia perked up, her mouth full of noodles. She had been not paying attention. "Please, double check the access lists for both my office and the biology lab."

She bit off her noodles and swallowed everything in her mouth. "You don't trust Harvey?"

"I'm tired of being too trusting," said Pierre.

"Scary and paranoid."

"Just verify it." Pierre lowered his voice. "We need to go back to the cave."

"What? Why?" said Alicia.

"Why should we believe Chin was able to clean out the cave when everyone was half-blind from blowing sand?"

"What makes you think they missed anything?"

"They didn't discover the source of the EMPs." Pierre sat back. "If they had discovered it, they would have claimed it. Nor did they find the cause of the blight. So our mission hasn't changed."

"And the skeletons?" she said.

"Chin has done us a favor," said Pierre. "They were a distraction. We would have spent a lot of time cataloging the bones, trying to extract genetic material, running tests, and taking measurements. Would have been great for science but wouldn't get us closer to saving the colony."

"That's smug of you."

"Chin is not done with us."

"And back to paranoid."

"What day is it?"

"December 24th."

"Christmas Eve," he said. "Everyone will be taking tomorrow off."

"I have a feeling everyone won't be us."

Pierre looked over his shoulder, out the window. "The storm is dying down. It should be over by tomorrow. You and I need to go back to the cave tomorrow morning while everyone is still asleep."

* * *

The sun pierced the horizon in the distance. A strong wind blew sand about but nothing like the fury of a sandstorm. Pierre and Alicia were back at the cave. Empty cardboard boxes, flattened and crushed by the storm, littered the base of the scree.

172

Pierre was disappointed but not surprised. "Let's go up," he said, then started the climb up the incline of the scree. The storm had partially filled the pathway. Trudging through the sand, he followed the path to the mouth of the cave.

When he reached the mouth, he looked inside. Darkness shrouded the recess in the escarpment. He reached into his pocket and pulled out a light stick. With both hands, he cracked the glass vial inside the plastic tube and shook it hard. A green chemical light shone brightly. Pierre stepped into the cave. This was his first time inside. The cave was only about twelve feet deep and ten feet wide. Chisel marks on the walls revealed how the cave had been carved out and expanded. A smoothed stone wall was at the back of the cave.

"They were quite thorough about cleaning out the bones," said Alicia.

He turned a full circle, and his shoulders slumped. "Completely empty. Everything's gone."

"They missed something." Alicia bent and picked up a white ceramic shard. She turned it over. Unfortunately, no writing on the piece. "Don't know how helpful a broken piece of ceramic will be."

"One with writing would be better, but I'll be grateful if they missed anything." Pierre set down his backpack. He opened the zipper and pulled out a roll of specimen bags, which he handed to Alicia. He also pulled out the notebook of illustrations that Jasmine had drawn. He flipped through the book that was nearly full. He admired Jasmine's obvious speed and skill at drawing. He went back in the book to the point where the cave was fully excavated. He stopped at a drawing of the smoothed wall. There had been large calligraphic writing on the wall.

Pierre inspected the wall. The burnt umber surface was blank. The texture was polished with a slight gloss like it had been burnished and glazed.

"I'm surprised how shiny it is," said Alicia. She followed close behind Pierre.

"That's desert varnish. Clay mixed with metal oxides, usually manganese and iron, embedded into the surface of the stone until polished. I've seen it on limestone as well as flints." Pierre ran his hand over the wall. The desert varnish had been stripped away where the writing had been, the glassy surface replaced with rough stone. He found a piece of steel wire embedded in the wall. "The bastards used wire brushes to erase all the writing."

Alicia muttered to herself.

Pierre flipped through the illustrations some more until one caught his eye. He brought it over to Alicia. The illustration showed a skeleton laying on its side. Its left arm reaching up against the smoothed wall.

"Do you remember this illustration?" He handed the book to Alicia and held the glow stick over the drawing.

Alicia nodded her head. "That one was strange."

"Can you be more specific?"

"The skeleton had an arm that reached up and against the wall at the back."

"Jasmine is remarkably accurate with her drawings." He flipped a few pages back. He pointed to a small spot on the drawing. "Is that a hand?"

"I believe so."

"Are those the hand bones to that skeleton?" Something about the hand bones did not seem right to Pierre.

"Probably."

"Where are the metacarpals?"

"What do you mean?"

"The hand in the drawing has no fingers. Were any finger bones found in the sand?"

"I don't know." Alicia shrugged. "We were in such a rush to empty the cave. It was confusion."

"I wonder." Pierre reached into the backpack and pulled out a satchel and a mineral hammer. He went over to the wall and kneeled. "Was it in this spot?"

Alicia replied with a nod.

Pierre opened the satchel. He rolled open a selection of fine brushes and picks. His original archaeological tools had been lost in the transport accident. But he cobbled a set of tools from dental picks, scavenged paint brushes, and other improvised implements made from sheet metal in the tool shop. He pulled out a brush and swept over the wall. He found four small indents—each was a circle within a circle.

He took a small dental pick from the satchel and picked at the stone beside the circles. The stone chipped away in small flecks. He pulled out a small chisel and mineral hammer. He gently tapped out the stone matrix. The circle extended into the stone forming a small cylinder in the rock. He loosened the cylinder. He put the chisel back in the satchel and pulled out a set of large tweezers. He grabbed the edge of the cylinder and wiggled it free from the stone.

"What is it?"

"A finger bone." Pierre motioned for a sample bag. Alicia handed him a bag. He put the specimen in the bag and put the bag in his jacket pocket.

"How did fingers get embedded into solid rock?"

"Maybe it wasn't always solid."

"Seems pretty solid to me."

"Concrete can seem like solid rock too." Pierre put the rest of his tools away then grabbed the mineral hammer. He stood up still facing the wall. He felt the wall with the left hand. He tapped the wall with the mineral hammer. He noticed nothing. He cracked the wall *hard* with the hammer. The percussion reverberated with a metallic clang.

"What are you doing?" Alicia protested.

"Listening." Pierre held up the index finger of his left hand. He waited for a moment. "Don't worry. It's fine. Chin's goons destroyed any archaeological value this wall may have had."

He hammered the wall again and immediately grabbed the head of the hammer to stop any sympathetic ringing from the tool. The metallic ring waned.

"Interesting." A broad smile grew across Pierre's face. "Very, very interesting."

"What?"

"This wall."

"What about the wall?"

"It's not a wall. At least it's not a real *stone* wall."

"What do you mean?"

"In Egyptian tombs, you sometimes find false doors. Decorative images of doors on walls that symbolize passage into the spirit world. On rare occasions, false doors were used to hide real passages. A passage could be sealed up with mudbrick and clay, covered in plaster, and a false door painted over top."

"Are you saying this is a false wall?"

"It's hollow. Got to be."

Pierre drew the mineral hammer over his head. Repeatedly, he pummeled the wall with as much force as he could muster. Fragments of stone flew back. Alicia stepped back, hiding her face to prevent getting beamed by the flying pieces of stone.

A one-foot rock slab, two inches thick, broke and fell to the floor. A smooth surface of metal appeared from behind the slab.

"We need to go back," said Pierre out of breath.

"Why?" said Alicia. "We found something."

"I need a bigger hammer."

* * *

The sledgehammer leaned against the far wall of the cave. It took three days to clear away the faux stone. A metal door was behind the false wall. No hinges were visible, but the metal panel was clearly recessed into a door frame. Pierre dumped the fragments of stone into a bucket.

Alicia entered the cave with an empty bucket. They were both wearing rebreathers. It was the middle of the night. They had to sneak in and out of the colony so as not to alert Chin and his men.

176

"How does it open?" she said, setting the empty bucket on the cave floor.

"I don't know, but I think it has to do with that." Pierre pointed to a three-inch disk with six divots. "That's where the embedded fingers would have been."

"What was it trying to do?"

"Maybe it was trying to open the door," said Pierre, "or close it… before the stone façade solidified. For every answered question, another unanswered question appears."

"Isn't it obvious? We know that there were two types of aliens. They built a fake wall over a metal door, wrote a strange language, and built an EMP device."

"I hope you're being facetious." Pierre raised an eyebrow.

"Did you ever doubt it?" said Alicia.

"That's not helping." Pierre stepped over to the metal door. "What kind of metal do you think this is?"

"Looks like nickel-silver, but that could be the tint of the chemlight." Alicia lingered by the cave entrance.

"Or a sign of its age." Pierre took out his tool satchel and selected the chisel. He went to a discrete spot on the door. He pressed the edge of the chisel against the metal door and tried taking a shaving off the metal surface for analysis. The metal was harder than he expected. Harder than alumasteel. He tried a few more times but was unable to get any filings off the metal door. Pierre tossed the chisel down. "No way are we going to get a sample off the door."

"Why not open the door?" said Alicia. "I mean it *is* a door."

Pierre weighed his options. It did seem the most obvious course of action. "Okay, I'll try to open the door."

He stepped over to what seemed to be the door's mechanism. The silver disk had no buttons or controls. The metal was cold to the touch and felt solid. He tried to turn it, but the disk did not move. The stone-like substance had gotten into the mechanism.

Pierre grabbed the mineral hammer from his bag. He gave the circular disk a light tap. He tapped the metal door all around the disk. He tried the disk again and wiggled it loose. Turning it to the right, the disk jammed instantly. Then counterclockwise. The wheel turned. Pierre heard a groan inside the door. He looked up.

"It's an Archimedes mechanism." He looked back at Alicia still standing at the cave entrance. "Small gears release energy stored up and perfectly balanced in larger mechanisms. It's a bit like going to a library with rolling stacks. You turn a crank and can move a stack weighing tens of thousands of pounds."

Pierre gave it a quarter turn. A slight grinding sound. He gave it another quarter turn. A wisp of green gas puffed out from behind the door. He quickly turned the disk clockwise, closing the door.

Pierre shot up. His eyes watered. He turned and ran out of the cave, pushing past Alicia. As soon as his foot hit the scree, he tumbled down the incline. When he reached the bottom, he ripped the rebreather off his face and fell onto all fours. He vomited black bile and nosedived into the sand.

* * *

Pierre woke up. An intubator was down his throat. He looked around. He was lying on a cot in the infirmary. A physician in a blue lab coat, noticing Pierre was awake, came over to him.

"You're lucky to be alive," said Doc Jones, a stooped man in his 80s and nearly bald. He removed the intubator from Pierre's throat. Pierre felt like throwing up as the physician removed the plastic tube. When Jones was done, Pierre realized there was nothing in his stomach and his nausea immediately subsided.

Pierre's mouth was dry. He smacked his parched lips. "What day is it?"

"It's the second of Intercalarus."

He recalled the events leading up to that moment. "I've been down for nine days."

"At least you can still count," said Jones with a grim sense of humor. "That's a better prospect than I gave you."

"How did I get here?"

"Your assistant carried you back to your rover." The Doc pulled out a tablet with Pierre's medical record. "I don't know what happened to you and neither does Alicia. But you had several baseball-sized holes in your lungs. You've lost a quarter of your lung capacity. You will probably never again go outside without a rebreather. The air is thin enough at the best of times."

Alicia entered the infirmary and walked over to Pierre's bedside. He tried to get up. Pain jolted across the surgical incision on his chest.

"No!" said Jones. "You'll undo my fancy stitching. You're going to be in that bed for the next three days."

"How are you feeling?" said Alicia. She sat beside Pierre.

"Like I've been trampled by a herd of *gamusa*." Pierre was looking for anything resembling a bottle of water, but nothing was on his side table.

"What's a *gamusa*?"

"Water buffalo." Pierre looked at her. "You okay?"

"I'm fine. You're just lucky I do a lot of weight training," she said. "What happened?"

"Not exactly sure." Pierre's memory was fogged by the strong meds the Doc had prescribed. "I nudged the door open. Some sort of vapor. I have been in many tombs and smelled a lot of rot and decay. Not the smell of decomposition. It was inhaling death itself."

Alicia frowned. "How are we going to get in there?"

"Let me think about that," said Pierre. "A problem for another day."

"It won't do any good if you're dead."

"If I don't get back on my feet soon, we'll all be dead." The dryness of Pierre's mouth began to hurt. "Can I have some water?"

Alicia went to the sink in the infirmary and returned with a drinking cup and a straw. She held it up to Pierre's mouth, and he took a few sips.

"What does Gardiner know about what happened?"

"He had me in his office. I told him we found a door and what happened. He has ordered everyone to stay away from the cave."

"I won't be following that order."

"Don't think that applies to us," she said.

"What are the other colonists saying?"

"No one wants to go to the cave. That's good."

"Nobody wants to lose a lung? Hard to believe."

Alicia pulled a rebreather out of her pocket. The plastic on the intake vents had melted. "That's your rebreather. Probably, the one thing that stood between you and death. Nobody wants to go near an environment that melts plastic."

Pierre picked up the rebreather and felt the intake vents. It reminded him of melted cheese. "While I'm down, I need a favor," said Pierre. "Please, work with Dutch and Vladomyr to improvise an old-fashioned analog camera."

"Can that be done?"

"Twentieth century cameras were mostly analog, not digital." Pierre motioned for another drink. "At some of my digs, I occasionally found discarded antique cameras." He paused for a moment. "They used glass lenses and cartridges of plastic strips covered with silver halide, requiring a chemical development process. I don't know the details, but Dutch and Vladomyr should be able to figure it out."

"Anything they should know?"

"Yes, tell them I need something better than a pinhole camera. The colony database should have model files of camera bodies, which can be 3D printed. I'll need also a selection of lenses and some sort of flash."

* * *

180

A week later Pierre was back in the lab. He was sitting at an examination table going over the photos and the handful of samples that survived Chin's purge: the photo of Gardiner's ceramic shard, Jasmine's drawings, his photos of the reassembled skeletons, a single finger bone, and a bunch of burnt-out electronics. Then there was that metal door you couldn't enter.

Vladomyr walked into the lab. He stepped over to Pierre.

"How is the camera coming along?" asked Pierre.

"I wanted to talk to you about that," said Vladomyr. He rubbed his jaw. "It's proving more difficult than we thought."

Pierre squinted and turned to Valodmyr.

"We have a lot of designs and 3D models for a staggering variety of camera parts." Vladomyr shook his head. "We have printed out the frames of a dozen different cameras and nothing seems to fit together. It's going to take more time than we expected."

"Surely, you have the documentation and plans, don't you?"

"Sure, we can send a list of parts to the printer and out comes a bunch of parts. And you have three hundred parts in front of you. But you have no instructions on how to assemble the parts. No one here has used, let alone seen, an intact photo-chemical camera. Reverse engineering the assembly instructions is proving difficult."

"How long?"

"We might have a classic 35mm camera for you in three months."

"I need it sooner than that."

"Kind of figured," said Vladomyr. "That's why I want to propose an alternative to get you over the hump."

"What?"

"Ever heard of a glass plate camera?"

"You mean those cameras that look like small accordions?"

"Exactly," said Vladomyr. "The body is easy to construct. And we can easily make plates for it."

"Don't we need to use glass for that?" said Pierre. "Isn't there a high possibility of breakage?"

"No one said we had to use the exact same materials from the 19th century?" Vladomyr pointed his finger into the steel top of the examination table. "Let's use plastoglass for the negatives. Chemical resistant, strong as steel, and lighter too."

"And the lenses?"

"Plastoglass for them too. The 3D printer can make the lens blanks. This will be your great-great-great grandad's camera on steroids. Dutch and I did have one concern though."

"And that is?"

"The atmosphere behind that door." He straightened up. "We would prefer not to put a lot of work into making you cameras only have them melt when you enter the cave."

"I share that concern," said Pierre.

"We need you to go back to the cave and take a sample of the atmosphere."

Pierre turned pale. "How do you expect me to do that?"

Vladomyr grinned. "Go to environmental control. They can fit you out with a hazmat suit. Dutch can give you a gas extractor."

* * *

Alicia and Pierre were encased in multi-layered yellow hazmat suits as they ventured back into the cave. Each suit was a composite of redundant layers of chemical and gas resistant materials. Plastoglass helmets covered their heads—each helmet was completely transparent and allowed 360 degrees of view. Flat backpacks containing oxygen canisters with three hours of air were built into the suits, and exhale vents were located over the back.

"Pierre," said Alicia, "why are we doing this?"

"Because no one else volunteered." He dropped a duffle bag on the ground. He knelt and opened the zipper of the bag.

"Were we born stupid, or do we have a death wish?"

"Why does it have to be one or the other?"

182

"You would pick apart my logic," said Alicia with a huff. "But I'm serious. Why isn't an android here doing this work?"

"Because androids are outlawed."

"Not true, I've seen them on military bases."

"Okay, so they're restricted."

"But why?" She shuffled from foot to foot anxiously. "Why are we doing this dangerous task? Why can't an android do this job?"

"Because of World War IV."

Pierre pulled out a gas extractor from the duffle bag. The extractor could sample gas and compress it to thousands of pounds of pressure, storing the gas in clear plastoglass cylinders about eight inches in length.

He grabbed a pair of empty gas cylinders. "In 2317 an android, indistinguishable from a human being, joined a tour group, walked into the White House, and blew up the entire building. Androids were used for terrorism, biological weapons, and all manner of war crimes. They supplanted the role of drones in warfare. Most countries declared androids restricted weapons."

"Too bad. They would be ideal for work like this."

"Androids, especially those with AI nets, while incredibly intelligent, were also equally credulous. Ridiculously easy to fool into doing things that can hurt others."

"Can't they be programmed not to do harm?"

"Not that simple." Pierre loaded the first cylinder into the gas extractor. "You can train an android to be a coffee barista and then have it poison large numbers of people with tainted coffee."

"Couldn't a human be manipulated to do the same crimes?"

"Sure, psychopathy exists." Pierre stepped up to the metal door. "The difference is, when people get sick and start falling over, most humans start asking what's wrong, call for help, and may question their instructions. Androids don't question… they continue serving coffee. They do what they are told. It was simply easier to outlaw androids."

"But don't some colonies have androids?"

"Yes, some colonies have androids, but those colonies are also military installations that have other restricted weapons." He turned the circular mechanism on the door and continued to do so until a half-inch space appeared between the door and the frame. Green gas billowed out.

"Why don't we have androids?"

"Arish is not a military installation." He fed the collection tube into the gap. When the tube went as deep as it would go, he pumped the trigger on the extractor. The clear cylinder filled with green gas.

"Does Basra have any androids?"

"I'm not sure." When the canister was full, Pierre pulled the cylinder out of the extractor and replaced it with a second. He pumped the trigger again. "They might. Hard to say." When the canister was full, he pulled the extractor out and turned the mechanism to shut the door. Pierre removed the cylinder out of the extractor and packed everything back into the duffle bag. "We're done here. Let's go back."

Back at the colony dome, Pierre entered the chemistry lab. Dutch was at his desk looking over some papers. Pierre placed the duffle bag on the lab bench.

"You're back," said Dutch, looking over his shoulder.

"Got a couple of cylinders of the gas from the cave," said Pierre. "Be careful with that stuff."

"I suppose." Dutch seemed unconcerned, glancing over to the fume hood in the corner.

"Well, if you've got this," said Pierre. "I'm going to grab some lunch."

"I'll let you know when I've got results."

* * *

"I can't believe how bland the food is." Pierre held up a fork of spaghetti tinged with pallid yellow sauce. "What is this? It's not butter sauce. It's not Hollandaise. It's not even mayonnaise. I would kill for an honest-to-God ripe red tomato. Or even an expired packet of pepper from a gas station sandwich."

184

"Pierre's food review, yet again." Alicia rolled her eyes. "Stop whining and keep it down. You want Madi to hear you?"

"Experts from every scientific field work here but not a single person who can cook. Are you serious?"

"She's not an Earther."

"If she were," said Pierre, "at least she'd have actually tasted something not resembling poison."

"Cut it out."

"Just one tomato," he said. "Is that too much to ask?"

The lights dimmed and were replaced with red illumination. A siren wailed. Everyone stood up and rushed about. Pierre shoveled the food in his mouth. He hated every mouthful, but claxons could not mean anything good, and he might not be eating for a while.

"General quarters!" said Alicia.

"What are we supposed to do?" said Pierre.

"Report to our assigned emergency stations." Alicia stood up. "I need to go to fire control."

"Where do I go?"

"Upper management. That's you, by the way. Go to the situation room."

"Where's that?"

"The security offices." Alicia ran off with Pierre still sitting there.

Ten minutes later Pierre entered the situation room, which was little more than a security office filled with three stacked rows of video monitors. A bunch of people were gathered over the shoulders of security chief Okeli as he tried to patch into the relevant video cameras.

"Glad you could join us," sneered Gardiner. "Perhaps, be more prompt next time?"

"Had trouble finding the place," said Pierre. "What's going on?"

"A situation in the chemistry lab," said Gardiner. "Anyone know what Dutch was working on?"

"He was trying to re-create chemically based photographic film," said Vladomyr.

"No," said Pierre. Video streams from the lab appeared on the monitors. Dutch was lying on the floor motionless, blood seeped out of all his orifices. "He was analyzing gas samples from the cave."

"Must have escaped containment," said Vladomyr. "We need a level three purge."

"What's that?" said Pierre.

"The entire lab is flooded with accelerants, consumed in fire, and everything is pumped outside."

"Won't that destroy all the equipment?"

"That's the point," said Vladomyr. "To destroy everything in the lab so it cannot harm the colony."

"I need any data from the test machines," said Pierre. "The life of every colonist depends upon it." Deep down he hoped that Dutch would stir and that he was not dead, and they could forgo the purge. Was it too much to hope for?

Vladomyr looked at Gardiner.

"Ten minutes," said Gardiner.

"Listen up!" said Vladomyr to everyone in the room. "Do a memory dump of every machine in the lab: the mass spectrometer to the ultrasonic cleaner. I want everything. We only have nine minutes to do it." Several scientists sat at workstations and began typing to access the equipment. It was the first time, as long as anyone could remember, they worked as a team.

"Okeli," said Vladomyr. "Hack into Dutch's personal terminal and download everything."

"Could take more time than we got," said the chief.

"Do what you can," said Vladomyr.

Everyone raced against the clock. Pierre found himself isolated in the middle of the room, as everyone worked furiously at the edges. All this was above his level of computer skills. No scientific training to any appreciable degree. For the first time, he felt inadequate around those who had failed to find the source of the blight. Those around him whirled about in a blur while time lost all meaning.

As they worked, Pierre watched the monitors in disbelief. Dutch's body liquified into a ruddy puddle of goo before his eyes. He found it hard to breath and clutched the incision on his chest where the Doc had stitched him up.

"Time's up," announced Gardiner. Everyone stopped working knowing further effort would be futile. Gardiner turned to Okeli. "Ignite the purge."

Okeli turned the key and pressed a red button.

Pierre swallowed hard and shuffled closer to Vladomyr. He whispered, "What would prevent them from doing this to someone that's still alive?"

"Nothing," said Vladomyr. "This is about destroying pathogens as much as containing biohazards."

Fire engulfed the room and every monitor went black. Pierre eyes grew wide. "What happens next?"

"The fire will burn for thirty minutes, incinerating everything in the room to ash. Then the outside wall of the lab will fall open. All the ash will then be dispersed to the desert. Next week maintenance will reconstruct the lab with what few pieces of equipment we have left."

"And a new chemist?" Pierre was never going to sleep soundly ever again.

"Will have to be requisitioned from Earth."

Pierre recalled that, without a docking station and with all the transport ships being diverted, a new chemist would be a long time in coming. A generation could pass by until they get a new chemist. "And until then?"

"We must make do with our other scientific staff. We'll probably end up dividing the duties among us."

"The emergency is over," declared Gardiner. The lights were restored, and the siren was turned off. "Resume your duties."

"Did we get any data from Dutch's tests?" said Pierre to Vladomyr.

"I don't know." Vladomyr went over to a computer terminal and read the screen. "We got something, but not yet sure what. It's going to take me a few hours to sort out what we have and see if anything's usable."

"I appreciate it," said Pierre. The tone in the room withered as it set in that a colleague was dead.

"Pretty awful to do," said Vladomyr, "going through a dead man's data."

"Perhaps it's a field specific thing. Eventually, all men leave nothing but their data."

"That's sounds very Russian."

* * *

Pierre was in his office, updating his log files, when a knock came from the door. He looked down. The sand tray he had placed for his scatterbug was now so congested with vegetation Maat could no longer move comfortably among the weeds. He placed a second sand tray beside the first for the bug. Later that evening, he was going to move the old tray into the biology lab for further observation.

"Enter," said Pierre.

The door opened, and Vladomyr drifted into the room like a specter. His features were sallow. He didn't say anything.

"That's not the face of good news."

Vladomyr shook his head. He put a single sheet with half a page of print on Pierre's desk. "All we got."

"That's it?"

"Nothing from his personal terminal."

"What's this?"

"Partial results from the gas chromatograph."

"Partial?"

Vladomyr nodded. "The samples from the cave contained high amounts of hydrogen that caused the heating coil in the unit to ignite, burst, and leak the sample into the lab."

Pierre sighed at hearing the news. He shook his head.

Vladomyr took a seat. "The sample contained chlorine, cyanogen, acetone vapor, gaseous sulfuric acid, nerve agents, and hemotoxins. Plus, a variety of enzymes that can eat away organic compounds like I've never seen before. You are very lucky to be alive."

"Sobering," said Pierre.

"I wish Dutch had been so lucky." Vladomyr hit the desk with his fist and stood up.

"Right now, one person is dead on the deck." Pierre stood up. "If we don't get back into that cave and figure out what's happening, this incident will be a mere nosebleed. And their deaths will be on our heads for not figuring this out."

"Well, you can't go back into the cave. There's no way the hazmat suits will survive those conditions. And you can forget about a flash for your camera. The gas is too flammable."

"Would it be possible to vent the cave?" said Pierre.

"Vent the cave?" The Ukrainian man paused to consider it. "Maybe. The door would have to be wide open, and you'd have to pump fresh air in and vent bad air out. Depending upon the volumes involved, it could take weeks. But it's not impossible."

"Wouldn't an exhaust fan get destroyed by the gas?"

"Don't use a fan," said Vladomyr. "Use a magneto-pump instead. It is essentially a set of magnetic coils placed outside of an exhaust tube. Start with an ionizer unit covered in a ceramic film, which will make it corrosion resistant. The ionizer adds an electric charge to the gases, and then the magnetic coils pull the charged gases through the exhaust tube and out of the cave. And I even think we can do this without having to use a single semiconductor."

"EMP resistant too?" Pierre was impressed at Vladomyr's technical prowess.

"It could work. However, no one should go near the cave for the next couple of weeks while it airs out."

* * *

"Did you see Dutch die?" asked Alicia, setting up a blower fan at the cave entrance. Pierre laid out two-foot-wide ventilation tubing inside the cave. They both wore yellow hazmat suits. Glow sticks littered the floor lighting up the cave. It took nearly a week to get all the components working without the semiconductor parts.

189

"He was dead by the time anyone could do anything," said Pierre. "And I don't want to describe what I saw."

"Was it the gas?"

"Oh yes, it was the gas," said Pierre. "But what killed Dutch was carelessness."

"Horrible. What happened?"

"He pumped the gas sample directly into a chromatograph. He didn't test it for hydrogen or chemicals that eat plastic." Pierre grabbed the ionizer and attached it to the far end of the tubing. "Arish is 152 years old. The colony has never had an armed conflict. Never had a serious plague or even the flu. Hasn't ever been a chemical spill or nuclear accident. Imagine a nearly perfect safety record for over a hundred years."

"Lax safety standards."

"Exactly."

"Maybe, he was distracted by the time of year," said Alicia. She stretched the ventilation tubing, tugging on it to extend it outside the cave. "You do know the 21st of Intercalarus is in two days? Any plans for New Year's Eve?"

"I never celebrated New Year's Eve on Earth. Why should I start now?"

"The colony is throwing a party."

"I'm not a party person." Pierre attached the second tube to the ionizer. He strapped the magneto-pump coils to the exterior of the exhaust tubing and shook the coils to make certain they were snuggly attached. He dragged the remainder of the tubing out of the cave a good twenty feet. Any gas pumped out would be swept away by the desert winds. "Alicia, could you turn on the input fan?"

She left the cave and scaled up to where the mini-reactor was planted. Mini-reactors were compact, slow fusion reactors that behaved more like nuclear batteries. Clean, safe, light, and portable. Best of all they contained few semiconductor electronic components—they were a sophisticated device of magnets, slow flow media, and thermocouples.

Vladomyr replaced the power regulator, the only part of the reactor that had a semiconductor. He modified the device with a vacuum tube, which made the mini-reactor EMP resistant. When she flipped on the power, a strong inrush of air blasted into the cave, followed by an eardrum-splitting whine.

Pierre snorted. They call this a fan? More of a jet turbine. He stepped out of the cave. He attached power to the ionizer and magneto-pump. The exhaust apparatus was a bit slower to get going. Unlike the input fan, the ionizer needed to warm up before reaching peak efficiency.

"Looks good." Pierre raised his thumb. "I'm ready to open the metal door."

"Awesome." She climbed from the perch with the mini-reactor and joined Pierre in front of the cave.

"I want you to wait at the bottom of the scree."

"Why?"

"What I am about to do is dangerous even though we're both wearing hazmat suits," said Pierre. "If I don't exit the cave, you aren't to come in after me. Got it?"

"Do you actually expect me to follow those instructions?"

"Yes, I do," said Pierre emphatically. The entrance glowed dimly from all the light sticks still inside. "If I'm dead in there, don't come back until the cave is safe. I need you alive to report that the cave is properly being ventilated."

"How will I know that?"

"When you see green gas coming out of the exhaust tube, you'll know it's ventilating." Pierre put his hand on Alicia's shoulder. "Time to do this."

Alicia scaled down the scree until she reached the bottom while Pierre re-entered the cave.

Pierre stepped over to the metal door. He was not looking forward to doing this. But what was the alternative? He stretched out his gloved hand. Sand was being blown around the cave by the intake fan. He touched the latch and turned the metal disk. The door cracked open.

Green gas seeped out of the gap only to be wicked away by the hurricane in the cave. Pierre cranked on the speed, turning the disk ever faster. The door quickly pulled away from the right-most side of the frame, receding into the wall.

The door snagged, and he put his hand on the edge of the door to tug it along. The backside of the door was completely smooth. He checked again. The turning disk was only on the outside, not the inside of the door.

Once the door was opened as far as it would go, Pierre stepped back. Inside the door was pitch black, a green light flickered in the darkness. Pierre picked up the exhaust vent and draped it inside the door frame. He turned around and exited the cave with haste.

As he stepped outside, the exhaust vent spewed toxic green gas.

A broad smile appeared on Alicia's face as he reached the bottom of the scree. "You made it?"

"Seems so." Pierre laughed. "Strange thing. The Archimedes mechanism is only on the outside of the door." No sooner had he said that than he saw a glint in the distance in the foothills to the north. "Alicia, binoculars, now!"

She handed him her binoculars.

Pierre ripped off his helmet.

"What're you doing?" screamed Alicia. "The gas!"

"Wind is blowing away from us." Pierre held the binoculars up to his eyes. He squinted to focus. Far off in the foothills, he could swear he saw a person. He removed the binoculars to figure out where in the foothills he saw it. He put the binoculars back up to his eyes. The figure was now gone.

"What is it?" said Alicia.

"Trouble."

CHAPTER TWELVE

The MegaAI Sigma A017 was launched in AD 2355 from the Indigo Hypercube shipyard. The frame of the vessel is a dreadnought A-type design. The dimensions of the ship are 35 kilometers long and 9 kilometers wide with a max flank-speed 0.73 C. The ship is equipped with three antimatter reactors and twelve pulse engines. — **"Jain's MegaAI Starships and Space Stations"**

When Pierre returned to the colony, he went through decontamination and then marched directly to the cafeteria. Alicia tagged behind him, trying to keep up.

"What are you doing?" she said.

"What I've needed to do since day one," said Pierre. He rolled up his sleeves.

As soon as Pierre entered the cafeteria, he found Chin and his goons eating and laughing it up.

"Chin!"

The table immediately grew silent.

"What's the meaning of sending your goons after me today?" said Pierre.

"No idea what you are talking about," said Chin. His face contorted into a smirk.

"I saw your guy following me."

"You're paranoid."

"Are you telling me that wasn't your guy?"

"Right, I'm not telling you anything." Chin laughed his ass off. "I'm living rent-free in your head."

"You can't tell me you aren't trying to destroy my reputation."

"Past tense, bud." Chin composed himself.

"What?"

"Destroyed…deh. As in the past tense." Chin leaned back and picked up a dinner knife and played with it. "You only burn down a house that's still standing. I need not do anything to a house already turned to ash. Although I think Terry might still have some plans for you." His buddies all began to laugh together.

"Let's go," said Alicia. She pulled Pierre along with her. When they got to the far end of the cafeteria and out of earshot, he stopped.

"He didn't do it," said Pierre, "did he?"

"Don't think so." Alicia looked back. Chin's table had resumed the conversation they were having before being interrupted.

"This is much more concerning." Pierre was thinking about the implications.

"An exile?"

"Or Basra."

"You need to report this to the Governor."

"A momentary sighting of a blurry figure?"

"Yes," said Alicia. "Make the report, and let Gardiner decide what to do about it."

Pierre shook his head.

"At least report that Chin has been in contact with Basra."

"And say what? I don't have any hard evidence, except a couple suggestive off-hand remarks. And if I did report it, Chin could say he's just trying to re-establish contact with Basra. Despite how everyone acts around here, Arish is technically not at war with Basra and has been trying to reach out to them for years. So Chin hasn't done anything illegal by contacting Terry. Moreover, Gardiner would simply use my report to claim I was jealous to provoke more competition between his senior staff."

* * *

Because of crowding, colonies were normally noisy places. Yet, the need for privacy remained a universal human need, and to satisfy that need colonists found creative ways to be alone. Some found moments of solace in the dark underground passages. Some found abandoned rooms. Management had private offices. Pierre found respite in the biology lab. It was relatively quiet and few thought of looking for him there.

Pierre placed the first sand tray from his pet scatterbug on the examination table. He picked up a set of tweezers and poked through the long grass, lush and thick. The alder seedling was now nearly 30 inches and was quickly outgrowing its container. The weeds concealed new kinds of vegetation. When he cataloged all the life, he set the tray down on the ground.

Alicia walked into the biology lab. She was the one exception—somehow she always knew where to find Pierre. "What are you doing?"

"Working," said Pierre. "When do I not work?"

"Why aren't you in the mess hall?"

"I'd rather work."

"It's 11pm on New Year's Eve."

"That's supposed to mean something?"

"Yes, it means this colony has survived one more year. That's an achievement."

"They won't survive one more if I don't figure this out."

"Are you telling me working through midnight, one entire hour, is going to bring you the insight you need and change the destiny of this colony?"

"It might," said Pierre weakly. He wasn't getting anywhere, and he knew it. But because he was not getting anywhere, he did not want to be sociable either.

"You are the deputy governor of the emergency," said Alicia. "You need to show them everything is under control. The best way you can do that is to go to the party, eat some fake shrimp wrapped in fake bacon dipped in fake seafood sauce, and cheer when everyone else does. They need this."

"If I must." Pierre stood up from the examination table.

"And for pity's sake, smile. You're going to a party, not a wake."

When Pierre arrived at the cafeteria, the mess hall was packed with people, many of whom he had never met even though the colony was only about 300 people. Pierre was reticent to introduce himself and was uncomfortable in social situations. The music died, replaced with stark silence. Everyone stopped when they noticed Pierre had entered the room. He scanned the room. The entire colony must have been there.

"Whatcha looking at?" said Pierre. "The life of the party is here. Play on."

The music wound up again and people resumed mingling and dancing. Pierre went over to what might be called a buffet. It was more decoration than food, a sign of the times. He picked out a single piece of bacon-wrapped shrimp substitute. Each "shrimp" had square edges like it had been pressed into a mold. They were rubbery like real shrimp that had been boiled too long—perhaps the only resemblance it had to the real thing. That so many were left at this point of the night should have warned him they couldn't be good.

Vladomyr came up to Pierre. "I've got news," he said.

"He's eating," said Alicia. "Something he doesn't do nearly enough."

"This'll be quick," said Vladomyr.

"It's fine," said Pierre to Alicia. "Go enjoy the party. I won't be long."

Alicia quickly snatched a plate of food and went off to a table.

"What is it?" said Pierre.

"Got a response from the MegaAI. It has confirmed receipt of our request and will be entering orbit on March 9th to begin repairs on the orbital docking station."

"That's great news." Pierre almost felt like smiling.

"While it's in orbit, we can use its AI facilities. Maybe, it can lend some insight into our problem."

"The more resources we can devote the better."

"That gives you eleven weeks to figure out what information you are going to send up to the MegaAI."

"I've never worked with a MegaAI," said Pierre. "Is there anything special I need to know? Formatting instructions?"

"Not really," said Vladomyr. "As far as AIs go, MegaAIs are among the most intelligent we have. All you need to do is upload a data dump, then ask your questions after. It's like using any other AI. The only difference is they are smarter than your average AI. Any progress on the cave?"

Pierre turned around, stepping away from the table. He took a bite of the shrimp. The first taste was sharp and bitter. He spat out the mouthful. "That's disgusting."

"Yeah, you shouldn't eat that."

Pierre wiped his mouth with a napkin and tossed the entire plate into the trash. "We need to wait until January 12th until we can go back. But we went back yesterday, and the pumps are still working."

"When you opened the door, did you see anything?"

"Not really," said Pierre. "It was pitch black. There was something inside."

"How do you know?"

"Saw a green flash of light."

"As in a reflection or a transmitted light?"

"Not sure," said Pierre. "How's the camera coming?"

"Dutch's death has been a setback for creating the photographic plates. He knew the chemistry better than anyone. I've turned my lab into a dark room. I'm confident we can provide you with black and white silver halide plates in a couple of weeks. I'm trying to come up with some subtractive color plates as well, but they're more difficult to make."

"What about the camera body?"

"A bellows camera body will be ready for you this week. That was the easy part once we figured out how all the pieces worked with each other."

"Sounds like progress."

Their conversation was stopped by a whistle. Gardiner took center stage. Vladomyr noted the time, about a minute till midnight. "I better get back to my wife, or she'll never forgive me."

"We are seconds away from midnight!" shouted Gardiner. "Partner up with your significant other as we count down to midnight. And if you don't have a partner, what're ya waiting for?"

Pierre stood oblivious to those around him. A group of colonists crowded in as the seconds vanished.

Gardiner shouted out the countdown: "10, 9, 8…" But the colonists quickly took over.

"3, 2, 1… Happy New Year!" They all yelled.

A blonde woman grabbed Pierre and kissed him on the lips. He didn't recognize her. She was young, probably in her early twenties and most likely native-born to Gliese. "Happy Gliese Epoch 154," she said, smiling broadly. She stepped backwards from Pierre and wiped her lips with a napkin. Taking a few more steps back, she disappeared into a crowd of dancers. Pierre looked over his shoulder. Alicia scowled.

* * *

A week had passed since the party, and another sandstorm raged outside. Blowing sheets of sand whooshed in waves across the picture view window of Pierre's office. Pierre's feet were kicked up on a desk and he was reading. Alicia sat at her desk, tinkering with paperclips turning them into a chain. Meanwhile, Maat skittered across the floor—its new sandbox was already turning green with algae and moss.

"I hate waiting," she said.

"So you've said repeatedly." Pierre tried to ignore her, focusing on his book.

"What are you reading?"

"I'm reading a book on the gods and goddesses of ancient Egypt."

"Why? It's not like you're ever going to Egypt again."

"Just because I won't again see the sands of Egypt doesn't mean that I don't find the subject interesting."

"Yeah, I don't get that," said Alicia. "You have a Ph.D. in Egyptology."

"Yes…"

"You did all that study in one subject."

"Where's this going?"

"You know everything there is to know about your subject, and you're still interested in it. Don't you find it boring?"

"I learned all this about ancient Egypt so I can learn what I don't know." Pierre put the reading pad down for a moment. "Or to learn something new nobody has ever discovered. Take for example, our discovery of alien life. Has such a discovery been made on any of the forty-eight colony worlds?"

"No."

"What do we know about them?"

"Almost nothing."

"Yes, and that's exciting. We know nothing about their civilization. We know they were physically about our size, and they had technology and a writing system, but that's about it. We know everything that is known about them. But that leaves all sorts of other interesting questions. Did they dwell in cities or caves? What were the limits of their technology? What did they eat? What were their lives like? How did they organize themselves? What did they value? Did they have any existential or religious beliefs?"

"And that's why you are reading about the gods and goddesses of Egypt?" She said with a raised eyebrow.

"History does not repeat," said Pierre. "But as Mark Twain said, 'history does rhyme.' We don't know what we're going to encounter in that cave. And when you don't know something, you read more. So I have been reading up on excavation methods and theory, hypothetical exobiology, toxicology and biohazard containment, antique photography, primitive anthropology, and the sociology of institutions. Frankly, I'm tired of reading all that stuff. So I'm sitting back and reading something I like to read—Egyptian religion."

"Fair enough," said Alicia. "Can I ask you about something else?"

Pierre hummed in reply. He picked up his tablet and resumed reading.

"Have you thought about the 22-month rule?"

Pierre rolled his eyes. "You mean the couple up and start producing babies within two years or you're out of here rule?"

"Yes."

"Nope, not for a moment." He disliked where the conversation was heading.

"What are you going to do about it?"

"Sod all."

"You're joking, right?"

Pierre peered over the top of his pad. He squinted at her. "Do the math. We arrived here in June, and we've already been here six months. Between ten to twelve months from now, all the food will run out. There'll be rioting and a breakdown of civil order even in a small colony such as this. Do you seriously think Gardiner is going to be able to hold this all together when things start flying apart?"

"What if you find the problem and solve the mystery?"

"Let's say that I do. Let's say I find the cause today. Maybe in eleven months we will get the next crop. Will those crops be enough to feed everyone? I doubt it. Order will still break down. Let's face it. We were called in years too late."

"But what if there was someone special? Someone who might need you."

"No thanks." Pierre thought back to Sarah, his relationship with her, and his last conversation with her at that dive bar. He seethed with nothing but hatred for her. He was never again going to let himself be manipulated in such a way. "I've had a relationship where I was needed. As soon as that person no longer needs you, it's over. I have no interest in being used and discarded like last week's leftovers."

"What about the 22-month rule?"

"I can survive fine in the desert as an exile if it comes to it," said Pierre. "I'm only here to discover what's causing the terraforming blight. My entire worth rests in my ability to see what others cannot, find what others cannot find, and do it this time without a major screw up."

"Is that how you see yourself?"

"A man is only as good as his next victory. Only as good as his ability to kill the next wooly mammoth for the clan. Only as good as his foresight to navigate through the dangers that imperil our path."

"I see."

"Admittedly, I haven't always done well doing that." Pierre said downcast. He recounted all his failures, particularly the botched excavation at the Naqada fortress he had been working on. He should never have mentioned the possibility of an early dynastic foundation deposit at the temple inside the fort. The possibility of finding another Narmer Palette incited his poorly trained subordinates, and particularly that wretched nephew of Gerard's, to tear up the site without any consideration for proper archaeological methods or documentation. As a result, much of the context of the site had been destroyed by local workers who were out of control. He ran his finger along the side of the tablet and looked Alicia straight in the eyes. "I am no one's hero. I'm not Gardiner's hero, Melissa's hero, or your hero. I'm only doing this fool's errand to vindicate myself, and that's all."

* * *

"I'm surprised you joined us," Pierre said to Vladomyr. Vladomyr hiked out in the sand alongside Pierre and Alicia. The temperature was cool with the post-sandstorm golden hue where everything radiated a warm glow—definitely, autumn weather. "This hasn't been the most popular destination since the death of Dutch."

"That's a good thing," said Vladomyr. He wore fatigues while the other two wore yellow hazmat suits. Vladomyr carried a backpack while the other two lugged duffle bags. Alicia also had a rifle slung over

201

her shoulder. "The colonists needed a good scare that what we're dealing with is dangerous. Nothing communicates that better than a dead man."

Pierre looked askance at Vladomyr.

"Don't get me wrong," said Vladomyr. "Dutch was a friend, but he was also sloppy and took the threat all too casually. He got what was coming. My only regret was it didn't happen to Chin instead."

"Wow, that's cold," said Alicia.

"Colony life is short. Best get used to it." Vladomyr grinned in response. "Is that it ahead?"

"Sure is," said Pierre. "Don't get too close."

"Hey, I'm here for technical support, and because I'm curious… but officially for technical support." He dropped the backpack onto the sand.

"Technical support?"

Vladomyr opened the backpack and pulled out a tripod and two baggies. One baggie contained a camera. The other contained photographic plates. "I brought gifts. We're still working on color film, but I've got a bellows camera and six photographic plates." He unbagged the camera and mounted the camera onto the tripod. He then removed one caddy from the film bag and handed the rest to Pierre.

Pierre looked for extra pockets on the hazmat suit to stuff the film caddies into. Two on each leg, one on his vest.

"Okay, pay attention." Vladomyr showed Pierre the camera from the rear end of the body. "There's no LCD on the back. You load a film caddy into the top slot and pull out the protective plastic cover. That exposes the plate. Then move the bellows to focus the camera. The prism on top will help you align the shot. The focus is somewhat guesswork. I've set the shutter for 3/4s of a second. Whatever you do, don't move the camera while the shutter is open. This cord dangling off the side is the shutter release. Press the end to trigger the shutter. When you have your shot, put the plastic cover back over the film caddy. Replace it with a new caddy, and you're ready for the next photo. Any questions?"

"No." Pierre grabbed the camera with the tripod. "It's heavier than it looks."

"Count yourself lucky. It's about half the weight of a real antique camera."

Alicia took the rifle off her shoulder and handed it to Vladomyr. "Here. You may need this," she said. "You do know how to use a rifle?"

"I'm from the Ukraine. We've been at war with the Russian Federation for over four hundred years. Our mothers give their babies vodka and an AK-47." Vladomyr took the rifle, opened the chamber, and loaded a round. "I think I can handle it."

"Sort of thought you could." Alicia nodded her head, recognizing Vladomyr was a man who had seen death.

"Okay, let's go," said Pierre. Pierre and Alicia marched up the scree into the cave. The door was still open but no longer billowed out green smoke. Pierre grabbed a handful of light sticks. He broke one and tossed it through the door. Light reflected off a variety of rough surfaces. He threw a few more light sticks into the area. He made out the contours of a passage.

"Time to go inside," said Pierre. He walked inside holding up a light stick. The passage descended into the earth. Their feet crunched as they took each step downwards.

Alicia followed Pierre. She looked at her feet. There was nothing but brown dirt. "What's that sound?"

"Bones," said Pierre.

"I don't see any bones," she said.

Pierre turned around. He moved the top sand aside with his boot. Slivers of white bone churned up to the surface. "See them now?"

"Oh…" She grimaced baring her teeth.

He turned back into the passage. They descended to the bottom of the passage and walked around the corner. They entered a large cavern. Large broken urns were along the walls, all of which had caved in and were now shambling piles of shards. The toxic gas had dissipated. It probably would have been safe at this point to enter the cavern without hazmat suits, but Pierre did not dare forego the added protection, which brought him security if nothing else.

In the center of the room, tens of thousands of scatterbugs carpeted the floor of the cavern. The little robots hobbled about, seeming only half alive, broken, enervated. From the left far corner of the room, a beam of sunlight entered the cavern from the ceiling above. Every bug struggled to renew its power from the diffuse light, a starvation ration.

A scatterbug limped up to Alicia. She gave it a solid kick sending the little robot flying meters away.

"What did you do that for?" said Pierre.

"Hate scatterbugs, and this place creeps me out."

"Scatterbugs may be the least of our concerns." Pierre walked over to the sunbeam and stood in its light. He could not see the sky through the hollow. "I bet you that tunnel leads to the Varney Ridge plateau. The tunnel was probably formed by erosion, then the scatterbugs fell through by accident and once here were stuck."

Pierre bent down to examine one of the broken urns. It looked like it had been intentionally smashed. He picked aside a potshard. Bone fragments and ash were inside.

Out of the corner of his eye, Pierre noticed the flash of green light again. A beam of laser light, probing, searching, reaching out for who knows what. This time Pierre could pinpoint it to the furthest recesses of the cavern to his right, about eighty meters away. Whatever was there was shrouded in complete darkness.

"I don't like this." Alicia grabbed his sleeve and pulled him back.

Pierre grabbed Alicia's hand and peeled it off his sleeve. He walked through the swarm of scatterbugs on the floor towards the farthest depths of the cavern. He held up a light stick over his head, then he saw it. Alicia shuffled to Pierre. Pierre set down the camera tripod. He checked the focus, then raised the tripod as high as it would go and pointed the camera downward. Reaching into his pocket, he pulled out six more glow sticks. He cracked each one and threw it to the floor.

With each additional light source, it appeared out of the darkness. A golden face with a jutting chin, long and distorted, with a large green gemstone embedded in its forehead. A few more light sticks. Pierre grabbed the camera cord and released the shutter.

Alicia bolted out the cave, leaving Pierre behind. Scatterbugs flew up into the air as she kicked her path ahead of her. She ran out of the cave, scrambled down the scree, and landed where Vladomyr was waiting. She ripped the plastoglass helmet off her head. She was hyperventilating. Her eyes were wide and wild.

"What happened?" said Vladomyr.

Alicia thrashed and struggled until Vladomyr caught her. Despite her raw power, she was no match for the strength of the Ukrainian. As he restrained her, she breathed heavily. Looking side to side, she tried to get her bearings. "What? Who was that?"

"Slow down," said Vladomyr. "Compose your thoughts."

"No, no, no!" screamed Alicia. Her eyes were wild with panic. "Don't send me back. No… No!"

Pierre appeared in the mouth of the cave. He had the camera and tripod in one hand and a scatterbug in the other. The legs of the scatterbug thrashed in the air, kicking to get free. He casually scaled the scree towards the other two.

"Did you find something in there?" said Vladomyr.

"You could say that." Pierre rested the tripod against his shoulder. "I found what looks like a massive gold sarcophagus from a third alien species."

"You serious?"

"And a cavern full of scatterbugs, including this little fellow," said Pierre. He held up the bug by the carapace. The scatterbug struggled and snapped its climbing claws at Pierre.

"Is it fighting you?"

"Can't seem to put it back into hibernation mode." Pierre set down the camera. He opened the duffle bag, stuffed the scatterbug into the bag, and zipped it shut. "It's clearly damaged."

"Well, hanging out where your hardware is constantly being zapped with EMP pulses can't help," said Vladomyr. He maintained control over Alicia as she squirmed. "If it wasn't for that metal shell, they would have been completely fried. When you get the scatterbug back, just make sure you have it refurbished by Habib."

"No." Pierre packed the camera away.

"What do you mean? You can't bring a wild scatterbug into the colony without decontamination."

"Has every scatterbug been decontaminated and refurbished?"

"Of course, it's safety procedure."

"Are you seriously telling me that—and I may remind you, as we try to investigate the terraforming failure—we've been decontaminating the scatterbugs, and *only then* tried to diagnose the problem?"

"It wasn't quite like that."

"That's what it sounds like." Pierre crossed his arms. "If they were decontaminated, how did the big brains rule out contamination?"

"They took samples from the bioreactors. They found no contaminating agents. And then found that the flora in the bioreactors was as expected, every species of bacteria, spore, and seed was accounted for."

"All that means is they missed something," said Pierre. "They discovered nothing, so they stopped looking. Sloppy. Just sloppy. All it takes is finding one shred of evidence or one exceptional circumstance to make that a mockery."

"That's the way we've always done it."

"Not feeling well," said Alicia. She pushed Vladomyr away and rolled over face first on the sand.

"Then why is my pet scatterbug Maat prodigiously terraforming my office?" Pierre sighed. "We know scatterbugs work fine when they are reset by the factory and their bioreactors are purged and reseeded. Studying scatterbugs out in the field has not told us what we need to know. I need to take this bug back to the lab and study it in a controlled environment."

"What about the risk to the greenhouses?"

"Are you telling me what's happening in the wild isn't also happening to the greenhouses?" Pierre waited for an answer from Vladomyr, but none was forthcoming. "That horse has already left the barn."

"The others are not going to like this—" said Vladomyr.

"I'm not feeling well." Alicia was on all fours on the sand.

"Then don't tell them," said Pierre. "The others would commit suicide by procedure if left to do so. Following procedure means not having to think, not having to take responsibility, and not having Gardiner always in your face. So, if they want to crucify me for breaking the rules, then hang me high for saving their worthless skins. But examining a damaged and contaminated scatterbug may be our only way to get to the truth."

Alicia threw up violently all over the sand.

* * *

Vladomyr strode into the biology lab. Pierre was sitting at a desk writing some notes.

"How's Alicia doing?" said the Ukrainian.

"Doc Jones says it was more than a panic attack," said Pierre. "She had a complete mental breakdown of some kind."

"How's that possible?" said Vladomyr. "She's a Marine Corps vet."

"I know what you mean. I thought she was tougher than me."

"What's her prognosis?"

"Doc says she's fine physically. She's still suffering from crying fits and the occasional panic attack, but he says the mood swings are now less severe."

"What the hell happened in that cave?"

"Wish I knew." Pierre shook his head. "I didn't experience anything I haven't seen in other ancient tombs."

"Have you visited her?"

"Doc says no visitors until she's stable."

"It's been three weeks."

"I know," said Pierre. "It's like I've lost my right hand. But Jones has prescribed another week of bed rest followed by two weeks of light duties."

Vladomyr put the developed film on the desk. "Here are your photos."

"Ah yes," said Pierre. He picked up a handful of prints and flipped through them. "Nice. Excellent. Good detail."

"What about your new scatterbug friend?"

"You mean Isfit?"

"You named that thing?"

"Isfit means *chaos*. A name well-earned. He's in a pen at the back of the lab." Pierre looked back over his shoulder. The scatterbug was rustling in the vegetation inside the sandbox Pierre had left there, the sandbox seeded by Maat. A second sandbox with fresh sand had been placed in the pen along with the first box. "I had to pen him up. He kept creeping up to me and pinching me with his climbing claws."

"Serves you right for bringing a contaminated scatterbug into the colony."

"Never seen a scatterbug act so aggressive." Pierre walked over to the pen. Vladomyr followed the Frenchman. The alder seedling wiggled for a moment. Then its stalk flipped up into the air and landed flat onto the floor of the pen.

"It's tearing up the vegetation," said Vladomyr. "I've never seen them do that."

"The behavior is not normal."

"Nothing at all about this is normal. How many scatterbugs were in the cavern?"

"I wasn't inside for long. But a lot of them."

"Hundreds? Thousands?"

"More," said Pierre. "Tens of thousands. Eighty-three percent of the 1.02 million scatterbugs are still in operation. One hundred and eighty-six thousand have been scrapped. That leaves one hundred forty-two thousand unaccounted for. If I was to do a Fermi estimate, given the size of the cavern and the density of the bugs, there are between eighty and one hundred thousand bugs in the cavern."

"That many?"

"At least eighty thousand," said Pierre. "But that's only an estimate. And given they might have been falling into the cavern for 153 years, figure only about fifteen hundred lost per year. When you manufacture seven thousand bugs per year, it's hardly surprising you wouldn't miss one or two thousand here and there. All they need is a little light to recharge their solar cells. They could survive for hundreds of years as long as their circuitry remained working."

"Suppose so," said Vladomyr. "And what exactly is in those photographs?"

Pierre went to his desk. He picked up the photographs and went to the examination table. He spread out the photos onto the examination table.

"It looks like a sarcophagus." Pierre pointed to the darkest photo. He traced an outline on the photo with the back of a pen. "It has a general bipedal form, feet, and a face."

He grabbed the photo of the face of the object. The photo showed an elongated square chin. The eyes had sharp corners with slits for pupils. The nose lacking nostrils was square with sharp corners. A large, faceted gemstone was in the center of the forehead.

"It looks Egyptian," said Vladomyr.

"But it's not," said Pierre. "Remarkable, isn't it? The style is reminiscent of the Amarna Period, but that similarity is only cosmetic. If this was Egyptian, there would be a beard on the sarcophagus. The eyes are also not human. And while the Egyptians wore amulets on their foreheads, those amulets are part of a headband. The gemstone looks embedded in the forehead."

"So not human."

"Another feature of Egyptian sarcophagi is they have hands." Pierre showed a close-up of the body of the object. "No hands but six wings."

"Aren't there wings painted on Egyptian coffins?"

"Indeed, but only two wings. They represent the transformation of the dead into godhood by Isis and Osiris." Pierre paused for a moment. "But this is different. Gods in Egypt didn't have six wings."

"So not Egyptian at all."

"It's not that simple," said Pierre. He pulled out a close-up of the writing that covered the object. "We found black writing covering the entire object. The writing appears to be the same as what we found on the door and the ceramic shard fragments. But we also found trapezoid shapes on the coffin that look like shrine cabinets, and inside those shapes appears to be Egyptian hieroglyphs." Pierre looked at the glyphs inside the trapezoid. "This one reads *neru-su-ra*, 'He who respects Re.'"

"Who is Re?"

"He's the Egyptian sun god from the earliest dynasties of Egypt," said Pierre.

"I'm confused." Vladomyr rubbed the back of his neck. "Is it Egyptian or not?"

"Something still seems wrong about all this." Pierre reflected for a moment.

"You have a flair for understatement. EMP pulses. Poison gas. A strange alien coffin. Psychotic scatterbugs. An obscure connection to ancient Egypt. What about this seems right to you?"

Pierre gathered all the photos. He walked over to the wall. His fingers danced over a touchpad, and the door to a wall safe swung open. He put the photos into a folder, placed the folder inside the safe, and locked it with all the evidence he gathered, including the ceramic shard, Jasmine's notebook, and the finger bone.

"Isn't a safe going overboard?" said Vladomyr.

"After what Chin did?" Pierre glared at Vladomyr. "What we have found so far is too important, not just for us, but for humanity."

"What are you saying?"

"If the lab undergoes a level three purge, the contents of the safe will remain intact." Pierre sat back at his desk. "We have the only evidence of alien life ever discovered. That discovery must survive us. It will be important for humanity as it expands across the stars."

"How humanitarian of you," said Vladomyr drolly.

"I'm going back to the cavern." Pierre wrote out notes. "I need to document each and every glyph on the sarcophagus to get a better idea of what we're dealing with." He handed a list to Vladomyr. "I'll need another dozen photographic plates. I also am going to need a hardened EMP meter, one with a faraday cage."

"Wouldn't that defeat the point of the meter?"

"I need to find the source of the EMP emissions without the meter burning out," said Pierre. "We know the scatterbugs are protected by their carapaces, but they are not impervious to EMP damage. I don't need an absolute EMP measurement. I only need to know if the signal is stronger or weaker."

"I'll have them for you in two weeks."

"I need them next week. Tomorrow is already the beginning of February. Winter is here, and time is against us."

CHAPTER THIRTEEN

The only practical difference between a dead world and one that is alive is some unlucky organism calls the latter home. And whether that world stays living is then only a matter of whether that unlucky organism can do what it needs to do to stay alive and reproduce. Exoplanets are inherently hostile to the formation of life, and no organism has ever been lucky enough to survive evolution on an exoplanet. — **"The Futile Search for Exoplanetary Life" by Joseph Barnett**

Pierre wrote in his logbook, "February 13th, GE 154," and closed it as the rover bounced along the northern perimeter of the Bite. They stopped at the normal parking area, which was marked by a ten-foot pole with a red flag, now tilting at a sixty-degree list. The weather had flipped from oppressive heat to bitter cold as winter set in, but that did not prevent sandstorms. Another sandstorm had been through the area for the past four days, moving everything around and keeping them from coming back any earlier.

Vladomyr exited the vehicle. He pulled the flag out of the sand and replanted the pole straight up. The two men headed back to the cave. Pierre was dressed in a hazmat suit. While that protected from noxious chemicals, it did nothing against the biting cold. Vladomyr was decked out in a full parka, balaclava, and many layers and gloves. Even though the cave had been vented for two months, there was still no telling what toxic residues remained. It was better to be safe than sorry.

When they arrived at the cave, a fresh layer of sand covered everything. Vladomyr gave Pierre a bag of equipment. The Ukrainian unslung his rifle and looked through the scope at the foothills in the distance.

Pierre opened the bag. From among camera equipment, he pulled out the EMP meter. The hardened meter was encased in a copper shell. A small silica window, covered with a copper mesh, allowed him to read the LCD. A strap was attached to the outer casing. "The meter reads 100 millivolts per meter."

"Good," said Vladomyr. "The Faraday shielding is mostly effective. The internals of the meter have a maximum rating of about 500 volts per meter. You can expect the unshielded reading to be about five magnitudes greater."

"Yikes! That means EMP bursts out here are around 1000 volts per meter." More than enough to fry practically anything with a microchip. Pierre hung the EMP meter around his neck. Then he slung the tool bag over his shoulder.

"Don't let anything bite you in the dark." Vladomyr continued to watch through the scope.

"See you in a couple of hours." Pierre shrugged and trotted up the scree to the cave.

At the mouth of the cave, he looked back over of the sandy expanse of the plain. He could finally visualize the civilization that once thrived on Gliese. This was not a unique talent among archaeologists. Anthropologists would frequently visualize the ice age landscape with Neandertals hurling stone spears at mammoths, extrapolating from the tooth of a cave bear and a stone tool. Egyptologists would visualize the small chapels festooned in brightly colored paint that once adorned the royal tomb entrances from the scattered pyramidions found in the Valley of the Kings. Pierre could now visualize the sand basin below teaming with life and its civilization based upon the few remains that he now possessed.

The cave and cavern were built hundreds of millions of years ago, cut and carved out of the natural limestone escarpment. Surrounding the cave was a bustling city, full of gardens, greenery, and life, buildings as far as the eye could see. Plazas with fountains, waterworks, and ornamental canals snaked alongside the streets back when the climate had bountiful amounts of water on the surface. A great city reduced to nothing, eroded away by epochs of water, wind, and sand. All destroyed. All gone. All that remained was a malevolent vestige of a civilization that once had been. At least that's how he visualized it.

He turned and disappeared into the dark mouth of the cave. As he stepped inside, the sound was half as loud as normal. The exhaust tube was moved to one side, and the magneto-pump coils were unplugged. He assumed it was the sandstorm, plugged the pump back in, and moved the exhaust vent inlet into the doorway of the passage.

He checked the EMP meter. Already the reading had jumped up 700 millivolts. He pulled a light stick out of his pocket and cracked it. A bright white light shone from the stick in his hand. He walked down the passage until he reached the cavern. The meter shot up to 20 volts. He looked across the cavern.

Gone! Almost all the scatterbugs were gone.

Pierre ventured onto what was now a practically empty cavern floor. Only a handful of the robots and a bunch of loose rocks remained in the cavern. Where did they all go? And then he remembered about the sarcophagus. With one eye on the EMP meter, he rushed to the back of the cavern. The audio warning inside the meter crackled. As he approached the back wall, the meter spiked to 91 volts per meter. The sarcophagus was still there.

He ignited several more sticks to give himself light to work with. He held the EMP meter in his hand and walked back and forth from the sarcophagus. Walking around the object, Pierre measured the fluctuations in the EMP. There was little doubt the EMP pulses came from the sarcophagus. But for what purpose?

He stuffed the EMP meter back in the bag and pulled out his satchel of archaeological tools. Pierre wanted a close look at the sarcophagus. He selected a brush. He swept the feet of the sarcophagus. He was surprised it only had a light film of dust. This was strange. He had found coffins before. They were often covered in layers of dirt and dust. Some, like the coffin of King Tutankhamun, were even completely encased in a mixture of tar and plaster. Finding a coffin that was practically pristine was unheard of.

He put the brush back in the satchel and pulled out a pick. He touched the point of the pick against the metal of the sarcophagus near the feet where there was little decoration or writing. When the point of the pick touched the metal, he could feel the metal was hard like steel. Might have looked like gold, but it was not soft like gold. He ran the pick down the side of the coffin. Metal against metal whined. He put the pick back into the satchel. How odd. No seam. He took his book out of his bag, jotted a quick note, and returned the satchel and his notebook to the bag.

However, Pierre was far from done with his agenda. He pulled out the tripod and camera. He spread the legs of the tripod and positioned the camera. He placed a stack of film caddies on the cavern floor, ready to be popped into the camera. His plan was to start on the left side of the coffin, moving top to bottom, then to the right. He focused the camera on the writing and took the first photo. He put the exposed film caddy in his hazmat suit pocket and replaced it with a fresh plate. As he took the photographs, he moved down the length of the sarcophagus. The plastoglass plates inside his pockets jangled as he positioned the camera for the next shot.

A sense of dread fell over Pierre, but he compartmentalized the fear. He had been in tombs thousands of times. He had only ever found dead people in tombs, and most mummies weigh less than a small rabbit. Hardly something to be afraid of.

I see you. Pierre heard a voice but not with his ears. The voice was outside of him but was in his head. He assumed it was an echo in the cavern. Pareidolia of the ears and mind. He resumed taking photographs, this time of the right side of the sarcophagus. A beam of green light from the stone in the sarcophagus' forehead scanned over Pierre's form.

Who are you? Pierre heard the voice a second time. A quiet male voice in tone, powerful, enticing, comforting, seductive. Pierre raised an eyebrow.

"I don't answer strange voices." Pierre stepped up the pace of his work. He ceased being careful about where he put the tripod. He planted it quickly and clicked the shutter and continued to stuff his pockets with exposed film plates. He moved the tripod again and clicked again.

I know what you are thinking.

"Do you?" He removed the camera from the tripod and threw the tripod aside. A conversation with a disembodied voice can't be good. He increased the shutter speed—any blur or exposure problem could be fixed in post. He deftly and with haste, focused, held still, and clicked. "What am I thinking?"

You are afraid. There's nothing to fear.

"What makes you think I'm afraid?"

I've encountered your kind.

"Really? And what was that like?" With one hand, Pierre changed the plate: open caddy, focus, click, close caddy, remove plate. "Did the encounter include tea and crumpets?"

The 300 souls at Arish are mine.

"Who told you that? You shouldn't believe everything you hear." But that did raise a question. Where did it get that information?

Why have you approached the Reliquary?

"Is that what you call yourself? Or did someone else name you?"

You haven't touched the Reliquary?

"I'm cautious."

It won't harm you.

Pierre thought about it. It didn't look harmful. He had already touched it with a metal pick with no consequences. He could gain knowledge through touch. How much mass did the object contain? Does it vibrate? Is it exothermic or endothermic? He heard himself breath heavily inside the hazmat suit. He reached out with a gloved hand. The glove pressed against the side of the sarcophagus.

He immediately pulled the hand back and looked at the palm. The glove turned from yellow to black and began to dissolve. Pierre tore off the glove and threw it to the ground. A tendril of liquid metal grew out of the base of the Reliquary and punched into the ground. Pierre noticed there were several of these roots at the base of the sarcophagus. Pierre stepped back. A moment later vents on the side of the Reliquary opened and green gas issued out.

With his hazmat suit compromised and his hand exposed, he had to get out *now*. He dropped everything and ran towards the exit as fast as he could. The ventilation would eventually evacuate the gas, but not before the toxins entered his skin and dissolved him from the inside out. He looked over his shoulder. The Reliquary was shrouded in a cloud of green gas. A green beam of light scanned through the cloud, searching for him. The deadly gas drifted slowly.

He fled up the passage and exited the cave, but Vladomyr was not waiting for him at the bottom of the scree.

"There you are." Vladomyr said from behind him. He scaled down the embankment. He had been on the shelf of the escarpment. When he reached Pierre just outside the mouth of the cave, Vladomyr said, "We have a problem."

"You have no idea," said Pierre.

"We're being watched," said Vladomyr.

Pierre squinted and shook his head.

"That's not what you're talking about, is it?" Vladomyr inhaled deeply. "Shit."

When they got back to the rover, Vladomyr sat in the driver's seat while Pierre took the passenger seat. The Ukrainian turned the engine over and put the rover into drive. Pierre looked out to the side as they made their way back to Arish.

"What would cause the scatterbugs to disappear?" said Pierre.

"Maybe, with the door open, they found their way out of the cave. Like when you open a bird cage, eventually all the birds fly out."

"Many of those scatterbugs could barely move. Even if they had found the exit, we are talking about tens of thousands of bugs finding their way out and into a sandstorm. There should be pieces of bug all over the landscape. But there was something else."

Vladomyr hummed indicating he was still listening.

"When I entered the cave, the ventilation ducting was moved, and the magneto-pump was unplugged."

"Sandstorms don't unplug magneto-pumps," said Vladomyr. "Were the scatterbugs stolen?"

"Stolen?" Pierre found the concept bizarre since no one owned a scatterbug. They were built then released into the wild to do their thing. "What do you mean?"

"Every world man has discovered has been a lifeless rock. Colonies need scatterbugs for terraforming. They can't survive without arable land for crops. So let's say you run a colony, and the mother is no longer able to build new scatterbugs, what would you do?"

Pierre shrugged. The concept of rustling scatterbugs struck him as peculiar.

"Scatterbugs don't home," said Vladomyr. "You can transplant bugs from place to place without difficulty."

"Basra?" said Pierre incredulously. "Could it not be exiles?"

"Don't think so," said Vladomyr. "When I was on the ridge, I observed a scouting party of three watching us. Well, they were watching you." He swerved the wheel to avoid a large rock. Their bodies swayed with the vehicle. "Exiles aren't that organized. They steal what they want quickly and then disappear. Exiles never hang around to see who comes back." The Ukrainian took another deep breath. "Also relocating eighty thousand scatterbugs is no mean feat. You need people and vehicles. People who are disciplined enough to move in and out during a sandstorm."

"Don't know what scares me more," said Pierre. "That Basra is stealing our scatterbugs or that they can raid our colony at any time under the cover of a sandstorm."

"Gardiner is not going to like this."

"And tell him what?" said Pierre. "We found the source of the EMP bursts, but we can't touch it because it quite literally melts anything organic it comes in contact with. Oh, and yes, Basra stole all our broken scatterbugs lost in a cave for a century that nobody even knew were there."

* * *

Three days later, Pierre was going over the most recent set of developed photos. Even though he had to abandon the camera in the cavern, at least he had the good sense to keep the exposed plates on his person. Pierre scanned the photos into his computer terminal and photo-merged them into one large composite image.

His right hand tremored uncontrollably. He pressed it against the top of the desk to make it stop. His hand had never done that before. Was this a side-effect from his encounter in the cavern?

"Stacy597: highlight and extract all trapezoid shapes on the image," Pierre said to the computer. The computer extracted images of each shrine shape from the composite.

"Eighty-four images extracted," said the computer terminal.

Pierre issued another command. "Stacy597: with the extracted images, use optical character recognition and pattern fitting. Find unique instances among the extracted images." As he said that, he regained control of his right hand.

"Computing," said Stacy597.

There was a soft knock at the door.

"Enter," said Pierre.

The door opened slowly, and Alicia entered the room. She was no longer the ruddy stout woman who saved Pierre from the transport ship. Her complexion was ashen gray, and she had lost about twenty pounds.

"Alicia?" said Pierre. "Good to see you. How are you doing?"

"I'm ready to resume work." Alicia's hand tremored.

"Don't lie to me." Pierre got up and poured her a glass of water from a thermos. "You're not a good liar."

"I didn't want to disturb you," she said.

"Please, have a seat. What can I do for you?" Pierre sat back at his desk.

"Do you want me back?" Alicia's face was downcast. She avoided all eye contact.

"Why wouldn't I want you back?"

"I failed in the cave."

"You failed no one," said Pierre. "Something odious is in that cave. And the sarcophagus is not what we think."

"Are you just saying that?"

"No, I'm not." Pierre frowned and picked up a pen. He twirled the pen. "First, it's not a sarcophagus. A sarcophagus is a vessel that holds a body. This object has no seam and was never designed to contain a body. Second, it is the source of the EMP bursts and poison gas. Third, it is the product of a third species that has figured out how to psychically manipulate other lifeforms. You weren't weak. You were psychically attacked."

"How do you know that?"

"Because the Reliquary attacked me too." Pierre eased back into his chair. "If I hadn't had twenty years of experience controlling irrational fears of death, darkness, and being buried alive, I might have acted as you." Pierre poured himself a glass of water. "In your case, the Reliquary had probably not encountered a sentient being in a half a billion years. It reached out to you to see if its base attack still worked.

It was successful with you, so it tried the same attack on me. When I didn't respond as expected, it spoke to me and tried to probe me for answers."

"It can speak?"

"After a fashion and not with an audible voice. It plants thoughts into your mind you perceive as speech."

"Is the Reliquary psychic? Did it read my mind?"

"No, it's not psychic in the way you think. It can't read minds. It didn't seem to gather any more information than I was willing to give it."

"But it can implant thoughts. Isn't that being psychic?"

"I suppose you could call it that," said Pierre. "But it's a kind of psychic ability that has limits. Imagine a transistor radio."

"Always with the antiques?"

"I am an archaeologist."

Alicia pursed her lips and conceded the point.

"Think of the human brain like a transistor radio," said Pierre. "Better at receiving messages than transmitting them. All the Reliquary has to do is find a frequency that resonates with the frequency of your brain to insert thoughts."

"But if it has a psychic ability, does that mean it's sentient?"

"Not like you or me."

"So is it alive?"

"It's not alive but has a rudimentary intelligence." Pierre held the end of his pen to his temple. "It's a machine. A bit like how some androids can communicate with each other using a psionic link."

"How do you know it's a machine?"

"It doesn't answer open-ended questions." Pierre tapped his pen against his notebook. "But it also seems to be following a script, a script that probes for weakness. It's probably less intelligent than an android. But it is modelling a pre-determined pattern of behavior. Think of it more as an engram."

"An engram?"

"It's a piece of cognitive information or an ability that has been imprinted into a physical substance. It can collect rudimentary information and identify the vulnerabilities of an intruder. Whoever made the Reliquary imprinted upon it cunning, deceit, and malice. But it is unable to respond with anything not within its imprint."

"Task complete," said Stacy597 in the background. "Eleven unique instances identified."

"Stacy597," said Pierre, "using the unique instances, identify individual glyphs according to the Egyptian hieroglyphic language, then scan the main text."

"Command running," said the computer terminal.

"What are you doing?" said Alicia.

"I'm trying to decipher the alien inscriptions."

"I'm confused," said Alicia. "You asked the computer to correlate the language to ancient Egyptian, but you also told me that the Reliquary is hundreds of millions of years old. Isn't ancient Egyptian only fifty-five hundred years old?"

"Ever looked at the Chinese writing system?"

"No."

"There are seven official dialects of Chinese. All pronounced differently, but all of them now use the Simplified Chinese writing system."

"So are you saying that the Egyptians used a logographic writing system that was taken from these aliens?"

"It might be safer to say that Species 3 had a priestly or royal language that was incredibly long lived. It's possible that Species 3 used a kind of proto hieroglyphic."

"How would the Egyptians have encountered the writing from Species 3?"

"It's not unusual for cultures to adapt writing systems for their own use. English had two writing systems, which it adapted from Latin. It used a printed script that is a combination of two other writing systems:

Old Roman majuscule cursive and Carolingian minuscule scripts. English also had a cursive script that was used for hundreds of years but is rarely used today."

"What are you saying?"

"We can't know how Species 3 spoke their royal language. But if their pictographs employed similar meanings, like a Chinese person who can read Japanese while being unable to understand the spoken language, we might be able to read a portion of Species 3's language without necessarily being able to understand the spoken language."

"And that is because hieroglyphs are pictographic?"

"To a large extent, yes." Pierre paused for a moment. "Unfortunately, only a small minority of the language uses hieroglyphs. The second script will be a greater challenge."

"How so?"

"It doesn't seem to be directly related to the proto hieroglyphs." Pierre pulled up a magnification of the composited image. "If you look at this writing system, it's not pictographic. Seems to use a system of forty-four letters."

"How do we figure this out?"

"Not sure we can," Pierre said prospectively. He zoomed into some of the trapezoids. "These trapezoids act like cartouches. They frame names. Some of the names have been substituted with the second script. Mapping those crossovers might give us a clue."

"So where do we start?" said Alicia. She moved her chair until she sat next to Pierre.

"You want to work with me on trying to crack the code?" said Pierre. "The process of deciphering a new language is seldom fast and is often a tedious struggle. You sure you want to do that?"

"Doc did say light duties."

"Task complete," said Stacy597 in the background. "Two hundred, eighty-three instances of hieroglyphs found in the main text."

"If you insist," said Pierre. He moved his chair up to the desk. "The first step is to try to translate symbols we can figure out. Names are often a good place to start."

Pierre selected the contents of the first trapezoid cartouche. He opened a notebook and with a pen carefully drew out the first name. He then transliterated the name and then translated it. One read *msdji-ef-ankh*, 'he who hates life.' The meaning of this was clear. Meanwhile, Alicia quietly watched him work.

He selected another: *netjer-iqu*, 'a god who destroys.' Pierre scratched his head.

"Are you translating those names right?" Alicia asked, reading over his shoulder.

"These are clearly names," said Pierre. "But what kind of civilization gives its offspring such terrible names?"

He flipped back earlier in his notebook to his first translation: *neru-su-ra*, 'He who respects the god Re.' Pierre repeated it out loud.

"That name seems perfectly reasonable," said Alicia. "If I was a king or something similar, I would want to show my support of the religious system. The opiate of the masses thing."

"How anachronistically Marxist," said Pierre dryly. Then he saw it. "Indeed, reasonable, if it weren't for my mistake."

"What mistake?"

Pierre ran a stroke through the translation. "I assumed that *neru*, 'fear' means the inverted 'fear of him,' which is how we render it in Egyptian royal texts. However, I did not properly consider the trailing pronoun. It should read *ra-neru-su*, not *neru-su-ra*."

He wrote his new translation beside the old, 'the sun fears him.' An endorphin hit of instant relief washed over him.

"There's a pattern," said Pierre. "Can you see it?"

"No."

"They are all blasphemous names."

"Why would anyone do that?"

"I don't know."

Pierre read the next name. *kher-pauty*, 'fallen of the primeval gods.' He paused to take it in.

"The primeval gods?" said Alicia. "What are primeval gods?"

"The stuff of legends," said Pierre. "Some ancient civilizations, like the Israelites, called them principalities and powers. Other civilizations called them foundation deities. Their function was to rule in the place of the supreme God after the chaos monsters were vanquished."

"Are they Nephilim?"

"No, Nephilim are also legendary, but they were the offspring of castes of fallen priests. The Nephilim were men. Primeval gods are much older than that. Beings billions of years old that were at the height of their power when the first multicellular life was getting its foothold on Earth. The primeval gods were said to be capricious and dangerous."

"You talk about them like they are real."

"Who knows?" shrugged Pierre. "*Legend* is a shifty concept. A legend can be a completely fictional story. But a legend can also be mytho-history where historical reality is transformed so that it intertwines with a religious narrative. And given that we found it among broken urns of what is likely to have been sacrificial victims, it might be wise to at least entertain the possibility there might be a grain of truth behind the primordial god legend. One culture's monster of legend is sometimes another culture's existential threat."

"If these names are any indication, they sound horrible." Alicia's right eyelid twitched as a tremor passed across her right hand. Was she having a flashback?

CHAPTER FOURTEEN

In the early 21st century, the Glaucom Corporation (based out of Milwaukee Wisconsin) began in the agricultural industry creating build to order replacement parts for tractors and combines. Their specialization was making parts for end-of-life and high-end farming equipment. During the Third World War, the company produced premium firearms with advanced features and missile components. – **"Armed and Profitable: Handgun Manufacturing in America" by George N. Ford**

"You know what day it is?" said Gardiner. He stood behind his desk. Pierre's reports were in his hand. "March 7th, and you've been at it for eight months. All you have to show for your efforts are some intellectual curiosities and a lot of speculation."

Pierre's heart sank. He had been in one-on-one meetings like this before. He knew exactly what was about to happen.

"I discovered the source of the EMP pulses," said Pierre.

"The EMP pulses are not a threat. The failure of the terraforming *is* a threat." Gardiner slammed the reports on his desk. "You were supposed to discover why our crops are failing and why the scatterbugs aren't doing their job, not go into speculation and conjecture over ancient alien civilizations."

"I believe the two are related," said Pierre.

"Well, Chin has convinced me otherwise," said Gardiner.

Pierre regretted not beating the shit out of Chin when he had the opportunity.

Gardiner sat at his desk. "In two days, the MegaAI will arrive in orbit. Chin has convinced me that, if we give the MegaAI all your data, it will figure out what you could not. And you will no longer be necessary for the colony's survival."

"So I collect all the raw data, and Chin decides how it gets used."

"I decide how it gets used," said Gardiner. He scowled at Pierre. "But Chin makes a good point."

"You mean when he isn't plagiarizing someone else's work?"

"Enough from you," Gardiner snapped. "You collected some data."

"Some?"

"Don't provoke me." The governor clenched a copper cup in his hand. The cup crumpled inward.

"Even if Chin gets a coherent answer out of the MegaAI, doesn't mean he will be able to understand it." Pierre exhaled. "Are you going to put the fate of the entire colony into the hands of its least competent person? Haven't you learned Chin promises big and delivers nothing?"

"What did you promise?"

"I didn't make you any promises."

"Exactly, that's why I like what he says more. You're done here. March 9th at 8am you will report to the situation room to upload all your data to the MegaAI. All you will do is hand over the data and leave. After that, Chin will ask the AI the appropriate questions. You will be officially stripped of your position as Deputy Governor and no longer hold a management position. Your assistant will be reassigned to scatterbug maintenance. The lab will return to Chin's control in one week. Finally, you will need to find yourself a new job. I recommend farming in the greenhouses as it would do something for that ego of yours."

Pierre stood, dusted himself off, and headed to the door.

"I'm not done," said Gardiner.

"Oh, you're done," said Pierre. "You've signed the death warrant of everyone here. You just don't know it yet."

* * *

Pierre was by himself in the mess hall. A metal tray of untouched food sat in front of him. In his hand was a shining clean fork. On the large video monitor, a loop reel of videos streamed from the MegaAI showed simulations of what the great ship was capable of: rebuilding space stations, in-orbit repairs, manufacturing specialized components that could be dropped to any colony in its vicinity. It was a robot metropolis of manufacturing, floating in space from colony to colony.

Vladomyr and Alicia came over to Pierre and sat across from him.

"We heard what happened," said Vladomyr. He covered his food in a thick black layer of artificial pepper. "Chin's been bragging about it all morning."

"He wins again," said Pierre. "The Chins of this world always win."

"Have you seen the mood around here?" said Alicia. "People are excited about the MegaAI."

"It's a big deal," said Vladomyr. "There's only twenty MegaAIs out there servicing the forty-eight colonies. Most are doing deep space exploration looking for habitable exoplanets. A MegaAI may visit a colony only once every fifty years. And usually, they provide a colony with well-needed relief."

"I hear some colonies even hold annual festivals based upon the last appearance of a MegaAI." Alicia took a fork full of food and shoveled it into her face. Her cheeks bulged like a chipmunk packing in too many nuts.

"Really isn't much to celebrate in deep space, is there?" said Pierre.

"How long is it expected to stay here?" Alicia had already devoured a third of her food.

Pierre shook his head. Could she have any taste buds at all? He was so done with colony food. He knew the exiles hunted rats and cobras. Could eating rats be worse than this?

"Given the damage to the orbital docking station, I would estimate it will be here for about three weeks," said Vladomyr. "Plenty of time to use its computer facilities."

"Good news I guess," said Pierre. "Although I won't have access to any of those facilities."

"You'll still have us," said Alicia.

"You're going back to scatterbug maintenance," said Pierre. "And Vladomyr, well, nothing they can do to him."

"What about you?" said Vladomyr.

"I'm going to explore a new career as a farmer." Pierre poked at the food on his plate but ate nothing.

"A Pol Pot solution if I've ever heard it," said the Ukrainian. He spooned his amorphous mush into his mouth like he was shoveling dirt. "Trust Gardiner to waste good material to placate the lowest common denominator."

Pierre set his fork on the metal cafeteria tray. He had more than enough to satisfy him for the next week. "I didn't think it could get much worse than my career on Earth."

"We aren't done," said Alicia. "You discovered something that changes everything we thought we knew about the universe."

"Gardiner is right," said Pierre, pushing his tray away. "What does any of that matter if we don't discover why our crops are failing?"

"That's not how discoveries are made," said Vladomyr. "You can't force someone to discover something on demand. Discoveries happen through diligence and no small amount of creativity and insight, all of which Chin lacks."

"A week from now, I'm not going to have a lab, an office, or even a computer terminal. It's going to be difficult for me to do anything resembling proper research."

"The colonies were not supposed to be about mere survival." Vladomyr shook his head. "But about science and discovery. You made the first interesting discovery on this desolate rock."

"And it was successfully suppressed." Pierre thought for a moment. "Look, I get it. The first alien life was not supposed to be discovered by an archaeologist on his first attempt. It was supposed to be discovered by someone in the scientific elite: a biologist, a chemist, or a physicist. Someone with the street cred, publication record, and collegiality as a scientist, not some disruptive outsider from the liberal arts."

"I wished that was unfair," said Vladomyr. He looked downcast. "The disciplines have had their share of professional hedge protection. We too often admire the position and the man more than the work and the truth."

Pierre stood up. He left his tray on the table, not even touched.

"You haven't eaten at all," said Alicia. She had seen the signs too many times not to notice.

"Not hungry," said Pierre. "Besides, I've still got papers I need to scan in for Tuesday. And the rest I need to toss to clean out my office." He slinked away and left the cafeteria.

Alicia reached over to grab Pierre's tray. Vladomyr grabbed her wrist.

"Halfsies," he said. Alicia agreed and split Pierre's meal. "I never knew one of the benefits of being his friend would be extra food."

"I worry about him," she said as she stuffed her face with the extra rations.

"Your concern is touching," said Vladomyr. "You're going to get fat."

"Like I care," she said, the edges of her mouth covered in orange-food-colored fake tomato sauce.

"And that's exactly the attitude I need for a certain favor." Vladomyr looked side to side. "A favor best not discussed here."

* * *

On the morning of March 9th, a little after 7am, Pierre sat in his office and waited. He looked out the picture window. People milled outside looking up into the sky. He looked up and could see the white reflection of the MegaAI in orbit around Gliese. The white smudge in the sky looked almost like a third moon.

Eight months of work were reduced to a single memory stick on his desk. All his notes and data had been photographed, scanned, and exported, ready for upload to the MegaAI. Two small baggies accompanied the stick: the finger bone and the shard of blank white ceramic. He was determined to keep those on his person for as long as possible. No way was he going to surrender the baggies to Chin so he could destroy them. But he doubted that Chin would even ask for them. If he did, questions would arise as to why the product of a "fraud" would be so important.

Beside his desk was a pile of paper ready for recycling. Per colony policy, anything scanned had to be recycled. This included his notebook and all the drawings Jasmine had done. Unfortunately, colony life did not value aesthetics. Pierre had already relocated Maat to his quarters. He did not know how long he would be able to keep his pet. In fourteen months, the 22-month rule would kick in. If by some miracle Chin and the MegaAI could figure this all out, he'd probably have to go into exile.

What will become of Maat? Pierre snorted. He faced exile and a probable violent death, and yet he was worried about what was going to happen to a robot designed to survive and thrive in a wilderness.

Vladomyr knocked on the door and entered Pierre's office. "It's time," he announced.

"Okay," said Pierre. He put the baggies in one pocket and the memory stick in the other. He stood up. The next time he would be back in this office it would only be to put the trash out.

Pierre left his office, and Vladomyr was waiting for him outside. They walked together down the hallway without saying a word. They arrived at the staircase leading up to the second floor. The security office and situation room were upstairs.

As Pierre was about to climb the stairs, Vladomyr stopped him.

"If you want to talk after," said Vladomyr.

"What's to talk about?" Pierre said to Vladomyr. "My life's work is once again being taken away from me and given to someone who did none of the work and has no aptitude. What can anyone say to that?"

"I understand."

"I doubt it." Pierre climbed the stairs past Vladomyr, and the Ukrainian followed.

The two men entered the situation room. The senior staff were around all the terminals. All the screens had changed since Pierre was last there. The monitor had video images focused on the MegaAI. Telemetry streamed across another screen. A variety of open terminals streamed data in and out. Chin hovered near the command terminal with Gardiner over his shoulder. Brian was yucking it up with the boys.

"An open data link has been established with the MegaAI," said Okeli. His broad muscular shoulders masked the command terminal from everyone's sight. Everyone cheered except for Pierre. The security chief stood up and surrendered the command terminal chair to Chin. The slight Taiwanese man took the chair and nestled into it. No one seemed bothered he was acting as Gardiner's right-hand man. The senior staff even seemed relieved the pecking order had been restored, which made Pierre's heart sink even deeper.

"Initiate text to voice so we can all hear what's happening," said Gardiner giddily. He bounced up and down like a small child. The atmosphere was like the coming of a demigod, fans coming face to face with their idol.

"Link protocol established with Arish… This is MegaAI *Sigma A017* of the National Space and Exploration Consortium. Repairs to the transport docking station initiated…. Estimated time to complete repairs is seventeen days. Waiting for next input request." The voice synthesizer added a deep metallic tone to *Sigma's* response.

"Send up our parts request list," said Gardiner. Chin uploaded the parts list.

"Parts list received. Automated manufacturing facilities activated. Processing parts requests." The MegaAI continued, "Estimated time to delivery is five days."

"Find out if Basra has established contact with the MegaAI," said Gardiner. Chin typed in the information request followed by the send command.

"Link protocol has not been established with Basra," said the MegaAI.

"That's strange," whispered Vladomyr. He and Pierre were standing at the back of the situation room.

"Why's that strange?" said Pierre. "Maybe the MegaAI can only work with one colony at a time."

"That's not the way they work," said Vladomyr. "They are massively parallel machines. They are designed to support hundreds of small colonies that are tens of thousands of people in size, and all at once."

"Maybe Basra didn't know the MegaAI was coming?"

"All colonies would have been alerted to the MegaAI's arrival. Strange that Basra hasn't initiated an uplink."

"Chin," said Gardiner, "what's next on the agenda?"

"That would be the scatterbug and terraforming problem," said Chin.

"Excellent. Initiate the query."

Chin typed in the query to the MegaAI. "Problem needs to be solved. Terraforming is failing inside and outside the colony setting. Ten months until the colony runs out of food. Situation critical. We have circumstantial evidence that may or may not be related. Preparing to upload all the data that we have."

"MegaAI *Sigma A017* has received an open query [Reference #Gliese-Arish-05]. Query pending data upload followed by 'Query complete' command," droned the voice of the terminal in undeviating monotone.

"Right," said Chin. "Uploading all the data and reports collected prior to September." He uploaded the data and reports submitted by the scientists prior to Pierre's arrival.

"MegaAI *Sigma A017* has received data dump #1 for open query [Reference #Gliese-Arish-05]," said the artificial intelligence.

"I now need the data from the dead weight." Chin eyes gleamed, and he rubbed his hands.

Gardiner looked back and spotted Pierre, making eye contact. "Gimme the data."

Pierre worked his way through the crowd of senior staff. When he reached the command console, he reached into his pocket and held up the memory stick.

"Is this it?" said Gardiner.

"I have a name," said Pierre giving the memory stick to Gardiner.

"Yeah, dead weight," said Chin laughing.

"You are no longer needed here. You can go now." Gardiner grabbed the memory stick and handed it to Chin. Chin plugged the memory stick into the console.

Pierre walked to the back of the room towards the door. He was blocked by Vladomyr.

"Stay," insisted Vladomyr quietly. "No one will notice you're still here. And you need to see the results from the MegaAI. Chin might steal the credit, but you need to know what you've achieved."

Pierre turned around and watched the monitor.

"Right," said Chin. "Uploading all the *worthless* data."

"MegaAI *Sigma A017* has received data dump #2 for open query [Reference #Gliese-Arish-05]," said the artificial intelligence.

"That should be everything for the upload," said Chin.

"Close the query," said Gardiner. "Finally, an end to our woes… once and for all."

"Closing the query." Chin grinned from ear to ear. He typed, "Query complete for Gliese-Arish-05," and hit the enter key.

"MegaAI *Sigma A017* link disconnected," spoke the command terminal.

"What happened?" said Gardiner. His eyes darted all over the command terminal. "Get the connection back."

Okeli checked the other monitors. "The MegaAI was disconnected at the source."

A collective cacophony could be heard from outside the situation room. Everyone inside hushed into complete silence. They could hear screams, crying, and yelling through the paper-thin walls of the security office.

"The colonists," said Okeli.

"Get me monitors to the outside," said Gardiner.

Okeli flipped the switch. The views changed on the monitors. People were running about. Some had fallen to their knees on the ground crying.

"Get the MegaAI back!" shouted Gardiner.

"I can't!" Okeli shouted, perspiration poured off his forehead. Chin sat in the chair of the command console listless and limp, clearly in shock. "The MegaAI is refusing to connect."

"Get me the MegaAI's telemetry."

Okeli checked the telemetry monitor. "The MegaAI is leaving orbit."

"Has a MegaAI ever abandoned a colony?" said Pavel Urbanovich. He paled to a ghostly white.

Vladomyr tapped Pierre on the shoulder. "Time for us to go," he said.

"I agree," said Pierre.

The two men darted down the stairs. Alicia waited at the bottom of the stairwell for them. "Were you able to do it?" said Vladomyr. "The guns *and* plastic explosives?"

"Just don't ask how I did it," said Alicia. She handed Vladomyr and Pierre each a handgun. "Three virgin Glaucom 17ZEs with an extra clip each. They have a fingerprint-lock ID system built into the grip. Electronics in the handle register your fingerprints. The pistol can only be fired by you and only if it can read your fingerprints. The plastic explosives are waiting in the biology lab."

"Convenient, but I don't know how to use a gun," said Pierre. He held the pistol in his right hand and heard the soft beep of his fingerprints registering with the ID locking system.

"Learn," said Vladomyr. "Other than the ID lock, it's like every other gun. Point the muzzle only at what you want to kill. And bullets only travel in straight lines. It is a 9mm standard colony-issued sidearm. Now, hide it in your clothing. And always keep it on your person."

"Even when I shower?"

"Especially when you shower and shower in your underwear with your pistol," said Vladomyr. "It is best right now no one knows we have these."

"How did you know this was going to happen?" said Pierre. He made sure the safety was on and stuffed the gun into his pants and closed his jacket over it.

"I didn't," said Vladomyr. "However, chances were pretty good something like it was going to happen. When people invest too much hope into a person, whether real or artificial, expectations can be easily dashed."

"Cynical," said Pierre. "I respect that."

"Pragmatic," Vladomyr corrected. "However, until you get a confirmation on your pending demotion, I would consider that postponed."

"What makes you think that?" They walked down the hallway.

"Gardiner is going to need to blame someone for this debacle."

"Fantastic."

"It is. The blame game is going to buy us some time."

They hurried to put as much distance as possible between them and the situation room.

"What the hell happened?" said Alicia. "I was outside with the others when a wave of panic swept over them. They pointed to the sky and screamed and cried."

"Didn't you see what happened?" said Pierre.

"Not really," said Alicia. "Those idiots have been pointing up into the sky all morning. Frankly, if you've seen one spaceship, you've seen them all."

"If you had been looking with the rest of them, you would have noticed the MegaAI high-tailed it out of Dodge."

"You're shitting me," she said.

"Wish he was," said Vladomyr. They rounded the corner but not without looking first to see if anyone else was armed.

"The MegaAI took off so fast it didn't bother to collect the service droids it sent out to repair the docking station," said Pierre crowding in from behind.

"What's going to happen to them?" asked Alicia.

"I'd worry more about what is going to happen to us," said Pierre. "The robots will take care of themselves. However, without the support of the MegaAI or shipments from Earth, things could get scarce here more sooner than later."

"Tip of the iceberg," said Vladomyr. "What is Basra going to do when they find out we were responsible for driving away the MegaAI?"

"Say what?" said Alicia.

"Yeah," said Pierre, "the MegaAI took off upon receiving my reports. Not sure why."

"Basra is likely to go from simply casing the joint to knocking on our front door," said Vladomyr. He ventured forward from the hallway to the archway of the mess hall. The cafeteria was vacant. A banner reading *Welcome MegaAI* was half-fallen from its ties, hanging limply. Plastic cups were strewn across the floor. No one even attended the breakfast service. It was the aftermath of a shindig that never took place like the Presidential campaign headquarters for the losing party. Vladomyr snuck over to the food service stations. He stepped behind the counters. The food was still piping hot. He stirred the trays with a ladle.

"What are you doing?" said Alicia.

"Eating." Vladomyr grabbed a tray and piled on some food. "I would suggest that you two do the same." He piled on a double ration. "I would eat as much as you can. Given the state of things, there might not be any lunch or dinner tonight either. And when the shock of what happens wears off, none of us are going to want to be here when the others come looking for food."

At that moment, the video screens came on with the face and upper body of the governor. "Dear Fellow Colonists," Gardiner spoke with a clear, authoritative tone. "You have undoubtedly heard that the MegaAI has made an unexpected early departure."

"The man certainly knows how to diminish his responsibility," said Pierre.

"No reason has been forthcoming from the MegaAI explaining its departure. Rest assured. We are pursuing every course of action to re-establish the data link. We are assuming a technical difficulty has caused the break in the uplink and that this will only be a temporary glitch." Gardiner's shirt was disheveled and stained with sweat, and even his moustache lacked the fine pointed tips he carefully styled.

"Yeah, sure. Like MegaAIs pick up and leave at the first data glitch." Vladomyr shook his head at the posturing.

"And I assure you, if there is any individual responsible for the break in transmission, that person or persons will be held to justice," said Gardiner.

"There's the rub," said Vladomyr. "Just like Gardiner, always giving himself a scapegoat when he can't find the problem. And there we see the real reason why the colony is on the brink of disaster."

Gardiner continued the broadcast, "We promise you we will get to the bottom of this. And with complete transparency, you will learn everything that we do. And we will survive despite every setback and every adversity. You have my promise on that." The screen went black, and the broadcast ended.

"Pierre." Vladomyr stopped piling food on his cafeteria tray. "Does the biology lab have a fridge?"

"Yes," said Pierre.

"Change of plan. Forget the trays. Fill as many takeaway containers as you can carry. We may need a few *days* of food." He turned to Alicia. "Alicia, carry only as much as you can in one arm. I want you to be ready with your pistol if we get stopped on the way to the lab."

Alicia pulled out her pistol and put a round in the chamber. They each filled as many takeaway containers as they could, and they left the mess hall with haste. They crept quickly down the darkened hallways.

"The lights have all been dimmed," whispered Pierre. He was afraid the echo in the hallway would resonate.

"Martial law. It's to keep people calm and prevent rioting," said Vladomyr in a low tone. "It also helps security to see if people are in the hallway against the lighting from the mess. We're in danger as long as we stay in the open."

"The lab is in the next wing."

When they arrived at the lab, Pierre unlocked the door and allowed the other two inside. He closed the door and locked it. All three went over to the fridge to put the food away. Pierre opened the fridge door and put his six takeaway containers into the fridge. When he backed away from the fridge, Alicia stowed her containers.

"Now, what?" said Pierre. "It's not like the biology lab is defensible. If Gardiner wants to kill us, all he needs to do is authorize a level three purge, and it's curtains for us." Alicia walked over to the pen with the scatterbug.

"He won't do that immediately," said Vladomyr. "This will buy us a few days—"

"Hey guys," said Alicia.

"What do you think he will do next—" Pierre ignored Alicia.

"Guys," said Alicia.

"What?" said Pierre, annoyed at being interrupted.

"Is the scatterbug's sandbox supposed to look like this?"

Pierre walked over to Isfit's pen and hovered over the bellicose robot. The sand tray that had been lush and green with life was now completely black with dead foliage. He took a metal probe and leaned over the sand tray. He poked at the dead foliage, gently lifting the dead leaves. He looked for insects and signs of fungus but found none.

"Is that significant?" said Vladomyr with a perplexed look on his face.

"I'll say," said Pierre standing upright. "We got the final piece of the puzzle." He turned to Alicia. "Bring me Pavel Urbanovich right now. And do so at gunpoint if he needs persuasion."

CHAPTER FIFTEEN

The origins of flight in animals are examples of convergent evolution. Flight has evolved independently in insects, reptiles, and birds, and each time it looks somewhat different. The phenomena has also been observed in the body plan of crab-like organisms that have evolved from at least a dozen unrelated phyla. Thus, it should not come as a surprise that we find a similar tendency in archaeology. Pyramids were developed independently in both Africa and the Americas. And even the trappings of Egyptian culture seem to have been recapitulated not only on Earth but somehow on an exoplanet like Gliese 832 c. — **"The Reliquary: Final Report" by Pierre Gulet**

A half-hour later, Pavel Urbanovich walked into the biology lab. He was observably flustered and annoyed at having been compelled to come to the lab. Alicia followed in after him, her loaded Glaucom under her jacket, ready to put a couple of rounds into Pavel if he did not comply.

"Are you completely unaware of what is going on out there?" blustered Pavel.

"Glad you could join us," said Pierre. "We just want a conversation."

"Was threatening me at gunpoint necessary?"

"The situation is urgent, and we needed to ensure your cooperation, especially as you said because of what is going on out there." Pierre paused for a moment. "That reminds me. Have you had anything to eat today with the early morning meeting and chaos breaking out immediately after?"

"Well… um… no," he stammered, "I guess not."

"We have food. Probably still warm," said Pierre. "Feel free to leave if you want. Or you can have a conversation with us while you eat. It might be the only solid meal you get in a while."

"What did you want to talk about?"

"Your field of expertise. No one here knows more about plants and plant biology than you." Pierre tried his best to be ingratiating.

Pavel glanced over at Vladomyr.

Vladomyr nodded at Pavel. Pierre observed there was no love lost between the two men. Alicia was behind them, observing and taking notes.

"I suppose a short conversation wouldn't hurt," Pavel relented. Pierre nodded to Alicia who went to the fridge and grabbed a food container and a disposable fork. Pierre escorted Pavel to Isfit's pen.

Pavel nodded. "So what? I've seen a lot of our plants look like that."

"Like that," said Pierre. "Black like that?"

"Yes, many times," insisted Pavel. "What's this about?"

"This scatterbug has not been decontaminated."

"What?" said Pavel.

"Don't look so surprised," said Vladomyr. "You've admitted that you've seen this kind of vegetative death many times. Your precious greenhouses are already contaminated."

"What are you getting at?"

"This tray was originally terraformed and planted by a factory fresh scatterbug isolated in my office," said Pierre. Alicia handed Pavel a tray of food that was still warm. "That bug, named Maat, is still happily terraforming to this day. Maat is our scientific control. I took a tray with lush vegetation from the control environment and put it in this pen with a scatterbug we extracted from the wild."

"Is this about your alien species nonsense?" said Pavel.

Vladomyr grabbed Pavel by the collar and drew his fist back to punch him.

"Gentlemen!" shouted Alicia from behind. She walked up to Pavel. She put her fingers on Vladomyr's chest and pushed him backwards. She looked Pavel in both eyes. "You have no idea what terror awaits. These gentlemen have kindly asked you for your help. They recognize your expertise, and you can do something like perhaps save the colony by being a little bit more collegial." Pierre grinned when he heard Alicia use academic jargon to garner Pavel's cooperation.

"May I continue?" asked Pierre.

Pavel nodded. He opened the takeaway tray and began to eat as he listened.

"The scatterbug in this pen, which we named Isfit, was introduced to the vegetation sixty-one days ago."

"Sixty days?" said Pavel.

"Three days ago, the plants were still alive. We noticed plant growth was inhibited around day five after Isfit's introduction."

"That's a long time," said Pavel. He scratched the back of his hand against his bristle covered chin. His deeply recessed eyes stared at the scatterbug, snapping its climbing claws at him. "But that's not uncommon with a fungal infection where the roots die first and then the rest of the plant starves to death."

"We thought about that. We figured that moving the sand tray from the control environment to the lab might have been the cause. However, I had moved the tray into the lab on the 18th of Intercalarus. So there were two full weeks between the introduction of the tray to the lab and the introduction of the contaminated scatterbug. Plant growth was observed preceding the introduction of the Isfit scatterbug. Besides, aren't the fungal species we introduced only supposed to be pathogenic as opportunistic secondary infections?"

"Yes," said Pavel.

"So that rules out fungi as the cause as even your own report noted," said Pierre. He placed a printout of Pavel's report beside him. "The experiment here in front of you has shown that Isfit is carrying something that is killing vegetation. Something that is killing plants at the root level by inhibiting nutrient uptake. And we know the scatterbug bioreactors did not contain herbicides, and the bacteria, fungi, and seeds inside were all the species expected."

"That's exactly what we found," said Pavel.

"Now, I have to ask," said Pierre. "In your analysis, did you find any plant viruses?"

"No, that would have been immediately detected by the presence of virus protein sheaths."

"What about exotic contagions that aren't viruses or bacteria?"

"What are you talking about?" said Vladomyr.

"Let Pavel answer the question," said Pierre. An uncomfortable pause filled the room.

Pavel nodded and sighed. He shook his head. "A prion. A proteinaceous infectious particle."

"A prion," repeated Pierre.

"What's that?" said Vladomyr.

"It's an intrinsically disordered protein that self-replicates," said Pavel. "It was best known in the 20th Century for an outbreak of spongiform encephalopathy, also known as Creutzfeldt-Jakob or Mad Cow Disease. But those diseases primarily affect animals."

"What would be the implications if a prion caused the death of these plants?"

"Well, it would be incredibly difficult to detect unless you were specifically looking for it. A prion can't be cultured with normal growth media. And the standard diagnostic tests to detect pathogens would be useless." Pavel's voice slowed down as he spoke. "It would probably reproduce in such a way that would block the plant root's ability to uptake nutrients. And the soil would end up being infertile for potentially generations."

"That sounds eerily like our situation. Does it not?" Pierre looked at Pavel. "And let's say our scatterbugs became infected with these prions when they took up water and soil nutrients for their bioreactors. The bacteria and microrrhiza inside would replicate the prions and spread the contagion all over."

"What was the source of that contagion?"

"You don't need to concern yourself with that," said Pierre. "What we need you to do is confirm the presence of self-replicating proteins." Pierre grabbed a sterile sample bag and a spoon. He scooped a sample of sand and dead plant material from the sand tray and filled the bag. "It sounds like you might want to focus on the plant roots."

"I will." Pavel took the bag and his food and left the biology lab. Pierre waited for the lab door to close. He stepped up to the door and listened for a few seconds to make sure Pavel was gone.

"The children have left," said Pierre. He walked over to Vladomyr and Alicia. "The adults can now talk."

"You didn't tell him the scatterbug was from the cavern." Vladomyr sat on a stool.

"You saw how he reacted to the notion of an alien species."

"Was he wrong?"

"No, but confirming that wouldn't have been helpful either."

"So you think the contamination is from the Reliquary?"

"I think Pavel completed the puzzle."

"Did you know about prions?" said Vladomyr.

"No," admitted Pierre. "I had no idea. But I also realize how difficult it is to consider every possibility. We needed to guide Pavel down a path he hadn't explored, and he gave us the answer. However, once Pavel said that, it wasn't difficult to connect the Reliquary to the blight. The Reliquary spews out every other kind of poison. Why not also prions?"

"If all that's true, what do we do about the terraforming problem?"

"Short term," said Pierre. "We need to isolate the greenhouse soil from the rest of the Gliesian surface. I would suggest installing a false floor, using decontaminated soil, and making isolation procedures more stringent. We will need to recall all the scatterbugs, and not only decontaminate them, but find a way to genetically modify the scatterbug biome to resist and denature the prion. With new scatterbugs, I think we could get a batch of bean plants growing in no time."

"We can't live off of the greenhouses," said Vladomyr. "Their capacity won't sustain what the colonists need."

"I know. But I think we have a bigger problem."

"Like what?"

"Like the Reliquary," said Pierre. "Have you not put two and two together yet?"

"Apparently not," admitted Vladomyr.

Pierre opened the scatterbug pen. He picked up Isfit. The scatterbug thrashed and snapped its climbing claws. "What is this?"

"It's a scatterbug."

"That's what we call the robot. But what's its function?"

"To terraform the planet. I would have thought that much would be obvious."

"You see, the answer to the Reliquary has been in front of your eyes all along."

"Sorry, I still don't get it."

"Why do we terraform a planet?" asked Pierre.

"To make it more suitable for humans," said Vladomyr.

"Any other reason?"

"I guess to make it so that other forms of life we find desirable can also thrive."

"Can you think of any reason to reverse the terraforming process?"

"I suppose if there's a form of life that threatens you. In those rare circumstances, you might want to make a planet uninhabitable."

"That's a good guess. Let's say you are the kind of life form whose domain is being taken over by living beings that will someday threaten your supremacy?" Pierre placed the scatterbug back and stepped out of the pen. "We send out scatterbugs in the millions to terraform entire worlds to be suitable for human life. But the Reliquary is the antithesis, one massive reverse terraforming device designed to transform worlds to make them sterile, utterly unsuitable for living beings. An artificial intelligence patterned after a legendary being, employing every imaginable approach to destroy life: prions and poisons, radiation, psychic attacks, and anything else that can lay waste to a planet."

"Do you realize what you are saying?" Vladomyr shifted uncomfortably.

"The implications are more shocking than that," said Pierre. "Hundreds of millions of years ago, two intelligent bipedal species evolved on this planet. They had their differences—wars and atrocities—like all cultures do. Then they had their first contact from another dimension that promised peace but concealed dark intent. Species 3 seemed only to desire being worshipped and organized the other two species to build great cities and great machines. The greatest was the Reliquary, a device designed to absorb nutrients and energy from organic compounds to empower it to dig its roots deep into the ground to poison the planet. The cavern was essentially its cult center."

"How do you know that?" said Vladomyr.

"Those urns we found are what was left of the sacrificed victims. The cavern is pretty much natural except for the metal door and the entrance. There's no lock on the metal door, and the opening mechanism was only on the outside. So it wasn't to lock the Reliquary in, but to keep people inside from leaving. When the Reliquary had reached full strength, I imagine the cavern was filled with living beings—some willing, some not—and they were entombed with the Reliquary that would continue to feed after the door was sealed."

Vladomyr shook his head. "Your evidence?"

"The bones in the passageway. Those people would have survived just long enough to know they were doomed. The cavern was never intended to be a locked vault to entomb the Reliquary. And the toxic gas? It was a carrier of nutrients. It dissolved organic compounds and delivered them back to the Reliquary in gaseous form to be absorbed. That's why it not just killed, but it melted and dissolved people. So what we are dealing with here is an ancient cult center, a doomsday cult dedicated to a primordial god."

Vladomyr shuddered. "If that's the case, why didn't it kill and absorb everyone from Basra who collected the scatterbugs?"

"Great question," said Pierre. "And I haven't figured that out yet."

"And the bodies outside of the cavern that were piled up in the entrance?"

"They probably found out what was happening and tried to stop it. By then it was too late. The door was sealed, and the Reliquary couldn't be stopped. They wrote warnings on the door to the cavern and piled their own bodies in front of the door to warn others to stay away."

"Why didn't they break down the stone wall like you did?" said Vladomyr.

"Time." Pierre shrugged. "It had weakened over millions of years. If the metal door is any indication, the fake stone was probably a lot stronger when it was first applied. One poor fellow even put his hand in the wet matrix to try to open the door, only to have it harden around his fingers. Imagine a substance harder than concrete that dries as fast as superglue."

"That's a lot to take in." Vladomyr sat down.

"No shit," said Alicia shaking her head.

"You see," Pierre continued. "We have colonized forty-eight worlds and our MegaAIs have explored hundreds more. And up till now, no life has been found on any other world. Every world found so far has been a Mars, a Venus, a Gliese. Barren, dead, poisoned. We know that Mars and Venus were not always the way they are today. Mars had oceans, and Venus was very much like Earth. We have assumed that life on rocky temperate worlds is the extreme exception. But what if that assumption is backwards? Life was the norm, but Species 3 moved from planet to planet to snuff life out wherever it was found."

"The MegaAI knew about the Reliquary, didn't it?" said Vladomyr. "That's why it abandoned us."

"That would be my guess," said Pierre.

"Okay, so how did Earth escape their reverse terraforming?"

"Who said it did? Earth went through several mass extinctions and perhaps more importantly tectonic churn. More so than other planets. What if, after one of those major extinctions, a Reliquary type device got inducted into the Earth's mantle and was burnt up? And then when the agents of the primeval gods returned to Earth to check on the progress, early humans, perhaps even the ancestors of the Egyptians, arranged a little welcoming party for them."

"So then," said Vladomyr. "What can we do about the Reliquary?"

"I'm not sure much can be done."

"Can we blow up the bastard?" said Alicia.

"Species 1 and 2 might have died out hundreds of millions of years ago, but they had metallurgy that would put our technology to shame. Their metals were stronger than alumasteel, and the Reliquary is made of similar materials." Pierre shook his head.

"A nuke in the 5-megaton range," said Alicia.

"Might be hot enough, but too close to the colony," said Vladomyr.

"A 12-kiloton atomic?"

"Not sure it would work. And it would contaminate the ground."

"Can we move it and launch it into space?"

"We can't move it," Pierre explained. "It has roots that probably go deep underground. You're thinking about the Reliquary like it is restricted to the sarcophagus. If the scatterbugs are like bacteria, which conquer by numbers, think of the Reliquary more like cancer. You might destroy the sarcophagus in the cavern, but the roots will grow back into a dozen new reliquaries."

Vladomyr stroked his chin. "Well, shit. What do we do?"

"I think our best bet is to isolate the Reliquary until it sleeps again."

"How long will that take?"

"I don't know. But without nutrients or stimulus, the Reliquary does eventually seem to hibernate. The colonists from Basra did us a favor by stealing all the scatterbugs. If we collapse the cavern and plug the hole in the roof, the remaining few scatterbugs will all shut down in a couple of weeks. With the Reliquary deprived of resources and stimulus, maybe a hundred thousand years."

"A hundred thousand years?"

"Could be sooner," said Pierre. "But the Reliquary is designed to operate on geologic time scales."

"I've got a different question," said Alicia. "Don't we have another serious problem if what we suspect about Basra is true?"

"What do you mean?" asked Vladomyr.

"Basra stole eighty thousand deranged scatterbugs from the cavern," she said. "And in doing so they may have destroyed all their fertile land. If they think we intentionally poisoned those scatterbugs, they might see that as an act of war."

"That's assuming they haven't found out already." Pierre rubbed the bottom of his chin. "They might have been stealing our scatterbugs for years, which would explain how we have lost the other sixty-two thousand unaccounted bugs. But with Pavel now knowing, the cat's out of the bag. Won't be long before everyone knows."

"If they follow procedure, won't they decontaminate the scatterbugs and replace the contents of their bioreactors?" Vladomyr rolled his shoulders and shrugged. "By the way, have you got anything to drink?"

Pierre stepped over to a cabinet and poured three beakers with the white whisky. He came back, gave one to Alicia, one to Vladomyr, and kept the one for himself. "Let's say they decontaminate and reseed just the eighty thousand scatterbugs from the cavern. How long would that take? A decade. If they don't have a scatterbug mother, even longer?"

"Is it likely they don't have a mother?"

"If they are stealing scatterbugs, it's highly likely." Pierre sat down on a stool. He swirled the drink in his hand. "But it doesn't matter. They've been into the cavern. I doubt they were wearing hazmat suits. The prion would be all over their shoes, inside their rovers, and on their clothes."

"How long before they start experiencing the effects of the contagion?" Vladomyr drank from the beaker.

"We now know the incubation period is about sixty days," said Pierre, leaning against a counter. "They stole the cavern scatterbugs sometime around February 1st. They're about two weeks from a mass die-off *if* they aren't experiencing symptoms of it already from the other bugs they stole. And when Basra's jungle starts dying in mass—"

"They'll show up on our doorstep with guns," said Alicia. "They will shoot first to soften up the colony. Breach an entrance. Then they will make their way to the situation room. Anyone who holes up in a reinforced room will face a level three purge."

"They're already lurking on the outskirts and probably even mobilized. Their next move could come anytime."

"How do we get everyone ready?"

"I'm not sure we can," said Vladomyr. "With the MegaAI abandoning us, the colony is in disarray and vulnerable. And leadership has lost control."

"What about the armory?" said Pierre.

"There's only enough weapons there to maintain security, not fend off an invasion."

"The real problem is the situation room," said Alicia. "If you control the situation room, you control the colony. Everything else can be reduced to guerilla tactics."

"That's not going to be easy," said Vladomyr. "Okeli and Gardiner both carry duplicate keys to operate the purges. Those keys operate switches that send encrypted signals that cannot be easily blocked. And either one of those men will cave when held to gun point."

"Whatever happens we cannot let them take the situation room." Pierre strolled to the back of the lab. He grabbed a tool bag and packed a high-pressure gas extractor, five empty gas canisters, and the dozen packs of plastic explosives with analog detonators Alicia had purloined from the armory.

"What are you going to do?" said Alicia.

"I'm going to check on our friend in the cavern one last time," he replied. "It has something we need."

"You can't go there alone," she said.

"I agree," said Vladomyr. "With Basra creeping out there and temperatures below minus 40° C, it's not safe."

"I wouldn't worry about me," said Pierre. "As I recall, there's a crow's nest on the top of the mess hall dome under the transmission tower."

"There is," said Vladomyr.

"I need you to install a large slingshot up on the crow's nest for lobbing these." He handed Vladomyr an empty gas canister. "It must be able to lob a cylinder to about 200 feet out. That shouldn't be too hard to manage since the crow's nest is about 40 feet up. If you use rubber, please make certain it's resistant to extreme cold."

"So, more or less, your projectile has to reach the outskirts of the colony huts," said Vladomyr.

"One other thing. If I come back from the cavern with a red flasher light on the rover blazing, have everyone inside the main colony domes armed and ready to fight." Pierre wrote a list of supplies and handed it to Alicia. "And Alicia, you meet me in the crow's nest wearing a hazmat suit and with every item on that list. Forget nothing." He took the handgun out of his pants and left it on the counter.

* * *

Pierre entered the mouth of the cave. He set his tool bag down and took off his parka. It was bone-chilling cold inside, but he needed to be able to work fast and the parka was too restrictive. At least there was no wind-chill factor to worry about in the cave and cavern.

He reached into the bag and pulled out a roll of vacuum tape and stuffed it into a pocket of the hazmat suit. He also grabbed a few light sticks. He picked up the tool bag and slung the strap over his left shoulder. He ignited a single light stick. And with light in his left hand, he entered the door and descended into the cavern. Broken pieces of camera and tripod, tools from his last visit, were strewn across the floor. A scatterbug slowly crawled up to Pierre. Somehow this bug got overlooked. Pierre picked up the scatterbug with his right hand and slowly walked towards the Reliquary.

"That's far enough." From out of the shadows strode a gun-wielding figure in thermal gear. Pierre recognized him immediately. Terry, the commander of the ESA mission to Gliese, certified murderer and overall son of a bitch.

"Look at what the snake dragged in. If it isn't my chum-buddy, Terry. Long time, no see. How you been?" said Pierre. He let the light stick and shoulder bag drop to the floor. He raised both hands up still holding the scatterbug. "You keep visiting our neighborhood, but you never stop in or write. How rude."

"That's Governor Brandt," corrected Terry. He remained the model of military discipline, strong and physically fit. He still had his buzz cut of blonde hair, and his uniform was perfectly tended even though now decorated with the insignia of colony command. His eyes were deep set pits of jealous envy and spiteful vengeance.

"Oh, is it now? Basra must be pretty damn desperate to have you as their leader."

"Shut the fuck up. No one disrespects me without paying the price."

"Failed to kill me on the transporter. Here to finish the job?"

"What do you know?"

"I know that Basra has bigger problems than Arish. Your terraforming is functioning right now, but all that is going to come crashing to an end soon."

"So you know about the Mother?"

"I had guessed about that too."

"That too?" Terry squinted at Pierre.

"You skulked about our perimeter, rustling scatterbugs for years, and just happened to come across our little archaeology project. After we vented all the toxic gas, you finally had the guts to venture inside and figured you found the motherload of scatterbugs all neatly corralled in one convenient spot. But that's not all. We also figured out that your situation room isn't functional."

"How did you figure that out?"

"You guys never uplinked to the MegaAI."

"Always think you're so smart. Always one step ahead." Terry kept the pistol pointed at Pierre. "Yes, and when the MegaAI sends its parts delivery, we'll be taking those off your hands."

"Why would Basra need the same parts as we do? Unless you had someone slip your parts onto our request list. Someone like Peter Chin?" Pierre played a likely hunch.

"What makes you think it was Chin?"

"Few other people had access to the list. Gardiner would never sell out to a cockroach like you. Okeli can be manipulated but is loyal to Gardiner. Brian has enough problems keeping everything running to get involved in another colony's drama. That leaves Chin, and Chin's only loyalty is to Chin. And besides, he speaks of you often. And you referred to him by his last name instead of denying any knowledge of him."

"Gotta try to one up." Terry was pallid and perspired like he was in a sauna even though it was well below freezing. His lower left eyelid twitched.

"With a rube like you, it's not hard. Terry, you're stupid and out of luck. There's not going to be parts for anyone. The MegaAI abandoned us to our fate. Chin didn't tell you that, did he? We're on our own."

"Doesn't matter," said Terry with a grin. "Our guys are massing in the foothills. We will reduce Arish to scrap and take the parts we need. No survivors. No witnesses."

"You would kill every man, woman, and child?" said Pierre.

"The Reliquary wants me to get it over with and kill you," the former soldier said. A tick in his left eye quivered out of control as if there was nerve damage.

"I see you've had a discussion with our mutual acquaintance," said Pierre. "Don't you get it? You've crawled into bed with a homicidal killing machine, a has-been engramatically programmed automaton that sees all life as either food or the enemy."

"This place. Can't you feel the energy in it? It's promised me power." Terry's eyes nearly rolled to the back of his head.

"Oh, I get it now." Pierre grinned. "That's why you're going to kill everyone at Arish. You don't just want the parts from the colony—you want the bodies too. You're going to feed that thing, aren't you?"

"You'll be the first to find out."

"You gave Arish's demographic information to that abomination, didn't you? Didn't you? That's why it didn't kill you when you came to collect the scatterbugs."

"Call it a strategic investment."

"That monstrosity is using you to plunder a larger but weaker colony." Pierre's bottom teeth were exposed. He squeezed the carapace of the scatterbug he was holding. "It won't stop with Arish, you know. Basra will be next. Once you feed that thing it will only grow. It's stronger than you. Smarter than you. It will dangle you like a weak-minded puppet on a psychic string."

"Watch what you say." Terry stretched out his arm with the pistol. His muscles became rigid, and his hand became hard. He tightened his grip on the pistol until his knuckles turned white. His cheeks flushed red. Pierre saw the rage in his eyes.

"Isn't that a Glaucom 17ZE?" said Pierre.

"You know your firearms."

"I know my electronics."

Terry pulled the trigger. The firing pin clicked. No shot.

"Oops!" Pierre pushed the pistol away and hit Terry in the face with the scatterbug. The hostile scatterbug latched onto Terry's face and clothing and clawed and scraped at human flesh. While Terry swatted at the scatterbug, Pierre punched him repeatedly. The Frenchman grabbed Terry's jacket and threw the man towards the Reliquary. The ex-soldier hit the ground, and the scatterbug rolled off.

Terry stood up and drew a combat knife. The gun may not have worked with all the EMP pulses from the Reliquary, but knives were deadly. And Pierre was in a hazmat suit. Terry had every advantage when it came to mobility and flexibility.

Pierre cautiously approached Terry, shortening the distance between himself and the knife-wielding man. Terry swung the knife at Pierre. Pierre stepped back and the blade missed. The laminated fabric of the hazmat suit would provide no protection from a sharpened blade.

"The Reliquary is twisting your mind." Pierre tried to keep clear of the knife.

Terry slashed again at Pierre.

Pierre was forced to take a step back. He held up both of his forearms to defend himself.

Terry crouched and lunged forward and drove the knife into Pierre's hazmat suit and into his left forearm. Pierre felt nothing to begin with. When the adrenaline subsided, he felt the sting of cut flesh. Pierre realized the error of his defense strategy.

Pierre responded by punching Terry in the face. Terry stumbled back. Pierre picked up a rock and threw it, hitting Terry on the head. Terry fell backwards lying beside the Reliquary. He sat up and blood trickled down his face. Pierre picked up another rock.

Terry wiped his forehead. He hopped to his feet and put his hand on the Reliquary to steady himself. He screamed and immediately fell dead beside the sarcophagus. His hand remained attached to the casing of the Reliquary. In seconds, the arm withered and turned black, and the life drained from all the flesh on Terry's face. His flesh desiccated, and in moments his entire body disintegrated into bone fragments and dust.

"Hypothesis confirmed," said Pierre.

More roots stretched out from the base of the Reliquary and green gas poured out of the vents. Pierre grabbed vacuum tape from his pocket and tightly wrapped the left forearm of his hazmat suit. The repair would not do much for his wound, but it would keep out the poison from the Reliquary.

He then hurried back to his shoulder bag. He picked up the bag and brought it closer to the Reliquary. He pulled out the gas extractor and loaded a canister. Pierre cautiously put the syphon directly up to the Reliquary gas vent without contacting the sarcophagus and filled a gas canister. He flipped a switch to overpressure the vessel.

What are you doing? said the Reliquary.

"I thought you knew what I was thinking," said Pierre. He looked at the pressure gauge. The pressure reached past 500 psi. The gas output began to trail off. Pierre bent and picked up a large stone. He banged on the side of the Reliquary with the stone. A loud metal gong echoed through the cavern. Gas billowed out the vents again. "That's it. Fuel that hate and contempt for life!"

What do you know about hate?

"You'd be amazed at what I know." As the pressure gauge needle pushed past 7000 psi, the green vapor inside the plastoglass canister condensed into a brown liquid. Pierre removed the first cylinder and fitted another. "And your new buddy is no longer available to do your dirty work. I think the pressure was too much for him. He completely went to pieces."

He served his purpose. We serve the Great Expiation.

"That what you're calling extermination these days?" As he filled the canister, he felt waves of fear and uncertainty, envy and loss, pride and hate wash over him.

Life brings chaos and cannot be caged. We bring changeless peace. Life is a disease. We are the cure. But you are not like the others.

"A bit late for flattery," said Pierre. He switched out the full canister and installed a third. Every time the gas outflow slowed, he banged on the Reliquary with a rock. Unfortunately, the Reliquary had more gas vents than he had syphons. The air was already thick with green gas. It wouldn't be long before the material of his hazmat suit would start to break down. "Can't resist the urge to kill, can you?"

I have been here for over 350 million years.

"Good to hear that you've been keeping count. Everyone should have a hobby."

You will never defeat me. The Reliquary pumped out even more poison gas.

"You are an engram. An impression. A computer program." Pierre changed the canister again. "What happened to the original? The real primordial god?"

So you know of me?

"You? Never heard of you. I've heard of your namesake." Pierre watched the outer layer of his hazmat suit peel back exposing the layers beneath. The gas was dissolving his suit faster than he expected. Even the slightest exposure to the gas was deadly. "The primordial gods once ruled to hold back the chaos monsters. Where are they now? Where are the chaos monsters? Gone! All obsolete relics."

You will pay for your insolence.

"Those are the words of your master." Pierre watched the pressure gauge. He did not want to remain in the cavern one second longer than necessary. "You are nothing but an imprint from a being that expired into the ether."

Primordial gods cannot die.

"There's more than one kind of death. Death of the body, death of agency, death of living memory, death of the name. No one remembers the names of the primordial gods." He kept watching the pressure gauge on the gas syphon as it compressed the gas into the canisters. "They have become utterly impotent and irrelevant as you have become predictable and pathetic."

Blue electric sparks leapt off the Reliquary and onto the body of the gas syphon. A flame flared out from the electrical discharge, igniting the hydrogen rich gas with a poof. The Reliquary just upped the ante. Pierre expected the voltage to eventually increase to a lethal dose. The rubber in the hazmat suit provided some protection from electric shock. But as the rubber layer deteriorated so did its protection. It was trying more tricks to kill him. He needed to provoke it while being careful not to goad it to the point where it got wise. When the canister was full, he removed the canister and loaded the fourth.

You will not leave here alive.

"Keep telling yourself that." Pierre watched as the rubber on the fingers of his gloves was stripped away. The second layer under the rubber was deteriorating even faster than the first. The poison gas reacted with the fabric, heating up his hazmat suit. Minutes at most before the suit would fail entirely.

I have destroyed worlds while your species was still burrowing in the ground.

Pierre felt another psychic attack. His thinking became clouded, confused. The cavern closed in on him like all the walls were falling in on him at once. He shook his head and tried to focus. He noticed that the gas extractor read "full." He pulled out the full canister and inserted the last empty.

I destroyed this world once, and I will do it again.

"I figured it was you." Pierre kept close tabs on the pressure gauge. "You are a Reliquary, a horde of malice, methods to destroy higher technology, and catalysts to manufacture pestilence, spew poison into the air, dry up the water, and contaminate the ground, a trove of every impure and evil thing. You are an artifact, a remnant with no future. Your posterity is extinct."

We will destroy you. There is no escape.

"You may have killed the other species on this world. But I can guarantee that you've never met any vermin as hard to eradicate as humans." The last canister was full. He threw everything into the tool bag. Pierre reached into his bag, pulled out a gray slab, and slapped a pack of plastic explosive with a detonator on the side of the Reliquary. It might not damage the artifact, but hopefully it would bring down the roof around it. "A parting gift."

Slinging the bag over his shoulder, he ran through the cavern fixing six more packs of plastic explosives to the walls of the cavern until he reached the entrance. Once at the entrance, he removed all the ventilation from the doorway. He placed three packs of plastic explosives on the roof of the passageway into the cavern. In the last pack, he inserted a detonator with a 45-minute analog timer similar to a spring-operated egg timer. He exited the passage and closed the metal door until it was once again sealed shut. He pulled out a large felt pen and wrote on the door, "Danger: Do Not Enter. Toxic Gas. Contains Killer Machine." After the message, he drew a skull and crossbones.

Pierre placed a couple more explosive packs in the entrance to the cave with a couple more detonators with timers. The timers were redundant. Once one explosive went off, the shock wave would trigger all the other detonators. He grabbed his tool bag and ran down the scree and back to the rover as fast as he could. He was almost back to the rover when two loud bangs shattered the cadence of his heavy breathing, followed by a string of concussive explosions.

He turned, looking back. Red light glowed briefly from the cave. His breath froze in the minus 40° C winter air. It always felt odd to him to be in a desert with such harsh cold. He had left his parka back in the cave, but with all the running it would have been too hot to wear.

Pierre was sure Basra's scout parties in the foothills would also hear the blasts, so he picked up the pace. At least he had a head start. When he reached the rover, he hopped in and turned over the engine. A whistle whizzed by him, followed by a second. They were shooting. He put the rover into high speed and got out of there as fast as possible. It would be less than an hour before they realized Pierre had collapsed the entrance of the cave and their governor was dead. They would never find any trace of Terry, and an invasion from Basra would quickly precipitate.

As he got within sight of Arish, Pierre turned on the red flasher. It was twenty minutes past sunset. Darkness was falling. Hopefully, the colonists would see his signal. Hopefully, they would have gotten their shit together, put aside their disappointment from earlier in the day, and organized some sort of defense.

When Pierre arrived at the colony, there was no one outside. He entered through the hatch to the mess hall. As he opened the door, a bunch of colonists pointed rifles at Pierre.

"Whoa, whoa, whoa! It's me. Pierre." He raised his hands.

Vladomyr stepped forward. Everyone lowered their guns. "We are as ready as we can be."

"Okay." Pierre lowered his hands. "A detachment from Basra is about twenty minutes behind me. Nobody starts shooting until they enter the building."

"We've got everyone at an assigned emergency station," said Vladomyr. "Gardiner is in the situation room along with a squad of colony security. Okeli has heavily fortified the entrance and will defend it with his life. Anyone wanting to take it will be up to their hips in their own blood. Pavel is in the fire control station. A few people are missing like Chin and Luke Bronson. And Alicia is waiting for you in the crow's nest wearing a hazmat suit completely confused as to what you are up to."

"I would expect that," said Pierre. "I couldn't tell her the real reason I went back to the cavern. I couldn't tell anyone. We had a mole."

"Who?"

"Chin. He was telling Basra everything that was happening here."

"How do you know?"

"I met their new governor in the cavern." Pierre took off his hazmat suit and tossed it to the floor. "Could one of you kind folks go get me a fresh hazmat suit? This one has seen better days." Pierre took a seat on one of the cafeteria benches wearing little more than his underwear. A young lady, the same one that kissed him on New Year's Eve, ran off to fetch him a new suit. Blood dripped from his left arm onto the floor. Melissa saw Pierre's wound and grabbed a first aid kit. Pierre's open wound was encrusted with black-caked blood.

"You'll need stitches for that," said Vladomyr.

Pierre shrugged in response. "Jones can stitch it up if we live to morning." He did not even feel it anymore. As Melissa worked on his arm, she kept soaking up gauzes and discarding them. Bloody gauzes piled up on the table.

"Morning? Don't you think that's being optimistic?"

"If we aren't successful fighting them off by morning, we won't make it to the afternoon."

"What did you learn?"

"Besides the fact that Basra is going to need a replacement governor?" Pierre leaned back for a moment. Finally, Melissa wrapped the whole forearm in several layers of gauze and taped it.

"He's dead?"

"The Reliquary is quite capricious about who it kills," said Pierre. "Chin was negotiating a deal with Basra's governor, Terry Brandt. Chin didn't tell Terry how bad our terraforming situation was, and Terry didn't tell Chin that their situation was worse than ours."

"How so?"

"They had some violent changes in leadership. That's the real reason they quarantined us. So we wouldn't find out how bad things were over there and pass that information back to Earth Central Command."

"That makes no sense," said Vladomyr. "We would have helped them gladly."

"They were paranoid and consumed by what they were planning. They thought we would do to them what they're going to do to us. Because of their infighting, they destroyed their scatterbug mother and their satellite equipment."

"So their terraforming was also living on borrowed time," said Vladomyr.

"Yeah, except they did it to themselves." Pierre looked at the floor of the mess hall. "I figured out their plan, which is to kill everyone here, feed our bodies to the Reliquary, and at their leisure harvest whatever technology they find."

Vladomyr's face blanched. He shook his head in disbelief as the report sunk in. The Ukrainian looked back at everyone in the mess hall and shouted for their attention. "If anyone here sees Peter Chin or Luke Bronson, shoot them on sight. They have sold the colony out to those who are coming to kill everyone. Do not hesitate and show them no mercy. Anyone got a problem with that?" Several rifle chambers were loaded with a round showing their approval.

"Something else I learned."

"What?"

"The Reliquary is not alone. It's got friends, and we're likely to encounter them again." Pierre took some deep breaths. It would be a while before he got to breathe fresh air again. And for the first time since arriving at the Colony eight months ago, he was hungry. "Are those hotdogs I smell?"

"Sure is." Madi walked up to Pierre and handed him a hotdog on a small tray.

Pierre picked up the hotdog and practically inhaled it in four bites.

"Slow down there, son," she said. "You'll choke if you eat too fast."

"After all this is over, I think we will need a report from you." Vladomyr shook his head, grimacing at Pierre's suggestion of possibly encountering more surprises from Species 3. The corners of his eyes twitched. He had every reason to be concerned.

The young woman from the party ran into the hall with a new hazmat suit. She was panting. She tossed Pierre the suit. "Ran into Okeli's messenger in the hall. Intruders spotted on the colony perimeter. Looks like about a hundred men."

"That's my queue," said Pierre. He put on the new hazmat suit. Vladomyr took off his BDUs and handed them to Pierre.

"Put these overtop the hazmat suit," said Vladomyr. All the women laughed at seeing Vladomyr wear nothing but his undershirt and boxer shorts. "You're going on the roof of the dome in the middle of the night."

"Are you kidding?"

"You are wearing a bright yellow hazmat suit," said the Ukrainian. "Do you want to paint a bright target on you? Until you get to the crow's nest, you will be easy pickings. Besides, it's freezing up there and an additional layer will help."

"Good point," said Pierre. He put the BDUs over the hazmat suit. Vladomyr was a much larger man than Pierre. The BDUs were loose. He buttoned up the jacket and grabbed his tool bag.

Fully suited up, Pierre left the others and went to a ladder leading to the roof of the dome. Once on top of the dome, Pierre kept low. A couple of bullets zipped past. He climbed the ladder of the satellite transmission tower and up into the crow's nest.

Alicia was huddled against the solid alumasteel cover of the nest. Despite the hazmat suit, she shivered and her lips were blue. It was the dead of a Gliesian winter night, close to 50° below. She clutched a hunting rifle that quaked in her arms, and beside her was the bag of supplies. An improvised slingshot was strung between the beams of the receiver tower.

"I thought you abandoned me." Alicia's voice stuttered from the extreme cold.

"You're not important enough to abandon," said Pierre. He opened the bag of supplies. He took out a pair of night-vision binoculars.

"You're still a shit," she said.

"Met an old acquaintance of ours on the way home."

"You don't mean Terry, do you?"

"The one and only."

"Should've killed that bastard when I had the chance." Her lips trembled as she spoke.

"I don't think he's going to be a problem going forward."

"Can't say I'm sad to hear that."

"What do we have down there?"

"A penetration team. About a hundred soldiers. Equipped with night-vision goggles and military grade rifles."

Pierre popped up his head and looked at the encroaching soldiers. "I don't see any of them with gas masks or hazmat suits."

"What have you got planned?"

"We're taking a page from WWI."

"You've got to be kidding."

"This is what I need you to do. There are five gas canisters. Take one M5 blast stick and cut the fuse to one inch, no more, no less."

"That's only ten seconds."

"That's enough."

"Tape a trimmed blast stick to each gas canister with vacuum tape." Pierre hid behind the alumasteel barrier. He could see the cold had affected Alicia's dexterity. He picked out an M5 stick and cut the fuse to length and handed it to Alicia who taped it to the gas canister. They repeated the process for the other four canisters.

Pierre popped his head back up to look. Soldiers were huddling at the base of the family domicile huts. They saw Pierre and took some shots at him. The alumasteel was more than strong enough to protect from the bullets.

"Now what?" said Alicia.

"Now, we give them a little party," said Pierre. "Are you still able to fire that rifle of yours to distract them?"

"Count on it."

"Okay, give them three shots, duck, and stay down."

Pierre loaded a canister in the slingshot. He had a lit lighter in his hand ready to go. Alicia leapt up, let off three shots, and ducked. Pierre lit the fuse and launched the gas canister into a spot between the huts. As he let go, a bullet ricocheted inside the crow's nest and hit Pierre in the shoulder. He dropped like a sack of rocks. Alicia scrambled towards him.

"Stay down!" said Pierre. He grabbed the vacuum tape and plugged the hole in the hazmat suit. A second later, a bang. The alumasteel of the transmission tower rattled from the shock wave.

A green fog moved between the buildings like the angel of death.